LONDON AFTER MIDNIGHT
Part Two

London after Midnight is a very special guided tour, far from the beaten track of the city's museums, galleries and monuments. It will take you down much darker routes which harbour secrets of the terrible deeds and awful villainies that accord London an infamous reputation in the annals of crime. This second volume contains a spine-chilling selection of tales by Agatha Christie, Sir Arthur Conan Doyle, Dorothy L. Sayers, and many more.

LONDON AFTER MIDNIGHT
Part Two

A Conducted Tour by
Peter Haining

Chivers Press • Thorndike Press
Bath, Avon, England • Thorndike, Maine USA

MA LS VZ BD BX MT
NW

This Large Print edition is published by Chivers Press, England, and by Thorndike Press, USA.

Published in 1997 in the U.K. by arrangement with Little, Brown (UK) Ltd.

Published in 1996 in the U.S. by arrangement with Seventh Zenith, Ltd.

U.K. Hardcover ISBN 0–7451–6911–2 (Chivers Large Print)
U.K. Softcover ISBN 0–7451–6912–0 (Camden Large Print)
U.S. Softcover ISBN 0–7862–0791–4 (General Series Edition)

The text of this Large Print edition is unabridged.
Other aspects of the book may vary from the original edition.

Set in 16 pt. New Times Roman.

Printed in Great Britain on acid-free paper.

British Library Cataloguing in Publication Data available

Library of Congress Catalog Card Number: 96–90281

For
John Kelly

CONTENTS

CONTENTS

ACKNOWLEDGEMENTS

The editor and publishers are grateful to the following authors, their agents and publishers for permission to include copyright stories in this collection: The Estate of John Rhode for 'The Elusive Bullet'; Victor Gollancz Ltd for 'The Bottle Party' by H.C. Bailey and 'The Cave of Ali Baba' by Dorothy L. Sayers; HarperCollins for 'Aces High' by Peter Cheyney; Aitken & Stone Ltd for 'Yellow Iris' by Agatha Christie; Random Publishing Group for 'Trent and the Fool-proof Lift' by E. C. Bentley; Chatto & Windus Ltd for 'The Border-line Case' by Margery Allingham; Curtis Brown Ltd for 'The Santa Claus Club' by Julian Symons; Express Newspapers Group for 'The Incautious Burglar' by John Dickson Carr.

While every care has been taken to establish the copyright holders of all the stories in this book, in case of any accidental infringement the Editor should be contacted in care of the publishers in order to correct this fact in any future editions.

PART TWO

CITY SLEUTHS

THE ELUSIVE BULLET

JOHN RHODE

By coincidence it is only a stone's throw from the last of London's black spots on our tour to the home of one of the city's formidable group of private detectives who have dedicated their lives to solving crime. The first of them is Dr Lancelot Priestley who lives in Westbourne Terrace just beside Paddington Station. Priestley is a somewhat humourless and academic figure who was once a Professor of Mathematics at a leading English university which he left after a fierce disagreement with the authorities. Since then he has been able to use his private means to live quietly in Westbourne Terrace and devote himself to solving crime problems which involve the use of mathematics or, more particularly, pure logic. He has, though, poor eyesight, a dislike of the telephone, and generally relies on his cases being brought to him by Inspector Hanslet—which he prefers, if at all possible, to solve without leaving his room. The armchair detective personified! Priestley does, though, often require the help of his daughter, April, and Harold Merefield, who is both his son-in-law and secretary. The Professor made his debut in the appropriately titled Paddington Mystery *(1925) in which he proved the innocence of*

3

Merefield and began their relationship, and thereafter built up a large readership for subsequent cases such as The Murders in Praed Street *(1928),* Mystery at Olympia *(1935),* Death in Harley Street *(1946),* Domestic Agency *(1955),* The Vanishing Diary *(1961) and over 70 other novels and short stories. Dorothy L. Sayers was a particular admirer of the Dr Priestley stories and included several in her anthologies.*

John Rhode (1884–1964) was almost as reclusive a figure as his creation: his real name was Cecil John Charles Street and he was a career army officer reaching the rank of major before his retirement. He was a prolific writer, too, and apart from the crime novels he also produced works of history, politics and biography as well as collaborating with Carter Dickson on Drop To His Death *(1939) in which the murder took place in a lift. For many years Rhode was a member of the Detection Club in London. Although Dr Priestley was described by the American crime fiction historians, Jacques Barzun and Wendell Taylor, as 'one of the most impressive detectives in British mystery fiction' only one of the books has been filmed,* The Murders in Praed Street, *as* Twelve Good Men *by Warner Brothers in 1936 starring Henry Kendall. In 'The Elusive Bullet', written in 1936, John Rhode is able to draw on his army experiences of the use of weapons as Priestley*

4

sets about solving the case of a man who has been shot on a train...

*   *   *

'By the way, professor, there's something in the evening papers that might interest you,' said Inspector Hanslet, handing over as he spoke the copy he had been holding in his hand. 'There you are, "Prominent City Merchant found dead". Read it, it sounds quite interesting.'

Dr Priestley adjusted his spectacles and began to read the paragraph. The professor and myself, Harold Merefield, who had been his secretary for a couple of years, had been sitting in the study of Dr Priestley's house in Westbourne Terrace, one fine June evening after dinner, when Inspector Hanslet had been announced. The inspector was an old friend of ours, who availed himself of the professor's hobby, which was the mathematical detection of crime, to discuss with him any investigations upon which he happened to be engaged. He had just finished giving the professor an outline of a recent burglary case, over which the police had confessed themselves puzzled, and had risen to go, when the item in the newspaper occurred to him.

'This does not appear to me to be particularly interesting,' said the professor. 'It merely states that on the arrival of the 3.20 train this afternoon at Tilbury station a porter,

5

in examining the carriages, found the dead body of a man, since identified as a Mr Farquharson, lying in a corner of a first-class carriage. This Mr Farquharson appears to have met his death through a blow on the side of the head although no weapon capable of inflicting such a blow has so far been found. I can only suggest that if the facts are as reported, there are at least a dozen theories which could be made to fit in with them.'

'Such as?' inquired Hanslet tentatively.

The professor frowned. 'You know perfectly well, inspector, that I most strongly deprecate all conjecture,' he replied severely. 'Conjecture, unsupported by a thorough examination of facts, has been responsible for more than half the errors made by mankind throughout the ages. But, to demonstrate my meaning, I will outline a couple of theories which fit in with all the reported facts. Mr Farquharson may have been struck by an assailant who left the train before its arrival at Tilbury, and who disposed of the weapon in some way. On the other hand, he may have leant out of the window, and been struck by some object at the side of the line, or even by a passing train, if he was at the right-hand side of the carriage, looking in the direction in which the train was going. Of course, as I wish to emphasize, a knowledge of *all* the facts, not only those contained in this brief paragraph, would probably render both these theories untenable.'

Hanslet smiled. He knew well enough from experience the professor's passion for facts and his horror of conjecture.

'Well, I don't suppose the case will come my way,' he said as he turned towards the door. 'But if it does I'll let you know what transpires. I shouldn't wonder if we know the whole story in a day or two. It looks simple enough. Well good night, sir.'

The professor waited till the front door had closed behind him. 'I have always remarked that Hanslet's difficulties are comparatively easy of solution, but that what he calls simple problems completely baffle his powers of reasoning. I should not be surprised if we heard from him again very shortly.'

As usual, the professor was right. Hanslet's first visit had been on Saturday evening. On the following Tuesday, at about the same time, he called again, with a peculiarly triumphant expression on his face.

'You remember that Farquharson business, don't you, professor?' he began without preliminary. 'Well, it did come my way, after all. The Essex police called Scotland Yard in, and I was put on to it. I've solved the whole thing in under forty-eight hours. Not a bad piece of work eh? Mr Farquharson was murdered by—'

Dr Priestley held up his hand protestingly. 'My dear inspector, I am not the least

7

concerned with the murderer of this Mr Farquharson. As I have repeatedly told you my interest in these matters is purely theoretical, and confined to the processes of deduction. You are beginning your story at the wrong end. If you wish me to listen to it, you must first tell me the full facts, then explain the course of your investigations, step by step.'

'Very well, sir,' replied Hanslet, somewhat crestfallen. 'The first fact I learnt was how Farquharson was killed. It appeared at first sight that he had been struck a terrific blow by some weapon like a pole-axe. There was a wound about two inches across on the right side of his head. But, at the post-mortem, this was found to have been caused by a bullet from an ordinary service rifle, which was found embedded in his brain.'

'Ah!' remarked the professor. 'A somewhat unusual instrument of murder, surely? What position did the body occupy in the carriage when it was found?'

'Oh, in the right-hand corner, facing the engine, I believe,' replied Hanslet impatiently. 'But that's of no importance, as you'll see. The next step, obviously, was to find out something about Farquharson, and why any one should want to murder him. The discovery of a motive is a very great help in an investigation like this. Farquharson lived with his daughter in a biggish house near a place called Stanford-le-Hope, on the line between Tilbury and

8

Southend. On Saturday last he left his office, which is close to Fenchurch Street station, about one o'clock. He lunched at a restaurant near by, and caught the 2.15 at Fenchurch Street. As this was the train in which his dead body was found, I need hardly detail the inquiries by which I discovered these facts.'

The professor nodded. 'I am prepared to take your word for them,' he said.

'Very well, now let us come to the motive,' continued Hanslet. 'Farquharson was in business with his nephew, a rather wild young fellow named Robert Halliday. It seems that this young man's mother, Farquharson's sister, had a good deal of money in the business, and was very anxious that her son should carry it on after Farquharson's death. She died a couple of years ago, leaving rather a curious will, by which all her money was to remain in her brother's business, and was to revert to her son only at her brother's death.'

The professor rubbed his hands. 'Ah, the indispensable motive begins to appear!' he exclaimed with a sarcastic smile. 'I am sure that you feel that no further facts are necessary, inspector. It follows, of course, that young Halliday murdered his uncle to secure the money. You described him as a wild young man, I think? Really, the evidence is most damning!'

'It's all very well for you to laugh at me, professor,' replied Hanslet indignantly. 'I'll admit that you've given me a line on things that I couldn't find for myself often enough. But in this case there's no possible shadow of doubt about what happened. What would you say if I told you that Halliday actually travelled in the very train in which his uncle's body was found?'

'Speaking without a full knowledge of the facts, I should say that this rather tended to establish his innocence,' said the professor gravely.

Hanslet winked knowingly. 'Ah, but that's by no means all,' he replied. 'Halliday is a Territorial, and he left the London on Saturday afternoon in uniform, and carrying a rifle. It seems that, although he's very keen, he's a shocking bad marksman, and a member of a sort of awkward squad which goes down occasionally to Purfleet ranges to practise. Purfleet is a station between London and Tilbury. Halliday got out there, fired a number of rounds, and returned to London in the evening.'

'Dear, dear, I'm sorry for that young man,' remarked the professor. 'First we have a motive, then an opportunity. Of course, he travelled in the same carriage as his uncle, levelled his musket at his head, inflicted a fearful wound, and decamped. Why, there's hardly a weak link in the whole chain.'

'It wasn't quite as simple as that,' replied Hanslet patiently. 'He certainly didn't travel in

10

the same carriage as his uncle, since that very morning they had quarrelled violently. Farquharson, who was rather a strict old boy, didn't approve of his nephew's ways. Not that I can find out much against him, but he's a bit of a young blood, and his uncle didn't like it. He travelled third class, and swears that he didn't know his uncle was on the train.'

'Oh, you have interviewed him already, have you?' said the professor quietly.

'I have,' replied Hanslet. 'His story is that he nearly missed the train, jumped into it at the last moment, in fact. Somewhere after Barking he found himself alone, and that's all he told me. When I asked him what he was doing scrambling along the footboard outside the train between Dagenham and Rainham, he became very confused, and explained that on putting his head out of the window he had seen another member of the awkward squad a few carriages away, and made up his mind to join him. He gave me the man's name, and when I saw him he confirmed Halliday's story.'

'Really, inspector, your methods are masterly,' said the professor. 'How did you know that he had been on the footboard?'

'A man working on the line had seen a soldier in uniform, with a rifle slung over his back, in this position,' replied Hanslet triumphantly.

'And you immediately concluded that this man must be Halliday,' commented the professor. 'Well, guesses must hit the truth sometimes, I suppose. What exactly is your theory of the crime?'

'It seems plain enough,' replied Hanslet. 'Halliday had watched his uncle enter the train, then jumped into a carriage close to his. At a predetermined spot he clambered along with his loaded rifle, shot him through the window, then, to avert suspicion, joined his friend, whom he had also seen enter the train, a little further on. It's as plain as a pikestaff to me.'

'So it appears,' remarked the professor dryly. 'What steps do you propose to take in the matter?'

'I propose to arrest Halliday at the termination of the inquest,' replied Hanslet complacently.

The professor made no reply to this for several seconds. 'I think it would be to everybody's advantage if you consulted me again before doing so,' he said at last.

A cloud passed for an instant over Hanslet's face. 'I will, if you think it would do any good,' he replied. 'But you must see for yourself that I have enough evidence to secure a conviction from any jury.'

'That is just what disquiets me,' returned the professor quickly. 'You cannot expect the average juryman to have an intelligence superior to yours, you know. I have your promise?'

'Certainly, if you wish it,' replied Hanslet

rather huffily. He changed the subject abruptly, and a few minutes later he rose and left the house.

In the course of our normal routine I forgot the death of Mr Farquharson entirely. It was not until the following afternoon, when Mary the parlourmaid entered the study with the announcement that a Miss Farquharson had called and begged that she might see the professor immediately, that the matter recurred to me.

'Miss Farquharson!' I exclaimed. 'Why, that must be the daughter of the fellow who was murdered the other day. Hanslet said he had a daughter, you remember.'

'The balance of probability would appear to favour that theory,' replied the professor acidly. 'Yes, I'll see her. Show Miss Farquharson in, please, Mary.'

Miss Farquharson came in, and the professor greeted her with his usual courtesy. 'To what do I owe the pleasure of this visit?' he inquired.

Miss Farquharson hesitated a moment or two before she replied. She was tall and fair, dressed in deep mourning with an elusive prettiness which I, at least, found most attractive. And even before she spoke, I guessed something of the truth from the flush which suffused her face at the professor's question.

'I'm afraid you may think this an

13

unpardonable intrusion,' she said at last. 'The truth is that Bob—Mr Halliday—who is my cousin, has heard of you and begged me to come and see you.'

The professor frowned. He hated his name becoming known in connection with any of the investigations which he undertook, but in spite of all his efforts, many people had come to know of his hobby. Miss Farquharson took his frown for a sign of disapproval, and continued with an irresistible tone of pleading in her voice.

'It was only as a last hope I came to you,' she said. 'It's all so awful that I feel desperate. I expect you know that my father was found dead last Saturday in a train at Tilbury, while he was on his way home?'

The professor nodded. 'I am aware of some of the facts,' he replied non-committally. 'I need not trouble you to repeat them. But in what way can I be of assistance to you?'

'It's too terrible!' she exclaimed with a sob. 'The police suspect Bob of having murdered him. They haven't said so, but they have been asking him all sorts of dreadful questions. Bob thought perhaps you might be able to do something—'

Her voice tailed away hopelessly under the professor's unwinking gaze.

'My dear young lady, I am not a magician,' he replied. 'I may as well tell you that I have seen Inspector Hanslet who has what he considers a convincing case against your cousin.'

'But you don't believe it, do you, Doctor Priestley?' interrupted Miss Farquharson eagerly.

'I can only accept the inspector's statements as he gave them to me,' replied the professor. 'I know nothing of the case beyond what he has told me. Perhaps you would allow me to ask you a few questions?'

'Of course!' she exclaimed. 'I'll tell you everything I can.'

The professor inclined his head with a gesture of thanks. 'Was your father in the habit of travelling by the 2.15 train from Fenchurch Street on Saturday afternoons?'

'No,' replied Miss Farquharson with decision. 'Only when he was kept later than usual at the office. His usual custom was to come home to a late lunch.'

'I see. Now, can you tell me the reason for the quarrel between him and your cousin?'

This time Miss Farquharson's reply was not so prompt. She lowered her head so that we could not see her face, and kept silence for a moment. Then, as though she had made up her mind, she spoke suddenly.

'I see no harm in telling you. As a matter of fact, Bob and I have been in love with one another for a long time, and Bob decided to tell my father on Saturday morning. Father was rather old-fashioned, and he didn't altogether

15

approve of Bob. Not that there was any harm in anything he did, but father couldn't understand that a young man liked to amuse himself. There was quite a scene when Bob told him, and father refused to hear anything about it until Bob had reformed, as he put it. But I know that Bob didn't kill him,' she concluded entreatingly. 'It's impossible for anybody who knew him to believe he could. You don't believe it, do you?'

'No, I do not believe it,' replied the professor slowly. 'If it is any consolation to you and Mr Halliday, I may tell you in confidence that I never have believed it. When is the inquest to be?'

A look of deep thankfulness overspread her features. 'I am more grateful to you than I can say, Doctor Priestley,' she said earnestly. 'The inquest? On Saturday morning. Will you be there?'

The professor shook his head. 'No, I shall not be there,' he replied. 'You see, it is not my business. But I shall take steps before then to make certain inquiries. I do not wish to raise your hopes unduly, but it is possible that I may be able to divert suspicion from Mr Halliday. More than that I cannot say.'

Tears of thankfulness came to her eyes. 'I can't tell you what this means to Bob and me,' she said. 'He has been terribly distressed. He quite understands that things look very black against him, and he cannot suggest who could

16

have wanted to kill my father. Father hadn't an enemy in the world, poor dear.'

'You are sure of that?' remarked the professor.

'Quite,' she replied positively. 'I knew every detail of his life, he never hid the smallest thing from me.'

And after a further short and unimportant conversation she took her leave of us.

The professor sat silent for some minutes after her departure. 'Poor girl!' he said at last. 'To lose her father so tragically, and then to see the man she loves accused of his murder! We must see what we can do to help her, Harold. Get me the one-inch map of the country between London and Tilbury, and a time-table of the Southend trains.'

I hastened to obey him, and for an hour or more he pored over the map, working upon it with a rule and a protractor. At the end of this period he looked up and spoke abruptly.

'This is remarkably interesting, more so than I imagined at first it would be. Run out and buy me the sheets of the six-inch survey which cover Rainham and Purfleet. I think we shall need them.'

I bought the maps he required and returned with them. For the rest of the day he busied himself with these, and it was not until late in the evening that he spoke to me again.

'Really, my boy, this problem is beginning to interest me,' he said. 'There are many points

17

about it which are distinctly baffling. We must examine the country on the spot. There is a train to Purfleet, I see, at 10.30 tomorrow morning.'

'Have you formed any theory, sir?' I inquired eagerly. The vision of Miss Farquharson, and her conviction of her cousin's innocence, had impressed me in her favour.

The professor scowled at me. 'How often am I to tell you that facts are all that matter?' he replied. 'Our journey tomorrow will be for the purpose of ascertaining facts. Until we know these, it would be waste of time to indulge in conjecture.'

He did not mention the subject again until the next morning, when we were seated in the train to Purfleet. He had chosen an empty first-class carriage, and himself took the right-hand corner facing the engine. He said nothing until the train was travelling at a good speed, and then he addressed me suddenly.

'You are a good shot with a rifle, are you not?' he inquired.

'I used to be pretty fair,' I replied in astonishment. 'But I don't think I've had a rifle in my hand since the war.'

'Well, take my stick, and hold it as you would a rifle. Now go to the far end of the carriage and lean against the door. That's right. Point your stick at my right eye, as though you were going to shoot at it. Stand like

18

that a minute. Thank you, that will do.'

He turned away from me, took a pair of field-glasses from a case he was carrying, and began to survey the country through the window on his side. This he continued to do until the train drew up at Purfleet and we dismounted on to the platform.

'Ah, a lovely day!' he exclaimed. 'Not too warm for a little walking. We will make our first call at Purfleet ranges. This was where young Halliday came to do his shooting, you remember.'

We made our way to the ranges, and were lucky enough to find the warden at home. Dr Priestley had, when he chose, a most ingratiating way with him, and he and the warden were very shortly engaged in an animated conversation.

'By the way,' inquired the professor earnestly, 'was there any firing going on here between half-past two and three on Saturday last?'

The range-warden scratched his head with a thoughtful expression on his face. 'Let me see, now, last Saturday afternoon? We had a squad of Territorials here on Saturday afternoon, but they didn't arrive till after three. Lord, they was queer hands with a rifle, some of them. Much as they could do to hit the target at all at three hundred. They won't never make marksmen, however hard they try.'

'Isn't it rather dangerous to allow such wild

19

shots to fire at all?' suggested the professor.

'God bless your heart, sir, it's safe enough,' replied the range-warden. 'There's never been an accident the whole time I've been here. They can't very well miss the butts, and even if they did, there's nobody allowed on the marshes when firing's going on.'

'That is comforting, certainly,' said the professor. 'Apart from this squad, you had nobody else?'

The range-warden shook his head. 'No, sir, they was the only people on the range that day.'

'I suppose it is part of your duty to issue ammunition?' inquired the professor.

'As a rule, sir. But, as it happens, this particular squad always brings their own with them.'

The professor continued his conversation for a little longer, then prepared to depart.

'I'm sure I'm very much obliged to you,' he said as he shook hands. 'By the way, I believe there are other ranges about here somewhere?'

'That's right, sir,' replied the range-warden. 'Over yonder, beyond the butts. Rainham ranges, they're called.'

'Is there any objection to my walking across the marshes to them?'

'Not a bit, sir. There's no firing today. Just keep straight on past the butts, and you'll come to them.'

The professor and I started on our tramp, the professor pausing every hundred yards or so to look about him through his field-glasses and to verify his position on the map. We reached the Rainham ranges at last, discovered the warden, who fell under the influence of the professor's charm as readily as his colleague at Purfleet had done, and opened the conversation with him in much the same style.

'On Saturday afternoon last, between half-past two and three?' replied the warden to the professor's inquiry. 'Well, sir, not what you might call any shooting. There was a party from Woolwich, with a new sort of light machine-gun, something like a Lewis. But they wasn't shooting, only testing.'

'What is the difference?' asked the professor.

'Well, sir, by testing I mean they had the thing held in a clamp, so that it couldn't move. The idea is to keep it pointing in exactly the same direction, instead of wobbling about as it might if a man was holding it. They use a special target, and measure up the distance between the various bullet-holes on it when they've finished.'

'I see,' replied the professor. 'I wonder if you would mind showing me where they were firing from?'

'Certainly, sir, it's close handy.' The range-warden led us to a firing-point near by, and pointed out the spot on which the stand had been erected.

'That's the place, sir. They were firing at number 10 target over yonder. A thousand yards it is, and wonderful accurate the new gun seemed. Shot the target to pieces they did.'

The professor made no reply, but took out his map and drew a line upon it from the firing-point to the butts. The line, when extended, led over a tract of desolate marshes until it met the river.

'There is very little danger on these ranges, it appears,' remarked the professor, with a note of annoyance in his voice. 'If a shot missed the butts altogether, it could only fall into the river, far away from any frequented spot.'

'That's what they were laid out for,' replied the range-warden. 'You see, on the other side there's a house or two, to say nothing of the road and the railway. It wouldn't do to have any stray rounds falling among them.'

'It certainly would not,' replied the professor absently. 'I see by the map that Rainham station is not far beyond the end of the ranges. Is there any objection to my walking to it past the butts?'

'None at all, sir, it's the best way to get there when there's no firing on. Thank you, sir, it's been no trouble at all.'

We started to walk down the ranges, a puzzled frown on the professor's face. Every few yards he stopped and examined the country through his glasses, or pulled out the map and stared at it with an absorbed expression. We had reached the butts before he said a word, and then it was not until we had climbed to the top of them that he spoke.

'Very puzzling, very!' he muttered. 'There must, of course, be some explanation. A mathematical deduction from facts can never be false. But I wish I could discover the explanation.'

He was looking through his field-glasses as he spoke, and suddenly his attention became riveted upon an object in front of him. Without waiting for me he hurried down the steep sides of the butts, and almost ran towards a flagstaff standing a couple of hundred yards on the far side of them. When he arrived at the base of it, he drew a couple of lines on the map, walked half round the flagstaff and gazed intently through his glasses. By the time I had caught up with him he had put the glasses back in their case, and was smiling benevolently.

'We can return to town by the next train, my boy,' he said cheerfully. 'I have ascertained everything I wished to know.'

He refused to say a word until our train was running into Fenchurch Street station. Then suddenly he turned to me.

'I am going to the War Office,' he said curtly. 'Will you go to Scotland Yard, see Inspector Hanslet, and ask him to come to Westbourne Terrace as soon as he can?'

I found Hanslet, after some little trouble, and gave him the professor's message.

'Something to do with the Farquharson business, I suppose?' he replied. 'Well, I'll come if the professor wants to see me. But I've got it all fixed up without his help.'

He turned up, true to his promise, and the professor greeted him with a pleasant smile.

'Good evening, inspector, I'm glad you were able to come. Will you be particularly busy tomorrow morning?'

'I don't think so, professor,' replied Hanslet in a puzzled voice. 'Do you want me to do anything?'

'Well, if you can spare the time, I should like to introduce you to the murderer of Mr Farquharson,' said the professor casually.

Hanslet lay back in his chair and laughed. 'Thanks very much, professor, but I've met him already,' he replied. 'It would be a waste of your time, I'm afraid.'

'Never mind,' said the professor, with a tolerant smile. 'I assure you that it will be worth your while to spend the morning with me. Will you meet me by the bookstall at Charing Cross at half-past ten?'

Hanslet reflected for a moment. The professor had never yet led him on a wild-goose chase, and it might be worth while to humour him.

'All right,' he replied reluctantly. 'I'll come. But I warn you it's no good.'

The professor smiled, but said nothing. Hanslet took his leave of us, and the professor appeared to put all thought of the Farquharson case out of his head.

24

We met again at Charing Cross the next day. The professor had taken tickets to Woolwich, and we got out of the train there and walked to the gates of the arsenal. The professor took an official letter out of his pocket, which he gave to the porter. In a few minutes we were led to an office, where a young officer rose to greet us.

'Good morning, Doctor Priestley,' he said. 'Colonel Conyngham rang me up to say that you were coming. You want to see the stand we use for testing the new automatic rifle? It happens to be in the yard below, being repaired.'

'Being repaired?' repeated the professor quickly. 'May I ask what is the matter with it?'

'Oh, nothing serious. We used it at Rainham the other day, and the clamp broke just as we were finishing a series. We had fired ninety-nine rounds out of a hundred, when the muzzle of the gun slipped up. I don't know what happened to the round. I suppose it went into the river somewhere. Beastly nuisance, we shall have to go down and start all over again.'

'Ah!' exclaimed the professor, in a satisfied tone. 'That explains it. But I wouldn't use number 10 target again, if I were you. Can we see this stand?'

'Certainly,' replied the officer. 'Come along.'

He led us into the yard, where a sort of tripod with a clamp at the head of it was standing. The professor looked at it earnestly for some moments, then turned to Hanslet.

25

'There you see the murderer of Mr Farquharson,' he said quietly.

Of course Hanslet, the officer, and myself bombarded him with questions, which he refused to answer until we had returned to London and were seated in his study. Then, fixing his eyes upon the ceiling and putting the tips of his fingers together, he began.

'It was, to any intelligent man, perfectly obvious that there are half a dozen reasons why young Halliday could not have shot his uncle. In the first place, he must have fired at very close range, from one side or other of the carriage, and a rifle bullet fired at such a range, although it very often makes a very extensive wound of entry, does not stay in a man's brain. It travels right through his head, with very slightly diminished velocity. Next, if Halliday fired at his uncle at all, it must have been from the left-hand side of the carriage. Had he fired from the right-hand side, the muzzle of the weapon would have been almost touching his victim, and there would have been signs of burning or blackening round the wound. Do you admit this, inspector?'

'Of course,' replied Hanslet. 'My theory always has been that he fired from the left-hand side.'

'Very well,' said the professor quickly. 'Now Halliday is notoriously a very bad shot, hence his journey to Purfleet. Harold, on the contrary, is a good shot. Yet, during our expedition of yesterday, I asked him to aim at my right eye with a stick while the train was in motion. I found that never for an instant could he point the stick at it. I find it impossible to believe that a bad shot, firing from the footboard and therefore compelled to use one hand at least to retain his hold, could shoot a man on the far side of the carriage exactly on the temple.'

The professor paused, and Hanslet looked at him doubtfully.

'It all sounds very plausible, professor, but until you can produce a better explanation I shall continue to believe that my own is the correct one.'

'Exactly. It was to verify a theory which I had formed that I carried out my investigations. It was perfectly obvious to me, from your description of the wound, that it had been inflicted by a bullet very near the end of its flight, and therefore possessing only enough velocity to penetrate the skull without passing through it. This meant that it had been fired from a considerable distance away. Upon consulting the map, I discovered that there were two rifle ranges near the railway between London and Tilbury. I could not help feeling that the source of the bullet was probably one of these ranges. It was, at all events, a possibility worth investigating.

'But at the outset I was faced with what seemed an insuperable objection. I deduced from the map, a deduction subsequently verified by examination of the ground, that a round fired at any of the targets on either range would take a direction away from the railway. I also discovered that the only rounds fired while the train in which Mr Farquharson's body was found was passing the ranges were by an experimental party from the arsenal. This party employed a special device which eliminated any inaccuracy due to the human element. At this point it occurred to me that my theory was incapable of proof, although I still adhered to my view that it was correct.'

The professor paused and Hanslet ventured to remark:

'I still do not see how you can prove that the breakage of the clamp could have been responsible,' he said. 'The direction of the bullet remained the same, and only its elevation was affected. By your own showing, the last shot fired from the machine must have landed in the marshes or the river.'

'I knew very well that notwithstanding the apparent impossibility, this must have been the bullet which killed Mr Farquharson,' replied the professor equably. 'I climbed the butts behind the target at which the arsenal party had been firing, and while there I made an interesting discovery which solved the difficulty at once. Directly in line with number 10 target and some distance behind it was a flagstaff. Further, upon examination of this flagstaff I discovered that it was made of steel.

'Now the map had told me that there was only a short stretch of line upon which a train could he struck by a bullet deflected by this flagstaff. If this had indeed been the case, I knew exactly where to look for traces, and at my first inspection I found them. High up on the staff is a scar where the paint has recently been removed. To my mind the cause of Mr Farquharson's death is adequately explained.'

Hanslet whistled softly. 'By Jove, there's something in it!' he exclaimed. 'Your theory, I take it, is that Farquharson was struck by a bullet deflected by the flagstaff?'

'Of course,' replied the professor. 'He was sitting on the right-hand side of the carriage, facing the engine. He was struck on the right side of the head, which supports the theory of a bullet coming through the open window. A bullet deflected in this way usually turns over and over for the rest of its flight, which accounts for the size of the wound. Have you any objection to offer?'

'Not at the moment,' said Hanslet cautiously. 'I shall have to verify all these facts, of course. For one thing, I must take the bullet to the arsenal and see if it is one of the same type as the experimental party were using.'

'Verify everything you can, certainly,' replied the professor. 'But remember that facts, not conjecture, are what should guide you.'

Hanslet nodded. 'I'll remember, professor,' he said. And with that he left us.

Two days later Mary announced Miss Farquharson and Mr Halliday. They entered the room, and Halliday walked straight up to the professor and grasped his hand.

'You have rendered me the greatest service one man can render to another, sir!' he exclaimed. 'Inspector Hanslet tells me that all suspicion that I murdered my uncle has been cleared away, and that this is due entirely to your efforts.'

Before the professor could reply, Miss Farquharson ran up to him and kissed him impulsively. 'Doctor Priestley, you're a darling!' she exclaimed.

The professor beamed at her through his spectacles. 'Really, my dear, you make me feel quite sorry that you are going to marry this young man,' he said.

THE ADVENTURE OF THE WORST MAN IN LONDON

SIR ARTHUR CONAN DOYLE

From Westbourne Grove, the walk to the address of the most famous detective of all is almost exactly a mile along Harrow Road and Marylebone Road to a turning within sight of the Planetarium and Madame Tussaud's Exhibition. Here, at 221B Baker Street, Sherlock Holmes—'consulting detective' according to his visiting card—lived and received those in trouble who came to enlist his extraordinary powers of observation and deduction. Almost invariably his close friend and companion, Doctor Watson, would be in attendance as well as their long-suffering housekeeper, Mrs Hudson. Although the site of 221B is generally thought to be that now occupied by the Abbey National Building Society, according to Edgar Wallace who once walked the length of Baker Street with Holmes' creator, Sir Arthur Conan Doyle (1859–1930), Doyle indicated he envisaged it on the opposite side of the road near the corner formed with George Street. (Interestingly, Granada Television also opted for this position when building their impressive reconstruction of Baker Street for the series of Sherlock Holmes

31

adventures starring the late Jeremy Brett which ran for ten years.)

There is, of course, no doubt about Holmes himself: his image was set by Sidney Paget in the Strand magazine, and all his attributes and foibles—from a predilection for drugs to a retirement plan rearing bees—have not only been carefully recorded by Dr Watson in the novels and short stories, but studied and argued over endlessly by Sherlockians all over the world. The sleuth of Baker Street is without doubt one of the world's immortals and so real is he to some people that the Abbey National employs a secretary to answer the mail which arrives each day addressed to 'Sherlock Holmes Esq' requesting his assistance in every kind of problem from the loss of a pet to the whereabouts of buried treasure! No mean accolade to a detective who never lived.

This story about Holmes is not, as some keen-eyed Sherlockians might think, a lost adventure because of the unfamiliar title, but the account of the detective's confrontation with another of his great adversaries, Charles Augustus Milverton. The reason for this title change is that it is the original one Conan Doyle wrote on his manuscript in 1904 and then crossed out to insert the more familiar 'Adventure of Charles Augustus Milverton'. I have this on the authority of the Holmesian expert Edgar W. Smith who owns the original holograph manuscript: 'On page one of this MS, Dr Doyle first wrote "The

Adventure of the Worst Man in London" then (how much later I do not know) he crossed this out and substituted the title eventually used for publication. I think this was definitely a change for the worse!' Most people would agree, and whether Doyle made the change of his own volition or on the instructions of the Editor of the Strand, I have no hesitation in restoring the original here. Milverton, whom Holmes described unequivocally as the 'worst man in London', lived in some style in Hampstead from where he exercised his power as the king of blackmailers. He had extorted thousands of pounds from unfortunate victims without the law being able to lay a finger on him—that is until Holmes was brought into the case. The story has been filmed several times, but undoubtedly the best version was the two-hour adaptation by Granada in 1992 with Robert Hardy as an evil, malevolent Milverton. It was also unique in that Jeremy Brett's Holmes was called upon to kiss a servant girl as part of his ploy to wheedle information from her—a scene which made newspaper stories worldwide! The story itself is all the more intriguing because Doyle admitted he based Milverton on a notorious Victorian blackmailer named Charles Augustus Howell who had earlier been found murdered in Chelsea—a fact which probably spared the author receiving the same treatment Howell's other victims had suffered!

It is years since the incidents of which I speak took place, and yet it is with diffidence that I allude to them. For a long time, even with the utmost discretion and reticence, it would have been impossible to make the facts public; but now the principal person concerned is beyond the reach of human law, and with due suppression the story may be told in such fashion as to injure no one. It records an absolutely unique experience in the career both of Mr Sherlock Holmes and of myself. The reader will excuse me if I conceal the date or any other fact by which he might trace the actual occurrence.

We had been out for one of our evening rambles, Holmes and I, and had returned about six o'clock on a cold, frosty winter's evening. As Holmes turned up the lamp the light fell upon a card on the table. He glanced at it, and then, with an ejaculation of disgust, threw it on the floor. I picked it up and read:

CHARLES AUGUSTUS MILVERTON,
APPLEDORE TOWERS,
HAMSTEAD.

Agent.

'Who is he?' I asked.

'The worst man in London,' Holmes answered, as he sat down and stretched his

34

legs before the fire. 'Is anything on the back of the card?'

I turned it over.

'Will call at 6.30—C.A.M.,' I read.

'Hum! He's about due. Do you feel a creeping, shrinking sensation, Watson, when you stand before the serpents in the Zoo and see the slithery, gliding, venomous creatures, with their deadly eyes and wicked, flattened faces? Well, that's how Milverton impresses me. I've had to do with fifty murderers in my career, but the worst of them never gave me the repulsion which I have for this fellow. And yet I can't get out of doing business with him— indeed, he is here at my invitation.'

'But who is he?'

'I'll tell you, Watson. He is the king of all the blackmailers. Heaven help the man, and still more the woman, whose secret and reputation come into the power of Milverton. With a smiling face and a heart of marble he will squeeze and squeeze until he has drained them dry. The fellow is a genius in his way, and would have made his mark in some more savoury trade. His method is as follows: He allows it to be known that he is prepared to pay very high sums for letters which compromise people of wealth or position. He receives these wares not only from treacherous valets or maids, but frequently from genteel ruffians who have gained the confidence and affection of trusting women. He deals with no niggard hand. I happen to know that he paid seven hundred pounds to a footman for a note two lines in length, and that the ruin of a noble family was the result. Everything which is in the market goes to Milverton, and there are hundreds in this great city who turn white at his name. No one knows where his grip may fall, for he is far too rich and far too cunning to work from hand to mouth. He will hold a card back for years in order to play it at the moment when the stake is best worth winning. I have said that he is the worst man in London, and I would ask you how could one compare the ruffian who in hot blood bludgeons his mate, with this man, who methodically and at his leisure tortures the soul and wrings the nerves in order to add to his already swollen money-bags?'

I had seldom heard my friend speak with such intensity of feeling.

'But surely,' said I, 'the fellow must be within the grasp of the law?'

'Technically, no doubt, but practically not. What would it profit a woman, for example, to get him a few months' imprisonment if her own ruin must immediately follow? His victims dare not hit back. If ever he blackmailed an innocent person, then, indeed, we should have him; but he is as cunning as the Evil One. No, no; we must find other ways to fight him.'

'And why is he here?'

'Because an illustrious client has placed her

piteous case in my hands. It is the Lady Eva Brackwell, the most beautiful *débutante* of last season. She is to be married in a fortnight to the Earl of Dovercourt. This fiend has several imprudent letters—imprudent, Watson, nothing worse—which were written to an impecunious young squire in the country. They would suffice to break off the match. Milverton will send the letters to the earl unless a large sum of money is paid him. I have been commissioned to meet him, and—to make the best terms I can.'

At that instant there was a clatter and a rattle in the street below. Looking down I saw a stately carriage and pair, the brilliant lamps gleaming on the glossy haunches of the noble chestnuts. A footman opened the door, and a small, stout man in a shaggy astrachan overcoat descended. A minute later he was in the room.

Charles Augustus Milverton was a man of fifty, with a large, intellectual head, a round, plump, hairless face, a perpetual frozen smile, and two keen grey eyes, which gleamed brightly from behind broad, golden-rimmed glasses. There was something of Mr Pickwick's benevolence in his appearance, marred only by the insincerity of the fixed smile and by the hard glitter of those restless and penetrating eyes. His voice was as smooth and suave as his countenance, as he advanced with a plump little hand extended, murmuring his regret for having missed us at his first visit.

Holmes disregarded the outstretched hand and looked at him with a face of granite. Milverton's smile broadened; he shrugged his shoulders, removed his overcoat, folded it with great deliberation over the back of a chair, and then took a seat.

'This gentleman,' said he, with a wave in my direction. 'Is it discreet? Is it right?'

'Dr Watson is my friend and partner.'

'Very good, Mr Holmes. It is only in your client's interests that I protested. The matter is so very delicate—'

'Dr Watson has already heard of it.'

'Then we can proceed to business. You say that you are acting for Lady Eva. Has she empowered you to accept my terms?'

'What are your terms?'

'Seven thousand pounds.'

'And the alternative?'

'My dear sir, it is painful to me to discuss it; but if the money is not paid on the fourteenth there certainly will be no marriage on the eighteenth.' His insufferable smile was more complacent than ever. Holmes thought for a little.

'You appear to me,' he said at last, 'to be taking matters too much for granted. I am, of course, familiar with the contents of these letters. My client will certainly do what I may advise. I shall counsel her to tell her future husband the whole story and to trust to his generosity.'

Milverton chuckled.

'You evidently do not know the earl,' said he.

From the baffled look upon Holmes' face I could clearly see that he did.

'What harm is there in the letters?' he asked.

'They are sprightly—very sprightly,' Milverton answered. 'The lady was a charming correspondent. But I can assure you that the Earl of Dovercourt would fail to appreciate them. However, since you think otherwise, we will let it rest at that. It is purely a matter of business. If you think that it is in the best interests of your client that these letters should be placed in the hands of the earl, then you would indeed be foolish to pay so large a sum of money to regain them.' He rose and seized his astrachan coat.

Holmes was grey with anger and mortification.

'Wait a little,' he said. 'You go too fast. We would certainly make every effort to avoid scandal in so delicate a matter.'

Milverton relapsed into his chair.

'I was sure that you would see it in that light,' he purred.

'At the same time,' Holmes continued, 'Lady Eva is not a wealthy woman. I assure you that two thousand pounds would be a drain upon her resources, and that the sum you name is utterly beyond her power. I beg, therefore, that you will moderate your demands, and that you will return the letters at the price I indicate, which is, I assure you, the highest that you can get.'

Milverton's smile broadened and his eyes twinkled humorously.

'I am aware that what you say is true about the lady's resources,' said he. 'At the same time, you must admit that the occasion of a lady's marriage is a very suitable time for her friends and relatives to make some little effort upon her behalf. They may hesitate as to an acceptable wedding present. Let me assure them that this little bundle of letters would give more joy than all the candelabra and butter-dishes in London.'

'It is impossible,' said Holmes.

'Dear me, dear me, how unfortunate!' cried Milverton, taking out a bulky pocket-book. 'I cannot help thinking that ladies are ill-advised in not making an effort. Look at this!' He held up a little note with a coat-of-arms upon the envelope. 'That belongs to—well, perhaps it is hardly fair to tell the name until tomorrow morning. But at that time it will be in the hands of the lady's husband. And all because she will not find a beggarly sum which she could get in an hour by turning her diamonds into paste. It *is* such a pity. Now, you remember the sudden end of the engagement between the Honourable Miss Miles and Colonel Dorking? Only two days before the wedding there was a paragraph in the *Morning Post* to say that it was all off. And why? It is almost incredible, but the absurd sum of twelve hundred pounds would have settled the whole question. Is it not pitiful? And there I find you, a man of sense, boggling about terms when your client's future and honour are at stake. You surprise me, Mr Holmes.'

'What I say is true,' Holmes answered. 'The money cannot be found. Surely it is better for you to take the substantial sum which I offer than to ruin this woman's career, which can profit you in no way?'

'There you make a mistake, Mr Holmes. An exposure would profit me indirectly to a considerable extent. I have eight or ten similar cases maturing. If it was circulated among them that I had made a severe example of the Lady Eva I should find all of them much more open to reason. You see my point?'

Holmes sprang from his chair.

'Get behind him, Watson. Don't let him out! Now, sir, let us see the contents of that notebook.'

Milverton had glided as quick as a rat to the side of the room, and stood with his back against the wall.

'Mr Holmes, Mr Holmes!' he said, turning the front of his coat and exhibiting the butt of a large revolver, which projected from the inside pocket. 'I have been expecting you to do something original. This has been done so

41

often, and what good has ever come from it? I assure you that I am armed to the teeth, and I am perfectly prepared to use my weapon, knowing that the law will support me. Besides, your supposition that I would bring the letters here in a notebook is entirely mistaken. I would do nothing so foolish. And now, gentlemen, I have one or two little interviews this evening, and it is a long drive to Hampstead.' He stepped forward, took up his coat, laid his hand on his revolver, and turned to the door. I picked up a chair, but Holmes shook his head, and I laid it down again. With a bow, a smile, and a twinkle Milverton was out of the room, and a few moments after we heard the slam of the carriage door and the rattle of the wheels as he drove away. Holmes sat motionless by the fire, his hands buried deep in his trouser pockets, his chin sunk upon his breast, his eyes fixed upon the glowing embers. For half an hour he was silent and still. Then, with the gesture of a man who has taken his decision, he sprang to his feet and passed into his bedroom. A little later a rakish young workman with a goatee beard and a swagger lit his clay pipe at the lamp before descending into the street. 'I'll be back some time, Watson,' said he, and vanished into the night. I understood that he had opened his campaign against Charles Augustus Milverton; but I little dreamed the strange shape which that campaign was destined to take.

For some days Holmes came and went at all hours in this attire, but beyond a remark that his time was spent at Hampstead, and that it was not wasted, I knew nothing of what he was doing. At last, however, on a wild, tempestuous evening, when the wind screamed and rattled against the windows, he returned from his last expedition, and, having removed his disguise, he sat before the fire and laughed heartily in his silent, inward fashion.

'You would not call me a marrying man, Watson?'

'No, indeed!'

'You will be interested to hear that I am engaged.'

'My dear fellow! I congrat—'

'To Milverton's housemaid.'

'Good heavens, Holmes!'

'I wanted information, Watson.'

'Surely you have gone too far?'

'It was a most necessary step. I am a plumber with a rising business, Escott by name. I have walked out with her each evening, and I have talked with her. Good heavens, those talks! However, I have got all I wanted. I know Milverton's house as I know the palm of my hand.'

'But the girl, Holmes?'

He shrugged his shoulders.

'You can't help it, my dear Watson. You must play your cards as best you can when such a stake is on the table. However, I rejoice to say that I have a hated rival who will certainly cut me out the instant that my back is turned. What a splendid night it is!'

'You like this weather?'

'It suits my purpose. Watson, I mean to burgle Milverton's house tonight.'

I had a catching of the breath, and my skin went cold at the words, which were slowly uttered in a tone of concentrated resolution. As a flash of lightning in the night shows up in an instant every detail of a wide landscape, so at one glance I seemed to see every possible result of such an action—the detection, the capture, the honoured career ending in irreparable failure and disgrace, my friend himself lying at the mercy of the odious Milverton.

'For Heaven's sake, Holmes, think what you are doing!' I cried.

'My dear fellow, I have given it every consideration. I am never precipitate in my actions, nor would I adopt so energetic and indeed so dangerous a course if any other were possible. Let us look at the matter clearly and fairly. I suppose that you will admit that the action is morally justifiable, though technically criminal. To burgle his house is no more than to forcibly take his pocket-book—an action in which you were prepared to aid me.'

I turned it over in my mind.

'Yes,' I said, 'it is morally justifiable so long as our object is to take no articles save those which are used for an illegal purpose.'

'Exactly. Since it is morally justifiable, I have only to consider the question of personal risk. Surely a gentleman should not lay much stress upon this when a lady is in most desperate need of his help?'

'You will be in such a false position.'

'Well, that is part of the risk. There is no other possible way of regaining these letters. The unfortunate lady has not the money, and there are none of her people in whom she could confide. Tomorrow is the last day of grace, and unless we can get the letters tonight this villain will be as good as his word, and will bring about her ruin. I must, therefore, abandon my client to her fate, or I must play this last card. Between ourselves, Watson, it's a sporting duel between this fellow Milverton and me. He had, as you saw, the best of the first exchanges; but my self-respect and my reputation are concerned to fight it to a finish.'

'Well, I don't like it; but I suppose it must be,' said I. 'When do we start?'

'You are not coming.'

'Then you are not going,' said I. 'I give you my word of honour—and I never broke it in my life—that I will take a cab straight to the police-station and give you away unless you let me share this adventure with you.'

'You can't help me.'

'How do you know that? You can't tell what may happen. Anyway, my resolution is taken. Other people besides you have self-respect and even reputations.'

Holmes had looked annoyed, but his brow cleared, and he clapped me on the shoulder.

'Well, well, my dear fellow, be it so. We have shared the same room for some years, and it would be amusing if we ended by sharing the same cell. You know, Watson, I don't mind confessing to you that I have always had an idea that I would have made a highly efficient criminal. This is the chance of my lifetime in that direction. See here!' He took a neat little leather case out of a drawer, and opening it he exhibited a number of shining instruments. 'This is a first-class, up-to-date burgling kit, with nickel-plated jemmy, diamond-tipped glass cutter, adaptable keys, and every modern improvement which the march of civilization demands. Here, too, is my dark lantern. Everything is in order. Have you a pair of silent shoes?'

'I have rubber-soled tennis shoes.'

'Excellent. And a mask?'

'I can make a couple out of black silk.'

'I can see that you have a strong natural turn for this sort of thing. Very good; do you make the masks. We shall have some cold supper before we start. It is now nine-thirty. At eleven we shall drive as far as Church Row. It is a quarter of an hour's walk from there to Appledore Towers. We shall be at work before midnight. Milverton is a heavy sleeper, and retires punctually at ten-thirty. With any luck

46

we should be back here by two, with the Lady Eva's letters in my pocket.'

Holmes and I put on our dress-clothes, so that we might appear to be two theatre-goers homeward bound. In Oxford Street we picked up a hansom and drove to an address in Hampstead. Here we paid off our cab, and with our great-coats buttoned up—for it was bitterly cold, and the wind seemed to blow through us—we walked along the edge of the Heath.

'It's a business that needs delicate treatment,' said Holmes. 'These documents are contained in a safe in the fellow's study, and the study is the ante-room of his bedchamber. On the other hand, like all these stout, little men who do themselves well, he is a plethoric sleeper. Agatha—that's my fiancée—says it is a joke in the servants' hall that it's impossible to wake the master. He has a secretary who is devoted to his interests, and never budges from the study all day. That's why we are going at night. Then he has a beast of a dog which roams the garden. I met Agatha late the last two evenings, and she locks the brute up so as to give me a clear run. This is the house, this big one in its own grounds. Through the gate— now to the right among the laurels. We might put on our masks here, I think. You see, there is not a glimmer of light in any of the windows, and everything is working splendidly.'

With our black silk face-coverings, which

47

turned us into two of the most truculent figures in London, we stole up to the silent, gloomy house. A sort of tiled veranda extended along one side of it, lined by several windows and two doors.

'That's his bedroom,' Holmes whispered. 'This door opens straight into the study. It would suit us best, but it is bolted as well as locked, and we should make too much noise getting in. Come round here. There's a greenhouse which opens into the drawing-room.'

The place was locked, but Holmes removed a circle of glass and turned the key from the inside. An instant afterwards he had closed the door behind us, and we had become felons in the eyes of the law. The thick warm air of the conservatory and the rich, choking fragrance of exotic plants took us by the throat. He seized my hand in the darkness and led me swiftly past banks of shrubs which brushed against our faces. Holmes had remarkable powers, carefully cultivated, of seeing in the dark. Still holding my hand in one of his, he opened a door, and I was vaguely conscious that we had entered a large room in which a cigar had been smoked not long before. He felt his way among the furniture, opened another door, and closed it behind us. Putting out my hand I felt several coats hanging from the wall, and I understood that I was in a passage. We passed along it, and Holmes very gently opened a door upon the right-hand side. Something rushed out at us, and my heart sprang into my mouth, but I could have laughed when I realized that it was the cat. A fire was burning in this new room, and again the air was heavy with tobacco smoke. Holmes entered on tiptoe, waited for me to follow, and then very gently closed the door. We were in Milverton's study, and a *portière* at the farther side showed the entrance to his bedroom.

It was a good fire, and the room was illuminated by it. Near the door I saw the gleam of an electric switch, but it was unnecessary, even if it had been safe, to turn it on. At one side of the fireplace was a heavy curtain, which covered the bay window we had seen from outside. On the other side was the door which communicated with the veranda. A desk stood in the centre, with a turning chair of shining red leather. Opposite was a large bookcase, with a marble bust of Athene on the top. In the corner between the bookcase and the wall there stood a tall green safe, the firelight flashing back from the polished brass knobs upon its face. Holmes stole across and looked at it. Then he crept to the door of the bedroom, and stood with slanting head listening intently. No sound came from within. Meanwhile it had struck me that it would be wise to secure our retreat through the outer door, so I examined it. To my amazement it was neither locked nor bolted! I touched

Holmes on the arm, and he turned his masked face in that direction. I saw him start, and he was evidently as surprised as I.

'I don't like it,' he whispered, putting his lips to my very ear. 'I can't quite make it out. Anyhow, we have no time to lose.'

'Can I do anything?'

'Yes; stand by the door. If you hear anyone come, bolt it on the inside, and we can get away as we came. If they come the other way, we can get through the door if our job is done, or hide behind these window curtains if it is not. Do you understand?'

I nodded and stood by the door. My first feeling of fear had passed away, and I thrilled now with a keener zest than I had ever enjoyed when we were the defenders of the law instead of its defiers. The high object of our mission, the consciousness that it was unselfish and chivalrous, the villainous character of our opponent, all added to the sporting interest of the adventure. Far from feeling guilty, I rejoiced and exulted in our dangers. With a glow of admiration I watched Holmes unrolling his case of instruments and choosing his tool with the calm, scientific accuracy of a surgeon who performs a delicate operation. I knew that the opening of safes was a particular hobby with him, and I understood the joy which it gave him to be confronted with this green and gold monster, the dragon which held in its maw the reputations of many fair ladies.

Turning up the cuffs of his dress-coat—he had placed his overcoat on a chair—Holmes laid out two drills, a jemmy, and several skeleton keys. I stood at the centre door with my eyes glancing at each of the others, ready for any emergency; though, indeed, my plans were somewhat vague as to what I should do if we were interrupted. For half an hour Holmes worked with concentrated energy, laying down one tool, picking up another, handling each with the strength and delicacy of the trained mechanic. Finally I heard a click, the broad green door swung open, and inside I had a glimpse of a number of paper packets, each tied, sealed, and inscribed. Holmes picked one out, but it was hard to read by the flickering fire, and he drew out his little dark lantern, for it was too dangerous, with Milverton in the next room, to switch on the electric light. Suddenly I saw him halt, listen intently, and then in an instant he had swung the door of the safe to, picked up his coat, stuffed his tools into the pockets, and darted behind the window curtain, motioning me to do the same.

It was only when I had joined him there that I heard what had alarmed his quicker senses. There was a noise somewhere within the house. A door slammed in the distance. Then a confused, dull murmur broke itself into the measured thud of heavy footsteps rapidly approaching. They were in the passage outside the room. They paused at the door. The door opened. There was a sharp snick as the electric light was turned on. The door closed once more, and the pungent reek of a strong cigar was borne to our nostrils. Then the footsteps continued backwards and forwards, backwards and forwards, within a few yards of us. Finally, there was a creak from a chair, and the footsteps ceased. Then a key clicked in a lock, and I heard the rustle of papers. So far I had not dared to look out, but now I gently parted the division of the curtains in front of me and peeped through. From the pressure of Holmes' shoulder against mine I knew that he was sharing my observations. Right in front of us, and almost within our reach, was the broad, rounded back of Milverton. It was evident that we had entirely miscalculated his movements, that he had never been to his bedroom, but that he had been sitting up in some smoking- or billiard-room in the farther wing of the house, the windows of which we had not seen. His broad, grizzled head, with its shining patch of baldness, was in the immediate foreground of our vision. He was leaning far back in the red leather chair, his legs outstretched, a long black cigar projecting at an angle from his mouth. He wore a semi-military smoking-jacket, claret-coloured, with a black velvet collar. In his hand he held a long legal document, which he was reading in an indolent fashion, blowing rings of tobacco smoke from his lip as he did so. There was no promise of a speedy departure in his composed bearing and his comfortable attitude.

I felt Holmes' hand steal into mine and give me a reassuring shake, as if to say that the situation was within his powers, and that he was easy in his mind. I was not sure whether he had seen what was only too obvious from my position—that the door of the safe was imperfectly closed, and that Milverton might at any moment observe it. In my own mind I had determined that if I were sure, from the rigidity of his gaze, that it had caught his eye, I would at once spring out, throw my greatcoat over his head, pinion him, and leave the rest to Holmes. But Milverton never looked up. He was languidly interested by the papers in his hand, and page after page was turned as he followed the argument of the lawyer. At least, I thought, when he has finished the document and the cigar he will go to his room; but before he had reached the end of either there came a remarkable development which turned our thoughts into quite another channel.

Several times I had observed that Milverton looked at his watch, and once he had risen and sat down again, with a gesture of impatience. The idea, however, that he might have an appointment at so strange an hour never occurred to me until a faint sound reached my ears from the veranda outside. Milverton dropped his papers and sat rigid in his chair. The sound was repeated, and then there came a gentle tap at the door. Milverton rose and opened it.

'Well,' said he curtly, 'you are nearly half an hour late.'

So this was the explanation of the unlocked door and of the nocturnal vigil of Milverton. There was the gentle rustle of a woman's dress. I had closed the slit between the curtains as Milverton's face turned in our direction, but now I ventured very carefully to open it once more. He had resumed his seat, the cigar still projecting at an insolent angle from the corner of his mouth. In front of him, in the full glare of the electric light, there stood a tall, slim, dark woman, a veil over her face, a mantle drawn round her chin. Her breath came quick and fast, and every inch of the lithe figure was quivering with strong emotion.

'Well,' said Milverton, 'you've made me lose a good night's rest, my dear. I hope you'll prove worth it. You couldn't come any other time—eh?'

The woman shook her head.

'Well, if you couldn't you couldn't. If the countess is a hard mistress you have your chance to get level with her now. Bless the girl, what are you shivering about? That's right! Pull yourself together! Now, let us get down to business.' He took a note from the drawer of his desk. 'You say that you have five letters which compromise the Countess d'Albert. You want to sell them. I want to buy them. So far so good. It only remains to fix a price. I should want to inspect the letters, of course. If they are really good specimens—Great heavens, is it you?'

The woman without a word had raised her veil and dropped the mantle from her chin. It was a 'dark, handsome, clear-cut face which confronted Milverton, a face with a curved nose, strong, dark eyebrows, shading hard, glittering eyes, and a straight, thin-lipped mouth set in a dangerous smile.

'It is I,' she said, 'the woman whose life you have ruined.'

Milverton laughed, but fear vibrated in his voice. 'You were so very obstinate,' said he. 'Why did you drive me to such extremities? I assure you I wouldn't hurt a fly of my own accord, but every man has his business, and what was I to do? I put the price well within your means. You would not pay.'

'So you sent the letters to my husband, and he—the noblest gentleman that ever lived, a man whose boots I was never worthy to lace—he broke his gallant heart and died. You remember that last night when I came through that door I begged and prayed you for mercy, and you laughed in my face as you are trying to laugh now, only your coward heart cannot keep your lips from twitching? Yes; you never thought to see me here again, but it was that night which taught me how I could meet you face to face, and alone. Well, Charles

55

Milverton, what have you to say?'

'Don't imagine that you can bully me,' said he, rising to his feet. 'I have only to raise my voice, and I could call my servants and have you arrested. But I will make allowance for your natural anger. Leave the room at once as you came, and I will say no more.'

The woman stood with her hand buried in her bosom, and the same deadly smile on her thin lips.

'You will ruin no more lives as you ruined mine. You will wring no more hearts as you wrung mine. I will free the world of a poisonous thing. Take that, you hound, and that!—and that!—and that!—and that!'

She had drawn a little gleaming revolver, and emptied barrel after barrel into Milverton's body, the muzzle within two feet of his shirt-front. He shrank away, and then fell forward upon the table, coughing furiously and clawing among the papers. Then he staggered to his feet, received another shot, and rolled upon the floor. 'You've done me,' he cried, and lay still. The woman looked at him intently and ground her heel into his upturned face. She looked again, but there was no sound or movement. I heard a sharp rustle, the night air blew into the heated room, and the avenger was gone.

No interference upon our part could have saved the man from his fate; but as the woman poured bullet after bullet into Milverton's

56

shrinking body, I was about to spring out, when I felt Holmes' cold, strong grasp upon my wrist. I understood the whole argument of that firm, restraining grip—that it was no affair of ours; that justice had overtaken a villain; that we had our own duties and our own objects which were not to be lost sight of. But hardly had the woman rushed from the room when Holmes, with swift, silent steps, was over at the other door. He turned the key in the lock. At the same instant we heard voices in the house and the sound of hurrying feet. The revolver shots had roused the household. With perfect coolness Holmes slipped across to the safe, filled his two arms with bundles of letters, and poured them all into the fire. Again and again he did it, until the safe was empty. Someone turned the handle and beat upon the outside of the door. Holmes looked swiftly round. The letter which had been the messenger of death for Milverton lay, all mottled with his blood, upon the table. Holmes tossed it in among the blazing papers. Then he drew the key from the outer door, passed through after me, and locked it on the outside. 'This way, Watson,' said he, 'we can scale the garden wall in this direction.'

I could not have believed that an alarm could have spread so swiftly. Looking back, the huge house was one blaze of light. The front door was open, and figures were rushing down the drive. The whole garden was alive with people, and one fellow raised a view-halloa as we emerged from the veranda and followed hard at our heels. Holmes seemed to know the ground perfectly, and he threaded his way swiftly among a plantation of small trees, I close at his heels, and our foremost pursuer panting behind us. It was a six-foot wall which barred our path, but he sprang to the top and over. As I did the same I felt the hand of the man behind me grab at my ankle; but I kicked myself free, and scrambled over a glass-strewn coping. I fell upon my face among some bushes; but Holmes had me on my feet in an instant, and together we dashed away across the huge expanse of Hampstead Heath. We had run two miles, I suppose, before Holmes at last halted and listened intently. All was absolutely silence behind us. We had shaken off our pursuers, and were safe.

*　　　*　　　*

We had breakfasted and were smoking our morning pipe, on the day after the remarkable experience which I have recorded, when Mr Lestrade, of Scotland Yard, very solemn and impressive, was ushered into our modest sitting-room.

'Good morning, Mr Holmes,' said he, 'good morning. May I ask if you are very busy just now?'

'Not too busy to listen to you.'

'I thought that, perhaps, if you had nothing particular on hand, you might care to assist us in a most remarkable case which occurred only last night at Hampstead.'

'Dear me!' said Holmes. 'What was that?'

'A murder—a most dramatic and remarkable murder. I know how keen you are upon these things, and I would take it as a great favour if you would step down to Appledore Towers and give us the benefit of your advice. It is no ordinary crime. We have had our eyes upon this Mr Milverton for some time, and, between ourselves, he was a bit of a villain. He is known to have held papers which he used for blackmailing purposes. These papers have all been burned by the murderers. No article of value was taken, as it is probable that the criminals were men of good position, whose sole object was to prevent social exposure.'

'Criminals!' exclaimed Holmes. 'Plural!'

'Yes, there were two of them. They were, as nearly as possible, captured red-handed. We have their footmarks, we have their description; it's ten to one that we trace them. The first fellow was a bit too active, but the second was caught by the under-gardener, and only got away after a struggle. He was a middle-sized, strongly built man—square jaw, thick neck, moustache, a mask over his eyes.'

'That's rather vague,' said Sherlock Holmes. 'Why, it might be a description of Watson.'

'It's true,' said the Inspector, with much

amusement. 'It might be a description of Watson.'

'Well, I am afraid I can't help you, Lestrade,' said Holmes. 'The fact is that I knew this fellow Milverton, that I considered him one of the most dangerous men in London, and that I think there are certain crimes which the law cannot touch, and which therefore, to some extent, justify private revenge. No, it's no use arguing. I have made up my mind. My sympathies are with the criminals rather than with the victim, and I will not handle this case.'

* * *

Holmes had not said one word to me about the tragedy which we had witnessed, but I observed all the morning that he was in the most thoughtful mood, and he gave me the impression, from his vacant eyes and his abstracted manner, of a man who is striving to recall something to his memory. We were in the middle of our lunch, when he suddenly sprang to his feet. 'By Jove, Watson! I've got it!' he cried. 'Take your hat! Come with me!' He hurried at his top speed down Baker Street and along Oxford Street, until we had almost reached Regent Circus. Here on the left hand there stands a shop window filled with photographs of the celebrities and beauties of the day. Holmes' eyes fixed themselves upon one of them, and following his gaze I saw the picture of a regal and stately lady in Court dress, with a high diamond tiara upon her noble head. I looked at that delicately curved nose, at the marked eyebrows, at the straight mouth, and the strong little chin beneath it. Then I caught my breath as I read the time-honoured title of the great nobleman and statesman whose wife she had been. My eyes met those of Holmes, and he put his finger to his lips as we turned away from the window.

THE BOTTLE PARTY

H. C. BAILEY

Only a few minutes walk from the junction of Baker Street and George Street lies Wimpole Street, another of the famous old London thoroughfares steeped in history. It is also where Reginald Fortune, the 'specialist in the surgery of crime', lives in a flat in Montmorency House. Although he is not often referred to as 'Doctor', Reggie Fortune is actually a practising physician and surgeon whose special knowledge of medicine and the human anatomy— particularly where violence or murder may have been used upon it—has resulted in his appointment as a special adviser to Scotland Yard. Notwithstanding this, he more often than not has to take a philosophical attitude when some of his triumphs are treated with resentment in certain police quarters. A Londoner by birth, Reggie qualified as a general practitioner, but when two criminal cases were brought to his attention in quick succession he found himself set on a career for life. Something of a gourmet, his gentle manner belies a tough physique and a painstaking method of sifting evidence. His usual associates from the Yard are the chief of the C.I.D., Stanley Lomas, and his assistant, Superintendent Bell. When he does not feel it

63

will appear too ostentatious, Reggie likes nothing better than driving his Rolls-Royce around London. Over twenty books recount his cases from Call Mr Fortune *(1920) to* Saving A Rope *(1948), which have inspired historian Otto Penzler to declare that he was 'probably the most popular sleuth in England between the two world wars'.*

Fortune's creator, Henry Christopher Bailey (1878–1961), was also born in London and received a classical education at Oxford. He joined the staff of the Daily Telegraph *where he worked as a drama critic, leader writer and war correspondent before achieving popular fame with the stories of his doctor-detective in the twenties. 'The Bottle Party' (1940) reveals Fortune at his most astute when the arrest of a drunken young man leads first to hints of drug-taking and then the discovery of the body of a young woman in a car nearby...*

*   *   *

Few are the cases which have given Mr Fortune so pure a pleasure.

When Carteret Square was built on a swamp, our ancient aristocracy bid against each other for its mansions and put their horses and carriages into a foul mews on the eastern side. The square is now a colossal quadrangle of flats inhabited by the new rich. The stables of the mews have been rebuilt to make garages for some of them and little houses for those who live upon them and renamed, to preserve the dignity of all, Carteret Place.

It is a narrow, prim street, empty, when the children of the chauffeurs dwelling over the garages have been put to bed, unless some knowing creature has left a car parked in one of the bulges provided to give a turning circle for the chariots of the past. But behind the curtains of the neat houses there is often some noise at night, and policemen stroll by from hour to hour.

About eleven on a misty autumn night a constable was pacing along Carteret Place from the southern end when he heard a police whistle blow at the other. He ran upon the sound and, reaching the northern end, found another breathless officer who had heard the whistle, but no one else. They hunted highways and byways in vain. The neighbourhood is prolific in bright young things who delight to take a rise out of the police.

About one o'clock he came down Carteret Place again. The little houses were quieter than usual. But by one of them a man bumped into him and when rebuked knocked his helmet off. They had a scuffle, the man fell, the constable picked him up and dragged him off, wambling in his walk, to the station, and charged him with assault. The man seemed dazed or drunk. With difficulty the inspector got a name out of him, which was Antony Cray, put him in a cell and sent for a doctor.

At nine o'clock next morning Mr Fortune was, as usual, in his bath. Mrs Fortune opened the door and exhorted him to come out. 'Why?' He sank deeper into the water. 'Why are wives?' She turned on the cold shower. 'Not for that, no,' he moaned.

'A lady has called to see you,' she said severely.

'My dear girl! Have a heart. Not before breakfast.'

'Parker says she wouldn't go away. And she's been here nearly an hour. Her name is Valerie Milburn.'

'Not guilty. Means nothing in my young life.'

'You've seen her. She plays the blondes that gentlemen prefer.'

'An actress? Before nine a.m.? Oh no, Joan.'

'I didn't say she could act,' said Mrs Fortune.

The secret of his eminence, he likes to explain, is a capacity to dress quicker than any man, thus making time for higher things. He ate half a cold partridge before he went to his consulting-room and yet half-past nine had not struck when Valerie Milburn sat down in front of him.

The silly, pretty face of the enchantress of light comedy was not at its best. Without make-up her fair complexion looked insipid. She tried her popular, yearning glance, but the

66

smile on the pale lips was a spasm.

'Oh, Mr Fortune, how kind you are!' She used the drawl of allure with which she spoke all her parts, though her voice could put no life into it.

'Not kind, no. Only curious. Who sent you to me, Miss Milburn?'

'Nobody. I came of myself.'

'Oh! Had a bad night?'

She laughed, rather too long. 'There's nothing the matter with me. It's someone else, Tony Cray, Antony Cray, you know, he's the nephew of Lord Frome.'

'I don't. Is he ill?'

'I believe he is, Mr Fortune. It's like this. I live in Carteret Place, you know the dinky little houses there. I had a bottle party last night, starting ten o'clock. Tony—Mr Cray was there on the dot. I'm sure he shouldn't have come at all. You can back him to be on top of the world at any show, but last night nobody could get a rise out of him. He just sat and gloomed. He owned up, about one, he didn't feel too good, he'd go home. Then the ghastly thing happened. Just outside my door a policeman barged into him, the silly brute, got rough with him, said he was drunk and ran him in. They've kept him at the station, they're going to charge him this morning. But he wasn't drunk, Mr Fortune. He couldn't have been. He wouldn't have a spot. He was sickly sober. But you know what the police are. If they get him convicted it'll break him. He hasn't a bean, except what he gets from Lord Frome. The old man was just going to wangle a Foreign Office job for him. That's right off, suppose Tony's in the news for drunk and scragging policemen. You see?'

'I wonder,' said Mr Fortune.

'You could stop it, you could, couldn't you?' she panted. 'He wasn't drunk, he's never violent. Do help him, do save him.'

'The police won't stop for me. Mustn't count on me to save anybody, Miss Milburn. Feeling this rather a lot, aren't you? However. Curious case. Interestin' case. As you put it. I'll see if they'll let me look it over.'

'Oh, thank you so much,' she started up and ran round the table to clutch his hands.

'Don't do that,' Mr Fortune withdrew them and rang the bell. 'Don't hope too much.' Valerie was shown out gurgling laughter and tears.

Mr Fortune rang up the Chief of the Criminal Investigation Department. 'Fortune speakin', Lomas. Most improperly. To foul the springs of justice. Any objection?'

'I've been pining to catch you at it for years, Reginald. Go on.'

'The woman tempted me. One Valerie Milburn.' He paused for a reply. None came. 'Know her?'

'Not officially,' said Lomas. 'On the stage, yes. The delight of callow youth and aged rips.

68

I thought you had better taste. When did she tempt you? And how? If it's fit for my ears.'

'When? She's only just gone.'

'Good God! Are you talking in your sleep? It's very early for temptation—and for you to be up.'

'I've been up an hour.'

'And fallen for a pretty lady already. Fie!'

'Didn't say fallen. Miss Milburn was woe on the top note. But points did emerge. Her trouble is one Antony Cray. Ever heard of him?'

Again the answer was delayed for some moments. Then Lomas repeated. 'Cray? Do you mean a nephew of old Lord Frome?'

'That's the fellow. Miss Milburn says you've pinched him for drunk and assaulting the constabulary which you didn't ought.' Reggie related precisely all that Valerie had told him . . .

'Do you believe her, Reginald?'

'What the lady said isn't evidence. However. Statement could be true.'

'Quite,' Lomas admitted. 'Some of these cases are the devil. It's hard measure to ruin a young fellow's career because he had a rough and tumble with the police. And if this fellow was seedy!'

'As you say,' Reggie murmured, but he contemplated the telephone with a small, satiric smile. 'Very fair, Lomas. Very human. May I look the case over?'

69

'By all means,' Lomas said heartily. 'You'd like to see the boy before he's charged?'

'Yes, please. And the police doctor. And the policeman.'

'I agree. I'll send Bell to meet you at the police station.' Lomas rang off.

'Well, well,' Reggie sighed to the dead telephone. ' "Barkis is willin'." '

Ten minutes later he entered the station and met the solid form of Superintendent Bell. 'This swift attention from the higher powers is gratifyin',' he returned thanks. 'Are you going to tell me things?'

'I don't know any more about the case than you do,' said Bell stolidly. 'But it wants checking up. This way, please.' Reggie was taken to the cell which contained Antony Cray.

He was dirty and tousled and of a yellow pallor, his eyes red rimmed and swollen, his shaking, twitching hands had bled from the knuckles. Yet reason for Valerie's interest in him could be detected. In good condition he might have been a fine fellow, at least a woman's man. He had long legs and a good pair of shoulders, the blurred features of the sickly face were well cut by nature.

'Sorry about this, Mr Cray,' said Reggie. 'I'm a doctor.'

'What do you want?' Cray's voice was hoarse. 'I'm not drunk. I wasn't drunk. The policeman did this,' he held out his damaged hands.

70

'No drink taken last night?'

'A small whisky at dinner. That's all.'

'Anything besides drink?'

'Yes. I had a splitting headache. I took some phenacetin tablets. They made me all the worse. I couldn't stand the row of the party. When I went out I was dizzy, and stumbled into the policeman, and he said I was drunk and beat me up.'

'Oh. Phenacetin. Often use that?'

'When I get a head.'

Reggie felt his pulse, murmuring: 'Any sickness? No? Rather depressed, what? Did you see things normal last night?'

'With a sick headache? Who does?'

Reggie looked into the swollen eyes and with his fingers on the chin tilted the head back.

Cray jerked it aside. 'Look out! My head's devilish sore.'

'Yes. It would be. That's all, Mr Cray.' Reggie left the cell.

The police doctor, he found, had been told the same tale, and sardonically pronounced it a good story.

'You don't believe it?'

'I never believe 'em. The young rascal wasn't drunk when I saw him, but he smelt of drink. He'd had more than one.'

'That could be, yes. But something else also, what?'

'I dare say. Certainly, I thought him rather down than up.'

71

'Still is. Not a drunk. No. Nerves all wrong.'

'Well, of course, your opinion is decisive, Mr Fortune,' the doctor was quick to answer. 'If I say neuralgic condition and an overdose of some sedative, that would be about right, I take it?'

'Yes. As near as we can get,' Reggie sighed.

The doctor bustled out.

'Everybody loves me,' Reggie complained to the empty room.

Bell entered. 'The doctor tells me, sir, you and him are agreed Cray was a sick man?'

'Why this kindly joy, Bell?'

'No joy from me one way or the other. I just want things straight.'

'What about the assaulted constable?'

'You want to talk to him, sir? Very good.'

An uncomfortable policeman was brought in. 'This Mr Cray,' Reggie asked, 'How did he collide with you?'

'Sort of staggered into me, sir. But I have to own he wasn't noisy. He caught hold of me, I reproached him. Then he got excited and hit out wild and I had to take him along.'

'Did him proud, didn't you?'

'Sir?' The policeman was aggrieved.

'Bruise under the chin?'

'Then it must have come from his falling down, sir. He did fall heavy. He barked his knuckles proper.'

'Well, well. Nothing more, thanks.'

The constable departed and Bell asked: 'Is

72

that all right, Mr Fortune?'

'My dear Bell. Splendid. Great force, the police force. However. I'd like to see this through.'

'Very good, sir. Come along into court. Cray's case'll be on any minute.'

It went with a rush. The policeman was mild, the doctor masterfully sympathetic. Reggie had just made out the wan face of Valerie watching Cray tell his tale of headache and phenacetin before the magistrate dismissed the charge with soft, paternal words.

'Sort of thing that makes England what she is,' Reggie murmured to Bell as they went out.

'We do know how to be fair,' Bell answered. 'Now would you come along with me? There's a big case turned up.'

Reggie looked up with wide, plaintive eyes. 'Big? What is big? Murder?'

'I want your opinion on that. There's a woman dead.'

'Where?'

'In the Westminster mortuary. Only five minutes' walk.'

'Walk?' Reggie's voice went up. 'My car's here.'

It brought them into the yard of the mortuary. A smaller car stood there, a coupé of class. 'She's inside that,' said Bell.

Reggie gave one glance within and turned. 'Why is she?' he complained.

'I couldn't say, sir.'

'Cautious fellow. Couldn't say whether it was murder! Look again.'

'I leave it to you, Mr Fortune,' Bell recoiled.

The woman's body lay huddled between the seat and the instrument board. Under that her head lolled back, the cheeks, the closed eyes bulged, the nose and lips spread flat. All the face was livid but for purple and yellow marks of bruising. A squirrel coat covered her from bent knees to chin. Reggie drew back its collar. Round the full neck bruises were black to the knot of red bronze hair behind.

He opened the coat wider. Beneath it was a green evening dress. He contemplated that with a pensive gaze which slowly extended to survey the whole of the car's interior before he turned to Bell.

'You don't want to look at her again? Not a cheerin' sight. Not a perfect world. Get your fellows to take her into the mortuary. When she's gone you might bear to look into the car. The higher intelligence could work out a fact or so.'

Bell glowered at him. 'I reckon I'll finish with the car before you're through. If you come back to the station I'll be there.'

Some hours later Reggie entered the bleak room where Bell sat writing, subsided on the only other chair and lit a pipe. 'Not to spoil the story,' he murmured and blew smoke rings. 'Dead woman was forty or so, in good health, well preserved. Married woman as per

74

wedding ring. Cause of death, asphyxia. From throttling with human hands. She died hard. Fought it out.'

'Ah. Clear case of murder,' Bell grunted.

'Oh yes. Not a nice murderer—or murderers. Things are what they seemed. On that point. Hands were almost clenched. Between the fingers of right hand light yellow hairs, from bobbed or shingled woman. On her teeth some scraps of human skin, colour indeterminate, bitten off assailant. Dress and other clothes not torn, not pulled about, but body and legs heavily bruised. She was on her back and somebody knelt on her to kill her. Murder therefore was not committed in the car. Time of murder indefinitely before midnight. That's the medical evidence. How do you like it?'

'Not so bad, Mr Fortune.'

'Always happy to gratify the higher powers. What is the story you're composin'?'

'I was just putting things together in order.'

'Order is a felt want. Yes. Got it?'

'Well, sir, fairly clearly. That car was found at three-fifteen this morning in Carteret Place.'

'Oh! Where Valerie Milburn gave her bottle party. Where Cray had his scrap with the policeman.'

'That's right. At least in a manner of speaking. The car wasn't at Miss Milburn's house but some way up the street, in a little sort of dead end. The constable who arrested Cray

75

says it wasn't there when he went up Carteret Place at eleven p.m. We can fix the time it was left between eleven and three.'

'As near as that! Better than me.'

'Ah! We might get nearer yet,' said Bell. 'At three another constable spotted the car. He didn't bother with it, being no obstruction. He came back about five and it was still there. Thinking that queer he looked in and saw the woman.'

'Oh my Bell!' Reggie protested. 'You haven't put things in order. How did it begin? Who is she?'

'Yes, sir. She's been identified. She's Mrs Arundel, a lady living just by where the car was found, and it's her car.'

Reggie blew one smoke ring inside another. 'Who is Mrs Arundel? What is she, that someone strangles her and dumps her in her own car by her own house? Is there a Mr Arundel?'

'Not to my knowledge,' said Bell solemnly, 'but she has had three real husbands.'

'Rather careless with spouses, what?'

'She was no better than she should be, Mr Fortune. A fast woman, half in society, more than half out.'

'The lady's—friends?' Reggie drawled. 'Are they known to the police?'

'She lived in a rackety crowd.'

Reggie smiled. 'Yes, Bell, Carteret Place was having frequent visits from the police at

76

night—eleven, one, three, five. Why?'

'We don't like that street, sir. We have nothing hard, but there is reason to believe it has snow falls. Cocaine, you know.'

'I do. Yes. Though not mentioned when I was introduced to your friend Cray. So Mrs Arundel was suspect of dope dealing?'

'We had her in view. But there have been other reasons for watching Carteret Place, complaints of rowdy parties there and spots of trouble in the neighbourhood. Only last night there was one.' He related the vain pursuit of a police whistle by the eleven o'clock constable.

Reggie sat up. His round face was plaintive and reproachful. 'My Bell! Oh my Bell! Is this puttin' things in order? No. Carteret Place was deprived of the eleven o'clock police inspection. Curious and interestin' fact. Yet I had to pull it out of you with forceps.'

'I'm sorry, sir. It don't signify. The constable went right along the street at eleven and he swears no car was in it. I told you.'

'But he left the street clear. So the car could have been brought along. The woman may have been killed some time before. He didn't come back till one and then he got busy arrestin' Cray. So we don't know whether she and the car were there then. Pity.'

'I grant you there is a look of tricks,' Bell frowned. 'But whistling to get a rise out of the police is a common game with the bright young things round there. I am giving you all the facts, Mr Fortune. When I went over the car I found this—' He displayed a scrap of pale blue silk. 'It was caught on the edge of the door the driver's side. From a woman's dress and not Mrs Arundel's dress. Hers was green.'

'As you say,' Reggie murmured. 'Not her colour. Dress probably worn by a blonde. Same like the hair in the fingers of the deceased. And Valerie of the bottle party is a blonde. Did you get her to look at Mrs Arundel?'

'Why no, sir. Mrs Arundel was recognised by the constable and then identified by her servant—she kept a house man, no maid, that was her style. I have no reason to think Miss Milburn was a special friend.'

'Till this,' Reggie held up the blue silk. 'Further conversation with Miss Milburn is required.'

'I was going to,' said Bell.

'My dear chap, we do agree beautiful.' Reggie stood up and looked at his watch. 'Help! Have you got a car? Mine has to go home.' He strolled out and, with brief instructions, sent his chauffeur away.

Bell joined him. 'We can walk it as quick as drive, sir.'

'Not me,' Reggie protested, hailing a taxi. But he stopped it at the beginning of Carteret Place. 'Walkin' is only justified when you can't get what is wanted otherwise. As now. In this nasty, neat little street. Where you have to show me things. Mrs Arundel's house. Dead end in which Mrs Arundel's car stood. After that, house of Miss Milburn.'

At that hour of the afternoon, the narrow street was a playground and a mixed club. Children of the chauffeurs who lodged over its garages sported across the roadway, chauffeurs and their wives clustered about the garage doors in gossip.

'That's where the car was found.' Bell glanced at a bulge in the roadway which went up between two houses to a blank wall. 'Used to be a turning circle when this was a mews, often used for parking.'

'Handy,' Reggie murmured, 'yet out of the way. Good and dark after dark.'

'That's right,' Bell nodded. 'Now the next house but one is Mrs Arundel's.'

It had an emerald green door and russet window frames and curtains of brown netting. 'Suits her complexion,' Reggie murmured. 'By the way, when did she leave the house yesterday?'

'Ah! You're asking something,' Bell grunted. 'Her man servant don't know. He was taking his weekly day off yesterday, and had leave for the night, he says. He went out at two o'clock, went to see his old dad at Kingston and didn't get back till eight this morning.'

'Do you believe him?'

'I have no reason not to. He hasn't been with Mrs Arundel long—only a month—and he's given us a story we can easily check.'

'Will aged father say son was with him at time of murder? Some check! However. Let's try Miss Milburn.'

'There's her house,' Bell pointed. It was some fifty yards from Mrs Arundel's on the same side, a little larger, double fronted, its door, and everything else that could be painted, white. All the windows had boxes of white flowers, geraniums and petunias.

The door was opened by an oldish maid who glared.

'If you please.' Bell stepped into the hall. 'Tell Miss Milburn I want to see her at once.' He held out his card.

'Madam's not at home.' The maid was shrill.

'Do as you're told,' Bell growled, and she slunk away into a room on the right and slammed the door, came out again looking malice sideways and went upstairs. She was not gone long. From the landing she beckoned them.

They were taken into a small room on the first floor, which was entirely white and cream but for two people in it. Valerie shimmered silver grey as she glided to meet them. The man behind her had put his lumpy form into bright blue tweeds and a honey-coloured beard and side whiskers grew on his large pink face.

Valerie was flushed out of insipidity. 'Superintendent Bell?' she smiled and the upward glance of allure had a gleam in it.

'Me too, Miss Milburn,' said Reggie.

80

'Oh, Mr Fortune. How too kind of you. It was splendid about poor old Tony.'

'Has he been here?'

'No, did you want him?'

'I wonder. Let's see. About your party last night, Miss Milburn—' Reggie stopped and glanced at the bearded man.

'I was here, sir.' The man's voice was high.

'You don't know each other,' Valerie giggled. 'How futile! On the left Mr Fortune, on the right Ned Patten.'

'Friend of Mr Cray's?' Reggie asked.

'I think so,' the man answered.

'Seen him since?'

'Since the party? No.'

'Mr Fortune!' Valerie cried. 'Has something happened to Tony?'

'What could happen? Charge dismissed. Revertin' to the party—' Valerie was staring at the stolid menace of Bell. 'Please—' Reggie waved her to a chair and sat down beside her. 'You told me it began at ten. When did Cray arrive?'

'With the first bunch,' Patten answered. 'So did I.'

'Many bunches? Lot of people?'

'Quite a crush,' said Patten.

'All in here?' Reggie looked round the little room.

'Heavens no,' Valerie giggled. 'The state apartments are beneath.'

'Oh! Do you mind—like to look at

81

actual scene.'

'Why?' Valerie gasped.

'Want to make sure where Cray was all the time.'

'But—but Tony's out now. You just said so.'

'Yes. He is. However.' Reggie moved to the door.

Valerie sprang up, slid past him downstairs and flung open the doors on either side the hall. Through one was a narrow dining-room of different gold shades, the other opened upon a lounge, with walls, carpet and furniture all white.

'There you are,' she cried. 'Now you know the worst, Mr Fortune. The lily house. Décor by Ned. Spirit by me.' She made him a curtsey, looking up under her eyelashes.

'Charmin' harmony. Yes.' Reggie glanced at the gold room and went into the white lounge. 'Bottle party buzzed about; what? But the main body here. Were you here all the time, Patten?'

'In and out from the gold room. That's where the drinks were.'

'And you, Miss Milburn?'

'I was here in the lounge from start to finish.'

'Where was Cray?'

'Down and dumb in the corner over there,' Patten pointed.

'Poor old Tony,' said Valerie. 'He was sick and hating himself for it.'

'Yet he stayed. Stayed from ten till one.'

'I couldn't shift him,' Valerie cried.

'Silly dam' fool,' said Patten. 'I tried to push him off.'

Reggie looked from one to the other. 'Who else was here?'

Valerie broke out laughing. 'Who wasn't? Hordes! Half my crowd.'

'Mrs Arundel among 'em?' Reggie asked.

That froze them both. Patten spoke first. 'Mrs Arundel was here hours.'

'It seemed like years,' said Valerie. 'She didn't go till after Tony's row with the policeman.'

'Oh. She was still here when he'd been arrested? Quite sure?' Reggie's eyes were set on Valerie.

'Absolutely.' Valerie stared back unflinching. 'She ragged us about it.'

Reggie strolled across the room to a settee. Its rough silk cover showed marks at one end as if it had been scraped by something hard. He bent over it, Bell came to look, they exchanged a glance. Valerie met them as they turned and gasped: 'What, what's the matter?'

'When did she go?' Reggie drawled.

'Mrs Arundel? Some time after Tony.'

'About ten past one,' said Patten.

'How?'

'What do you mean?' Patten scowled at him.

'On her own legs?'

'Of course,' Valerie gasped. 'She didn't have a car. Her house is only a few doors off.'

'I've seen it. So you say Mrs Arundel walked

83

out of your house soon after one. Cray bein' then in the hands of the police. Who remained here?'

Valerie and Patten consulted together with their eyes. 'I did,' said Patten.

'Nobody else?'

'Me of course,' Valerie cried. 'Only me.'

'And then?'

'Then I sat some time with Val and went home,' Patten answered.

'Which way?'

Patten was silent for a moment and grew pale before he answered: 'I live up the street.'

'Beyond Mrs Arundel's house. So you passed it. When did you know Mrs Arundel had been killed?'

'My housekeeper told me this morning.'

'Oh yes. Yes. But passin' Mrs Arundel's house last night, didn't you give an eye to her car?'

'I didn't see any car.'

'Of course we didn't,' Valerie giggled. 'We were only seeing ourselves.'

'Oh. You were with him?'

The giggle faded in a languishing smile. 'It is so hard to say good night. Hasn't anyone ever told you that, Mr Fortune? Give them a chance.'

'I have,' Reggie sighed. 'Good night, Miss Milburn.' He went out.

'You'll be required to make a further statement miss, and you, sir,' Bell told them. 'I warn you what you have said will be tested.'

Reggie had shut the door behind him, and when Bell emerged came from the inner recesses of the hall. 'This bein' thus,' he murmured. 'Passed to you.'

Bell did not answer till they were in the street. 'A pretty couple!'

'As you say.' Reggie stopped and contemplated the house.

'That minx with her goo-goo eyes!'

'Cloyin' damsel. Yes. Cloyin' house. All overdone.' Reggie made a weary gesture. 'Even the side door white.'

'Ah, overdone is right,' Bell chuckled. 'Such silly lying, they didn't know where to stop.'

Reggie looked up at him with pensive wonder. 'That is so. We do agree, Bell.'

'Ah! You got 'em over the car. They knew all about it.'

'One or both. Yes. Lies not so good on that. Smash the rest and all is gas and gaiters. Check the beastly bottle party.' Reggie hailed a taxi and drove off in it.

That night the Chief of the Criminal Investigation Department found him solitary at supper in one of their sprightlier clubs. A bottle of champagne was on his table, he was eating marrow bones.

'Reginald!' Lomas rebuked him. 'And you a married man! Is this domestic virtue?'

'No. Debauch. To preserve sanity. Sufferin' from a public dinner. Mass production food

85

and speeches. On top of your distressful case. The mind was hysterical.'

Lomas sat down with him and ordered a devilled sole and brandy and soda.

Reggie sipped his champagne. 'You may be right. Both equally coarse. Only a wine in name. What's your trouble?'

'Nothing but fatigue. We've done very well. We roped in some of the bottle party and got out of 'em it was an uncomfortable show. Valerie and Mrs Arundel on the edge of a flare up all the time. They've always been cats to each other, but last night well above themselves. They've had Cray in common for a boy friend and he funked both women hard. Mrs Arundel fed the party brimstone scandal about Valerie and Patten. When Cray left he looked dead to the world. On his scrap with the policeman the party broke up. The last of Mrs Arundel comes from a fellow who heard her ragging Valerie and Valerie scolding back. Not too clean, he says. So there's the motive. Then we have the damage to the settee. If the woman was thrown down and strangled there, her heels would have made marks like that.'

'As you say,' Reggie sighed. 'Strikin' and suggestive, the double scrape. Any more evidence?'

'That hair in Mrs Arundel's fingers matches Valerie's. The scrap of pale blue silk in the car was torn from the dress Valerie wore last night. We found finger-prints on the door and

86

window of the car and they're Patten's.'

'Careless animal. Futile liar. So you've taken his prints and searched her lily house. Charged 'em?'

'Not yet,' Lomas smiled. 'We got their prints on statements we handed them to sign. They are detained for enquiries. They'll be charged tomorrow.'

Reggie drank up his champagne. 'End of a perfect day,' he murmured. 'Began by gettin' one rackety fool off a twopenny crime, went on to lag two lying fools for murder. In sweet agreement with the higher intelligence.' He gazed at Lomas with heavy eyes. 'Pleasant dreams. Do you dream? I never could.' He wandered out.

Before eleven next morning Lomas heard his voice again. It came over the telephone. 'I want Bell,' it said. 'Bell in a fast car. With another hefty man or so. At the Oval tube station. Now.'

'Good Gad!' Lomas exclaimed. 'What—'

'I said now,' said Reggie, and rang off.

But when the car stopped by the Oval station, he was not there. Bell fumed for some minutes before a taxi crossed all the traffic lanes and Reggie sprang from it, ran to the police car, slammed the door which Bell opened and thrust himself between the driver and the other man in front. 'Camberwell Road. Let her out.' Between buses and trams the driver did wonders, but Reggie fidgeted and lifted up his voice. 'I asked for a fast car.' The driver flushed and scared all traffic over three busy miles.

Then he was directed into a glum, suburban avenue. 'Slow. Stop,' Reggie ordered. Bell frowned at rows of small houses, each asserting that it was different from the other but of a blinding uniformity.

A man loitering by the corner of a side street turned to look and went on looking.

'Come along, Bell,' Reggie jumped out.

Bell caught him up before he reached the corner, and received a wink from the man standing there. 'My oath!' he muttered, for he knew the man as Reggie's chauffeur. 'What's the idea, Mr Fortune?'

'All present and correct,' said the chauffeur out of the corner of his mouth.

'To see Killarney,' said Reggie. 'Leave your men here.' He turned down the side street.

The houses there were of still bleaker gentility and detached. Scrawny hedges of privet, laurel and aucuba protected each from neighbours and the vulgar world.

Killarney had its name in gold on a red gate. Inside that a monkey puzzler rose over straggling rhododendrons through which a curving path led to the lurid stained glass of the front door. Some noise came out of the house, petulant voices talking together. On a sudden both fell to silence. Reggie took Bell's arm and drew him from the door to a window beyond.

88

They looked in round aspidistras, upon a dowdy drawing room and a woman and a man standing close together. Reggie pushed up the window. 'Thanks very much, Cray,' he laughed.

Cray shrank and sagged and stumbled away from the woman. She stood fast. Her purple dress suited the maroon drawing-room, came near matching the mottled flush of her cheeks, but made a cruel discord with the bronze red hair above. She looked from Cray to Reggie and Bell, and they saw her eyes gleam dark.

'Good morning, Mrs Arundel,' Reggie cried, 'this is a pleasure.'

Bell thrust head and shoulders through the window. She clutched the table beside her, a table on which lay some woollen knitting. She looked again at Cray, who was white and dumb.

'Yes, kind of Cray to bring us along,' said Reggie. 'Superintendent Bell did want you.'

She picked up the knitting, she turned and flung herself at Cray and drove the needles into his face, into his throat.

Bell shouted; Bell clambered into the room. Cray had fallen and she was upon him, stabbing at him with the bestial strength of frenzy.

Bell dragged her off. She kicked and bit, till his men came through the window and mastered her. Reggie was kneeling by Cray. 'Don't be rough,' he said over his shoulder.

89

Handcuffs were put on her, her legs were tied.

'She has done you proud,' he said to Cray, whose throat was welling blood. 'However.' He rose and came to Mrs Arundel. 'Allow me.' He drew her long sleeves back from the handcuffs. On the right arm the skin had been torn and dents showed red. 'Oh yes. Where sister bit you,' he murmured, and the woman shrieked. 'Take her away. Me for the other victim.'

*   *   *

That afternoon he came into Lomas's room dreamy and benign. 'One of your larger cigars is indicated.' He helped himself and sank down in the easiest chair. 'Pleasin' case.'

Lomas took up his telephone. 'Come along, Bell. Mr Fortune's here at last.'

'My dear old thing!' Reggie protested. 'Only paused for a simple lunch.'

'Till half-past three,' Lomas rebuked him.

Bell strode in. 'What about Cray, Mr Fortune? Is he going to come through?'

'He thinks not. I didn't tell him he was wrong.'

'My oath!' Bell muttered.

'Had a confession from him?'

'Yes, sir. Him believing he wouldn't live.'

'Last dying speech,' Reggie smiled. 'Anything like the truth?'

'It's a queer story. He says Mrs Arundel was

90

in the dope business, and broke him down teaching him to take snow. She told him the dead woman was her sister and lived on her, passed her the dope and blackmailed her over it. The trade was bad lately. Money ran short and this sister turned nasty, threatened she'd give the whole game away. She came to Mrs Arundel's house day before yesterday. Mrs Arundel 'phoned him, and when he got there the woman was dead. Mrs Arundel said she'd had to kill her, the only way to stop her mouth; she was going to split on 'em both, but it would be all right if he helped get the body taken for Mrs Arundel's, she'd go off and pass as her sister. But he wouldn't stand for it; he wouldn't do a thing, and he quit. Then this morning he had a telegram: "Come Killarney," and he didn't dare not go for fear of her.'

'Fearful fellow. Yes. That's why he's such a brute. He helped to strangle the sister. Hence the bruise under his chin. Any confession from Mrs Arundel?'

'Not a word.'

'There will be. When she hears his. However. Don't matter. Been over Mrs Arundel's house yet?'

'We have, sir. What are you thinking of?'

'Oh my Bell. Settee, divan or bed. Scratches thereon, same like the white settee of Valerie.'

'That's pretty good.' Bell smiled grimly. 'We didn't find anything scratched. But Mrs Arundel's house man says there's an old

91

Persian rug gone from the couch in the drawing-room.'

'Splendid,' Reggie purred. 'Pleasin' case. Subtle female, Mrs Arundel. All clear.'

'Clear!' Lomas exclaimed. 'You flatter yourself, Reginald.'

'Not myself. No.' Reggie sank down in his chair. 'Do I flatter you? Surely not.'

'We can convict these two beauties now, but we don't know how the thing was worked.'

'Oh my Lomas. Think again. Believe the evidence. Cray and the Arundel strangled Mrs Jones and she left her mark on both of 'em, some time before ten. I told you she died earlier than midnight. Cray went off to Valerie's party at ten. The Arundel stripped dead sister and put on the body clothes of her own, evenin' dress matchin' the one she wore herself at the bottle party. Not a nice job. Not a nice woman. Twisted some of Valerie's hair in the dead fingers. Next event. Eleven o'clock constable called out of Carteret Place by a police whistle. No doubt Mrs Arundel blew that from her car. Him being gone, Cray slunk out of Valerie's lily house—I showed you the side door, Bell, it opens on a passage where the cloak room is. The Arundel brought her car round, Cray helped her put the body in the car, covered it with the missin' rug, so it wouldn't show and came back to party via side door and cloak room. The Arundel then arrived by the front door. Either of 'em could easily get a bit torn

92

off Valerie's blue dress to shove in the car, easily scratch the settee like the heels of the woman scratched the rug when they murdered her. When the one o'clock constable was due Cray barged out and got himself arrested, thus fakin' a perfect alibi for the murder of Mrs Arundel, then alive. After puttin' up a row with Valerie to make more evidence against her, the Arundel went off, dressed herself in dead sister's clothes, removed the rug from the body, proceeded to Killarney and became the sister. She is just like sister—to those who haven't had close ups of both. Cray was sweetly confident Valerie would swear he'd never left the party and Patten would back her through hell. Kindly nature, Cray's. Perfect trust in his friends. Patten took his good night walk with Valerie. They saw the car, knew it was Mrs Arundel's. They looked inside, Patten leavin' his fool prints on the door, and saw a dead woman. I should say he didn't recognise her. Not easy to see in the dark, not nice to investigate that face. They wouldn't think of it being Mrs Arundel as she'd only just left 'em. But there was a very dead woman in her car. Cray had behaved queer at the party, funking Valerie, lurking. They knew he might have slunk out and done the kill. They hated Mrs Arundel, they liked him, they knew she had him on a string. All they cared for was to save him. They left the woman for somebody else to find, and fixed up they'd give Cray his alibi, and Valerie came round bright and early to rub it in on me he was a poor, sick fellow under her eye all the time till arrested. Dear fools, Valerie and her Ned. Made for each other. Must have hit 'em cruel hard when they heard the dead woman was Mrs Arundel. And yet they stuck to their story. Very good effort. Bless 'em. Nice people. Hope you haven't charged 'em, Lomas?' Reggie smiled.

'We have not,' said Lomas with dignity. 'They were let go this morning.'

'Splendid. Not a blot on the official scutcheon. Now. I have my uses, Lomas.'

'Confound your impudence.' Lomas made a grimace. 'How did you know the Arundel woman had a sister?'

'By believin' evidence. Try sometime. I told you the dead woman was in good health, well preserved. Too good, too well for a woman who'd led a nasty life, as alleged of the Arundel. She shows wear and tear. Dead face so distorted, identification could only be from general likeness, hair, clothes and what not, and the identification was not made by intimates. So I wondered. I sent my chauffeur, Sam, to browse among the children of Carteret Place. Observant animals girl children. They told him Mrs Arundel wasn't always smart, quite shabby when she went on the buses. Some of 'em spotted her the day before descendin' from a Lewisham bus. Not the first time. Sam tried the Lewisham bus conductors, and heard of a lady like the Arundel who got on in those parts and got off at the stop by Carteret Square. Then the local milkman and postman gave him the glad news she was Mrs Jones, of Killarney. Quite the lady, kept herself to herself, most respectable, though only using a charwoman two days a week. Sam called as a tout and looked her over. Me too, from the adjacent aucubas. On which I 'phoned for the higher powers. There you are. All clear, as I said.'

'Is it?' Lomas put up his eyeglass. 'Why did Cray go to her?'

'My dear old thing!' Reggie stared back with large reproachful eyes. 'Use the evidence. Cray told you in his confession. He got a telegram: "Come Killarney." The Arundel had the wind up. Probably failed to like Sam's face. He will grin.'

'Failed to like Cray when he came,' Lomas answered. 'That's what broke her.'

'It could be,' Reggie murmured. 'Don't suppose he was comfortin'.'

'Who sent the telegram?' Lomas demanded.

'Oh my Lomas! Futile question. Answer obvious. Mrs Arundel.'

'She'll deny it.'

Over Reggie's face came a pensive smile. 'She may, yes. Nobody'll believe her.'

'Why should she telegraph? She was on the telephone.'

'Yet she couldn't get Cray? Nor Cray her?

Only wrong numbers. Too bad.'

'The line's broken on the wall of the house, Reginald. Who did that?'

'Take the goods the gods provide. Telegram's all right. Pleasin' case.'

ACES HIGH

PETER CHEYNEY

At the end of Wimpole Street, our route takes us across Oxford Street and into the imposing Mayfair landmark, Berkeley Square, where the nightingale was once reputed to have sung and which is now home to some of London's premier gambling clubs. There are quite a number of company offices here, too, and among them is to be found the rather less grandiose suite belonging to Slim Callaghan, described as 'fiction's most ruthless detective'. Callaghan is forty years old, sophisticated and ironic, and very tough. He likes a drink ('three or four fingers of whisky'), often starts the day nursing a hangover, and smokes cigarettes endlessly. He employs a young, attractive secretary, Effie Thompson, who is inclined to be cynical about her boss, and Windermere 'Windy' Nikolls, a Canadian-born assistant, who has an eye for 'the dames' and a wise crack forever ready on his lips. Slim Callaghan operates in and around the clubs of London's West End and is very au fait with the tricks of gambling and the traffic in illegal drugs and sex. Some of his cases, which began with The Urgent Hangman *(1938), were attacked by the critics for their excessive cruelty and violence, but this did nothing to halt*

97

Cheyney's huge sales on both sides of the Atlantic. A number of films were also made from the books including Uneasy Terms *(1948) with Michael Rennie as Callaghan,* Meet Mr Callaghan *(1954) starring Derrick de Marney, and* Diplomatic Courier *in which the American actor Tyrone Power made the detective less of a tough guy and more a handsome charmer.*

Peter Cheyney (1896–1951) was born in London and became familiar with the West End he was to depict so colourfully when he was still a boy by wandering all over Mayfair and the surrounding districts. Peter actually trained to be a lawyer, but soon grew tired of office routine and after a period of army service and some months as a special constable in Victoria, he opted for the life of a freelance journalist and writer. For a while he even owned and ran a detective agency, Cheyney Research and Investigations which, it is said, provided him with a lot of the raw material for his Slim Callaghan stories. 'Aces High' is typical of Callaghan at work in the surroundings he knows best when he is hired to help an aristocratic gambler who has got into debt and is now being threatened with scandal...

*   *   *

Lord Priorton—A perfect replica of the stage nobleman—rose from the desk and advanced to meet Callaghan. His face was long, lean,

98

distinguished; his drooping but well-trimmed grey moustache gave him the appearance, Callaghan thought of an unhappy seal.

He said: 'Sit down please, Mr Callaghan.' He opened a silver box of cigarettes, handed it to Callaghan. He went on: 'Like most other people of my class, Mr Callaghan, I've very little money. In fact I've nothing except this house, my cottage in the country, and, when I've paid my taxes, a few hundreds a year to live on. But I have one thing—my pride. And I'm afraid it has received a severe shock.'

Callaghan said: 'That's too bad! And you think I can do something to help about it?'

The peer nodded. 'It's not only a matter of pride, but of reputation,' he said, 'and also—' he paused for a second—'of some money.'

'I see,' said Callaghan. 'Supposing you tell me about it.'

Priorton said: 'As you probably know, Mr Callaghan, I used to be a great gambler. Well, I still gamble a little. From time to time I have a few friends in here, give them dinner and we play cards. Such a party was held here last week.' He sighed. 'Little did I realize when I arranged it,' he went on, 'what the results were to be.'

Callaghan said: 'So the results weren't so good, hey? I suppose you knew the people you were playing cards with?'

Lord Priorton nodded. 'I know them all very well,' he said. 'The party consisted of two men, a woman and myself. We were playing poker. One of the men was a rich American—George Vandeler—who is over here on business; the other man—a young man of thirty—Eustace Willhaven, the eldest son of my old friend Hubert Willhaven; the lady, a charming widow—Mrs Melody Vazeley—is the sister of another good friend of mine, Charles Venning. Last, there was, of course, myself. In other words,' continued the peer gloomily, 'there was no one who is not very well known to me. You understand?'

'I understand perfectly,' said Callaghan. 'Go on, Lord Priorton. And who did what to who?'

The other nodded. He said: 'Exactly! You've put it very succinctly, Mr Callaghan. Who did what to who! To cut a long story short, I was very lucky, and when the settlement came I had won just over three thousand pounds. The upshot of it was that Eustace Willhaven owed me three thousand five hundred—a very nice sum.'

'Did he mind losing the money?' asked Callaghan.

'Good heavens, no,' said Priorton. 'Anyway, he knew his father would pay—his father always does pay. He's a rich man and even if he does keep Eustace short of money he's only too glad to settle his gambling debts when he loses and even more delighted when his son wins.'

Callaghan asked: 'And did Eustace settle?'

100

'Not then,' said Priorton. 'He said laughingly that he couldn't give me a cheque on his own bank because he'd only a few pounds in his account, but that if I wouldn't mind he would arrange things with his father and send a cheque round to me in the course of the next day. Well ... he did so.'

'I see. And what happened?' asked Callaghan.

Priorton took a cigarette from the silver box on the table. He lit it. Callaghan noticed that the hand that held the lighter was shaking a little.

Priorton said: 'The cheque was an open cheque. I went round to Eustace's bank to cash it. Well, they wouldn't cash it. They marked it "Orders not to pay" and gave it back to me.'

Callaghan nodded. 'Not so good,' he said. 'So Eustace Willhaven had stopped payment of the cheque. Why?'

Priorton shook his head. 'I don't know,' he said gloomily.

Callaghan asked: 'I suppose Eustace's father—Hubert Willhaven—isn't hard up?'

Priorton smiled. 'Don't worry about that,' he said. 'Willhaven is practically a millionaire. Three thousand five hundred means nothing to him. That's what I can't understand.'

Callaghan said: 'I see. You mean that Eustace must have a really serious reason for stopping payment of this cheque?'

'Precisely,' said Priorton.

Callaghan drew on his cigarette. He said: 'It's odd, isn't it? I suppose Willhaven knew his son had been playing cards here?'

'Good heavens, yes,' said Priorton. 'Young Willhaven plays here at least once a month. Several times his father's been here and played with him, or stood by and watched the game.'

Callaghan said: 'What do you want me to do?'

'First of all,' said the peer. 'I'm fearfully worried about Willhaven having stopped that cheque. Quite obviously, he or his father must *think* they've got a good reason for doing so. They may think that I'm going to tell people that Eustace stopped payment of a cheque for a debt of honour, and he'll naturally want to defend himself against such an accusation. He may say things that will react against my character.

'Secondly, I want the money, Mr Callaghan. Three thousand five hundred pounds is a lot to me.'

Callaghan asked casually: 'Lord Priorton, did it ever occur to you to ring up Eustace Willhaven and ask him why he'd stopped payment of that cheque?'

Priorton nodded his head. 'It did occur to me,' he said. 'I rang up Eustace, and he said that he was fearfully sorry about it, but that he did it because his father *ordered* him to stop payment—he didn't know why.'

'I see,' said Callaghan. 'You didn't speak to

the father?'

'No,' said Priorton. 'I think it's his business to explain his action to *me*!'

Callaghan said: 'You're quite right.' He got up. 'Well, I'll do my best,' he said.

Priorton asked: 'What are you going to do, Mr Callaghan?'

Callaghan grinned. He said: 'Perhaps it would be better if I didn't tell you. What people don't know can't hurt 'em.'

Priorton nodded. He said: 'About your fee. You know I'm pretty hard up.'

Callaghan said: 'I'll take a chance on you, Lord Priorton. I think you've told me the truth. If I get that cheque paid, I'll take the odd five hundred. If I don't, I'll charge you nothing. How's that?'

'Very sportin'!' said the peer.

*　　　*　　　*

Callaghan stopped Eustace Willhaven on his way out of the Berkeley Buttery. He said: 'Excuse me, Mr Willhaven, my name's Callaghan. I'm a private detective. I'm trying to clear up a small point that's worrying a client of mine—Lord Priorton. It's about that cheque you gave him in settlement of your gambling losses.'

Eustace Willhaven said: 'Well, really! Do you think this is a good place to discuss it?'

'It's as good as any other, isn't it?' retorted

Callaghan. 'Do you know why your father told you to stop that cheque?'

Willhaven adjusted his eyeglass. He looked seriously at Callaghan. He said: 'To tell you the truth, Mr Callaghan, I don't. I don't know why my father told me to stop that cheque. But if you knew anything about my father, you'd know he's not likely to do a thing like that without good reason. Good-day to you!'

*   *   *

Hubert Willhaven—tall, distinguished, ascetic looking—listened attentively to what Callaghan had to say. When the detective had finished talking, Willhaven smoked silently for a few seconds. Then he said: 'What you have to say interests me very much, Mr Callaghan. And I appreciate your explanation as to why Lord Priorton should have employed you to try and settle this matter.'

Callaghan said: 'Let's not become confused about the issues at stake, Mr Willhaven. The position, to my mind, is quite simple.'

Willhaven raised his eyebrows. 'Is it?' he queried.

Callaghan said: 'To my mind, yes. A settlement was arrived at when this poker game was over—a general settlement. On this general settlement your son had to pay three thousand five hundred pounds to Lord Priorton. Quite obviously, when he left that house he intended to pay that debt. The proof of that is that he asked you for the money. The fact that *you* thought he owed it is proved by you having given him the money to put into his bank so that he could send a cheque to Lord Priorton.' Callaghan grinned. 'After that, of course,' he said, 'there's a snag.'

Willhaven smiled. He thought that Callaghan's grin was infectious.

'The snag being that I told Eustace to stop the cheque. Perhaps you can tell me something about that too, Mr Callaghan,' he suggested.

Callaghan said: 'I think I can. To my mind there is only one reason why you should have done that. There *could* only be one reason; that is that one of the other people who took part in that game besides Lord Priorton and your son have influenced you to have the payment of that cheque stopped. Lord Priorton *wanted* to receive the money. You *intended* it should be paid. Something made you alter your mind. My guess is, it was one of those two other people, and I'm going to find out. Either you tell me or I'll find some means of making them talk.'

Willhaven said: 'They might not *want* to talk, Mr Callaghan.'

Callaghan said: 'Whenever I want somebody to talk I find a means of making 'em talk.' He grinned. 'You'd be surprised,' he said.

Willhaven said: 'I probably shouldn't be. But I'll save them the inconvenience. You're

105

quite right in your supposition, because one of the other parties who took part in that game gave me some information which merited the payment being stopped.'

Callaghan said: 'One of the other parties? That would be Mr Vandeler or Mrs Vazeley.'

'Exactly,' said Willhaven. 'Mrs Vazeley wrote me a note and informed me that in her opinion the game had been crooked from start to finish.'

Callaghan said: 'Do you know Mrs Vazeley well?'

Willhaven shook his had. 'Not *very* well,' he said. 'I've met her.'

Callaghan nodded. 'You were prepared to accept this accusation from a woman who is merely an acquaintance, against the reputation of a man—Lord Priorton—whom you've known for years?'

Willhaven said: 'The point doesn't arise, Mr Callaghan. She was able to prove what she said!'

*   *   *

Mrs Vazeley was a delightful woman of about thirty-eight. Her clothes were simple but marvellous. She had *chic* and an extraordinary allure. Callaghan thought he could fall for Mrs Vazeley very easily. He said: 'You know, Mrs Vazeley, you're in rather a jam.'

She said airily: 'Am I, Mr Callaghan? How

exciting! My life is so uneventful that the idea of being in a jam almost appeals to me. Another thing, I ought to tell you that I'm absolutely *thrilled* at meeting a private detective. Please have a cigarette. And would you like a drink?'

Callaghan said he would. Whilst he was drinking the brandy and soda, she said:

'Do tell me about the jam I'm in. I think I ought to know, don't you?'

Callaghan said: 'You wrote a note to Hubert Willhaven, and you afterwards talked to him, either personally or on the telephone, and told him that the poker game at Lord Priorton's house was crooked. Quite obviously, as Willhaven told his son to stop payment of the cheque after that conversation with you, the suggestion was that Lord Priorton was the crook. Have you ever heard of the law of libel and slander, Mrs Vazeley? If you can't prove that Lord Priorton was responsible for that game being crooked you will be in a jam, and it might cost you a lot of money.'

She said: 'I know. I knew that when I told Mr Willhaven. But what else could I do? You see I *knew* that game was crooked, Mr Callaghan.'

Callaghan said: 'May I know how you knew?'

She said: 'It's fearfully simple. *I* had no reason to complain about the game. I won about fifty pounds. I won fifty pounds from Mr

107

Vandeler, and he settled that in bank-notes before the general settlement was made between the others. So you'll agree that I've no cause for complaint.'

Callaghan said: 'That's agreed. But how can you prove that that game was crooked and that Priorton was responsible?'

She said: 'I'll tell you. I was rather elated at winning fifty pounds, and when the game broke up I left my cigarette case behind. It's rather a valuable case. I'd left it on a little table by the side of my chair whilst I was playing. Next morning I had a very early appointment to leave London for Bangor on a train at seven-twenty, and I thought that on my way to the station I'd call in at Lord Priorton's house—I thought that possibly the servants would be up—and get my cigarette case. When I arrived at the house, the boot-boy let me in. I told him what I wanted and he said he'd go and look for my cigarette case. He seemed a rather stupid boy, so I told him not to bother but to go on with his work and I'd go and get the cigarette case because I knew exactly where it was. So I went up to the room on the first floor where we'd played, and there was my cigarette case. I picked it up. The card table was just as we'd left it the night before with the cards still lying on the table.

'The early morning sunlight was coming through the windows. It reflected on the glazed backs of the cards, and I saw something that

108

gave me rather a shock.'

Callaghan asked: 'What did you see?'

'Every one of those cards was marked,' said Mrs Vazeley. 'They'd been beautifully marked—cleverly marked—with a pin. Once you knew where to look you could see the little tiny pin-points, and if you were dealing you could tell the value of the card by the touch. Needless to say I was shocked. But I wanted to make quite certain. I examined all the cards. They were all marked. I took three or four of them and I showed them to Mr Willhaven when I talked to him about it. If that isn't proof, what is?'

Callaghan said: 'It looks as if there isn't a great deal of argument.' He picked up his hat. 'I'm afraid you won't have to worry about that action for slander.'

She said: 'No, I didn't think I should. Must you be going, Mr Callaghan?

*　　　*　　　*

Hubert Willhaven put down his newspaper as Callaghan was shown into the room. He said: 'Good morning, Mr Callaghan. What can I do for you?'

Callaghan lit a cigarette. He said casually: 'I think the easiest thing for you to do, Willhaven, would be to give me a cheque for three thousand five hundred pounds, and we'll call this business quits.'

Willhaven said: 'You're being funny, aren't you? I'm not in a frame of mind for humour this morning.'

Callaghan said: 'I'm not being funny. Just listen to me for a moment. When I'm handling a case I never look for clues. I leave that to the detectives in fiction. Usually I'm only interested in people. If I can find that somebody in a case has done something that seems to me incongruous, I wonder why.' Callaghan grinned. 'It usually gets me somewhere,' he said.

Willhaven said: 'It would have to be a hell of an incongruity to get you three thousand five hundred pounds from me, Callaghan.'

'I'll get it all right,' said Callaghan. 'Because it was a hell of an incongruity. Listen. I wondered why it was that Mrs Vazeley had to telephone *you* and tell *you* that that game was crooked. Why didn't she telephone your son? She knows him. He's a man. He's thirty years of age. The obvious thing for her to have done was to have telephoned to *him*. She didn't do it.'

Willhaven said: 'I don't see the point.'

'Of course you don't,' said Callaghan. 'I'll tell you what the point was. It was necessary for the success of your son's little plot that there should seem to be no connection between Mrs Vazeley and himself. That's why she telephoned you.'

Willhaven said: 'Are you suggesting that this

is a put-up job between my son and Mrs Vazeley?'

'I'm not suggesting anything. I'm *telling* you,' said Callaghan. 'Lord Priorton told me that you'd paid your son's gambling debts before. You're a rich man and you aren't going to have people saying that his debts of honour are unpaid. But quite obviously your son is often short of money—you keep him so because of his extravagance—otherwise he wouldn't have to go to you to pay money into his bank in order to give a cheque that would be met for a gambling debt.' He grinned. 'Not only has he been doing it on the people that he and Mrs Vazeley have played cards with, but he's also been doing it on *you*.'

Willhaven said: 'I think you're talking nonsense. I still don't understand what you mean.'

Callaghan said: 'I'll tell you what I mean. Your son and Mrs Vazeley went into that poker game at Lord Priorton's as partners. If they both won, it was going to be all right, but on this occasion Mrs Vazeley won fifty pounds, and your son dropped three thousand five hundred. So Mrs Vazeley leaves her cigarette case behind. The next morning, before anybody's up, she goes round to the house, rings the bell and asks for her cigarette case. She says she knows where she's left it. She probably tells the boot-boy to get on with his business and not bother to take her upstairs.

111

While she was up there she very quickly marked the cards with a pin. That was easy. She's used to doing it, and it would take her five or six minutes. Then she went off, taking four or five of the cards with her. She rang you up. She knew you'd tell your son; that he'd stop the cheque. And she also knew, as *he* knew, that you wouldn't ask him to return the three thousand five hundred pounds. Get it?'

Willhaven said: 'I see. You might be wrong, mightn't you?'

Callaghan said: 'I *might* be. But unfortunately for herself Mrs Vazeley told me that she got up early that morning in order to catch a train for Bangor in North Wales—the seven-twenty. Well, there wasn't a seven-twenty. That substantiates it a little bit, doesn't it?'

Willhaven nodded.

'The other thing is this,' said Callaghan, 'I understand from Lord Priorton that the last person to shuffle and deal the cards was your son. Therefore his thumb-prints should have been superimposed on practically every card in the pack. But that wasn't so. The most recent thumb-prints on every card in the pack were Mrs Vazeley's.' Callaghan grinned. 'I think that clinches it, don't you?' he said.

Willhaven said: 'I'm not going to argue. Anyway, I'll give you the cheque.'

He went to the desk, got his cheque book.

*　　*　　*

Lord Priorton handed Callaghan a large whisky and soda. He said: 'Very nice work, Mr Callaghan. I shall be delighted to pay you your fee. I congratulate you on your brilliant idea of checking the finger-prints on the back of the cards. I didn't know you had done that. That really was first class.'

Callaghan said: 'You can save your congratulations. I didn't check *any* finger-prints on *any* cards. I had a hunch and I played it.'

YELLOW IRIS

AGATHA CHRISTIE

Mayfair is also home territory to a detective very different to Slim Callaghan: the short, egocentric, rather effete but nevertheless brilliant former Belgian Sûreté police officer, Hercule Poirot. According to the accounts of his cases, Poirot initially shared a home with his friend and associate, Captain Arthur Hastings, at 14, Farraway Street, but after the Captain's marriage moved to Whitehaven Mansions, a modern block of flats near Park Lane. Here an efficient secretary, Miss Lemon, caters to his mercurial moods and receives his steady stream of clients and visitors—among whom is Mrs Ariadne Oliver, a detective novelist with a habit of stumbling across real-life crimes. Poirot with his egg-shaped head, fastidious tastes in food and clothes—not to mention his waxed and pointed moustache—is famous for his expression about using his 'little grey cells' to solve any problem. To millions of readers he is one of the most celebrated detectives in English crime fiction, though novelist and historian H. R. F. Keating says somewhat tongue-in-cheek that Poirot's taste for a tisane of thick sweet chocolate in preference to a cup of tea 'made him at one bound the detective all Englishmen loved

115

to hate'.

Arriving in England in 1914 after the German invasion of his homeland had forced him to flee, Poirot's first case, The Mysterious Affair at Styles *(1920) made him and his authoress famous. His subsequent appearance in 33 novels and ten collections of short stories guaranteed an enduring fame which was underlined when the cases were later adapted for the stage, cinema and television, starring such distinguished actors as Charles Laughton, Francis L. Sullivan, Tony Randall, Albert Finney, Peter Ustinov, Ian Holm and, arguably the definitive portrayal, by David Suchet in the current LWT series.*

Dame Agatha Christie (1890–1976) is one of the Queens of Crime Fiction and her books have probably sold more copies than any other author of the twentieth century. Her inspiration for Poirot may well have been Hercules Popeau, a short, vain, but shrewd and intuitive retired French detective living in England who appeared in several novels and short stories written by Marie Belloc Lowndes prior to 1920. All Agatha admitted was that she had chosen to make Poirot a Belgian after being deeply moved by the plight of some First World War refugees from that country who lived near her home in Torquay. 'Yellow Iris', written in the mid-Thirties, is an intriguing Poirot case combining his love of food with solving a seemingly unsolvable case of poisoning. Agatha Christie also re-wrote the basic idea into one of the most successful of all her novel-length Poirot cases, Sparkling Cyanide, *published in 1945.*

*   *   *

Hercule Poirot stretched out his feet towards the electric radiator set in the wall. Its neat arrangement of red-hot bars pleased his orderly mind.

'A coal fire,' he mused to himself, 'was always shapeless and haphazard! Never did it achieve the symmetry.'

The telephone bell rang. Poirot rose, glancing at his watch as he did so. The time was close on half-past eleven. He wondered who was ringing him up at this hour. It might, of course, be a wrong number.

'And it might,' he murmured to himself with a whimsical smile, 'be a millionaire newspaper proprietor, found dead in the library of his country house, with a spotted orchid clasped in his left hand and a page torn from a cookery book pinned to his breast.'

Smiling at the pleasing conceit, he lifted the receiver.

Immediately a voice spoke—a soft husky woman's voice with a kind of desperate urgency about it.

'Is that M. Hercule Poirot? Is that M. Hercule Poirot?'

'Hercule Poirot speaks.'

'M. Poirot—can you come at once—at

once—I'm in danger—in great danger—I know it...'

Poirot said sharply,

'Who are you? Where are you speaking from?'

The voice came more faintly but with an even greater urgency.

'At once...it's life or death...The Jardin des Cygnes...at once...table with yellow irises...'

There was a pause—a queer kind of gasp—the line went dead.

Hercule Poirot hung up. His face was puzzled. He murmured between his teeth:

'There is something here very curious.'

*   *   *

In the doorway of the Jardin des Cygnes, fat Luigi hurried forward.

'Buona sera, M. Poirot. You desire a table—yes?'

'No, no, my good Luigi. I seek here for some friends. I will look round—perhaps they are not here yet. Ah, let me see, that table there in the corner with the yellow irises—a little question by the way, if it is not indiscreet. On all the other tables there are tulips—pink tulips—why on that one table do you have yellow iris?'

Luigi shrugged his expressive shoulders.

'A command, Monsieur! A special order! Without doubt, the favourite flowers of one of

118

the ladies. That table, it is the table of Mr Barton Russell—an American—immensely rich.'

'Aha, one must study the whims of the ladies, must one not, Luigi?'

'Monsieur has said it,' said Luigi.

'I see at that table an acquaintance of mine. I must go and speak to him.'

Poirot skirted his way delicately round the dancing floor on which couples were revolving. The table in question was set for six, but it had at the moment only one occupant, a young man who was thoughtfully, and it seemed pessimistically, drinking champagne.

He was not at all the person that Poirot had expected to see. It seemed impossible to associate the idea of danger or melodrama with any party of which Tony Chapell was a member.

Poirot paused delicately by the table.

'Ah, it is, is it not, my friend Anthony Chapell?'

'By all that's wonderful—Poirot the police hound!' cried the young man. 'Not Anthony, my dear fellow—Tony to friends!'

He drew out a chair.

'Come, sit with me. Let us discourse of crime! Let us go further and drink to crime.' He poured champagne into an empty glass. 'But what are you doing in this haunt of song and dance and merriment, my dear Poirot? We have no bodies here, positively not a single body to offer you.'

Poirot sipped the champagne.

'You seem very gay, *mon cher*?'

'Gay? I am steeped in misery—wallowing in gloom. Tell me, you hear this tune they are playing. You recognize it?'

Poirot hazarded cautiously:

'Something perhaps to do with your baby having left you?'

'Not a bad guess,' said the young man, 'but wrong for once. "There's nothing like love for making you miserable!" That's what it's called.'

'Aha?'

'My favourite tune,' said Tony Chapell mournfully. 'And my favourite restaurant and my favourite band—and my favourite girl's here and she's dancing it with somebody else.'

'Hence the melancholy?' said Poirot.

'Exactly. Pauline and I, you see, have had what the vulgar call words. That is to say, she's had ninety-five words to five of mine out of every hundred. My five are: "*But, darling—I can explain.*" Then she starts in on her ninety-five again and we get no further. I think,' added Tony sadly, 'that I shall poison myself.'

'Pauline?' murmured Poirot.

'Pauline Weatherby. Barton Russell's young sister-in-law. Young, lovely, disgustingly rich. Tonight Barton Russell gives a party. You know him? Big Business, clean-shaven American—full of pep and personality. His

120

wife was Pauline's sister.'

'And who else is there at this party?'

'You'll meet 'em in a minute when the music stops. There's Lola Valdez—you know, the South American dancer in the new show at the Metropole, and there's Stephen Carter. D'you know Carter—he's in the diplomatic service. Very hush-hush. Known as silent Stephen. Sort of man who says, "*I am not at liberty to state, etc., etc.*" Hullo, here they come.'

Poirot rose. He was introduced to Barton Russell, to Stephen Carter, to Señora Lola Valdez, a dark and luscious creature, and to Pauline Weatherby, very young, very fair, with eyes like cornflowers.

Barton Russell said:

'What, is this the great M. Hercule Poirot? I am indeed pleased to meet you, sir. Won't you sit down and join us? That is, unless—'

Tony Chapell broke in.

'He's got an appointment with a body, I believe, or is it an absconding financier, or the Rajah of Borrioboolagah's great ruby?'

'Ah, my friend, do you think I am never off duty? Can I not, for once, seek only to amuse myself?'

'Perhaps you've got an appointment with Carter here. The latest from Geneva. International situation now acute. The stolen plans *must* be found or war will be declared tomorrow!'

Pauline Weatherby said cuttingly:

121

'Must you be so *completely* idiotic, Tony?'

'Sorry, Pauline.'

Tony Chapell relapsed into crestfallen silence.

'How severe you are, Mademoiselle.'

'I hate people who play the fool all the time!'

'I must be careful, I see. I must converse only of serious matters.'

'Oh, no, M. Poirot. I didn't mean you.'

She turned a smiling face to him and asked:

'Are you really a kind of Sherlock Holmes and do wonderful deductions?'

'Ah, the deductions—they are not so easy in real life. But shall I try? Now then, I deduce— that yellow irises are your favourite flowers?'

'Quite wrong, M. Poirot. Lilies of the valley or roses.'

Poirot sighed.

'A failure. I will try once more. This evening, not very long ago, you telephoned to someone.'

Pauline laughed and clapped her hands.

'Quite right.'

'It was not long after you arrived here?'

'Right again. I telephoned the minute I got inside the doors.'

'Ah—that is not so good. You telephoned *before* you came to this table?'

'Yes.'

'Decidedly very bad.'

'Oh, no, I think it was very clever of you. How did you know I had telephoned?'

122

'That, Mademoiselle, is the great detective's secret. And the person to whom you telephoned—does the name begin with a P—or perhaps with an H?'

Pauline laughed.

'Quite wrong. I telephoned to my maid to post some frightfully important letters that I'd never sent off. Her name's Louise.'

'I am confused—quite confused.'

The music began again.

'What about it, Pauline?' asked Tony.

'I don't think I want to dance again so soon, Tony.'

'Isn't that too bad?' said Tony bitterly to the world at large.

Poirot murmured to the South American girl on his other side:

'Señora, I would not dare to ask you to dance with me. I am too much of the antique.'

Lola Valdez said:

'Ah, it ees nonsense that you talk there! You are steel young. Your hair, eet is still black!'

Poirot winced slightly.

'Pauline, as your brother-in-law and your guardian,' Barton Russell spoke heavily, 'I'm just going to force you on to the floor! This one's a waltz and a waltz is about the only dance I really can do.'

'Why, of course, Barton, we'll take the floor right away.'

'Good girl, Pauline, that's swell of you.'

They went off together. Tony tipped back

his chair. Then he looked at Stephen Carter.

'Talkative little fellow, aren't you, Carter?' he remarked. 'Help to make a party go with your merry chatter, eh, what?'

'Really, Chapell, I don't know what you mean?'

'Oh, you don't—don't you?' Tony mimicked him.

'My dear fellow.'

'Drink, man, drink, if you won't talk.'

'No, thanks.'

'Then I will.'

Stephen Carter shrugged his shoulders.

'Excuse me, must just speak to a fellow I know over there. Fellow I was with at Eton.'

Stephen Carter got up and walked to a table a few places away.

Tony said gloomily:

'Somebody ought to drown old Etonians at birth.'

Hercule Poirot was still being gallant to the dark beauty beside him.

He murmured:

'I wonder, may I ask, what are the favourite flowers of Mademoiselle?'

'Ah, now, why ees eet you want to know?' Lola was arch.

'Mademoiselle, if I send flowers to a lady, I am particular that they should be flowers she likes.'

'That ees very charming of you, M. Poirot. I weel tell you—I adore the big dark red carnations—or the dark red roses.'

'Superb—yes, superb! You do not, then, like yellow flowers—yellow irises?'

'Yellow flowers—no—they do not accord with my temperament.'

'How wise ... Tell me, Mademoiselle, did you ring up a friend tonight, since you arrived here?'

'I? Ring up a friend? No, what a curious question!'

'Ah, but I, I am a very curious man.'

'I'm sure you are.' She rolled her dark eyes at him. 'A vairy *dan*gerous man.'

'No, no, not dangerous; say, a man who may be useful—in danger! You understand?'

Lola giggled. She showed white even teeth.

'No, no,' she laughed. 'You are dangerous.'

Hercule Poirot sighed.

'I see that you do not understand. All this is very strange.'

Tony came out of a fit of abstraction and said suddenly:

'Lola, what about a spot of swoop and dip? Come along.'

'I weel come—yes. Since M. Poirot ees not brave enough!'

Tony put an arm round her and remarked over his shoulder to Poirot as they glided off:

'You can meditate on crime yet to come, old boy!'

Poirot said: 'It is profound what you say there. Yes, it is profound...'

125

He sat meditatively for a minute or two, then he raised a finger. Luigi came promptly, his wide Italian face wreathed in smiles.

'*Mon vieux*,' said Poirot. 'I need some information.'

'Always at your service, Monsieur.'

'I desire to know how many of these people at this table here have used the telephone tonight?'

'I can tell you, Monsieur. The young lady, the one in white, she telephoned at once when she got here. Then she went to leave her cloak and while she was doing that the other lady came out of the cloakroom and went into the telephone box.'

'So the Señora *did* telephone! Was that *before* she came into the restaurant?'

'Yes, Monsieur.'

'Anyone else?'

'No, Monsieur.'

'All this, Luigi, gives me furiously to think!'

'Indeed, Monsieur.'

'Yes. I think, Luigi, that *tonight of all nights*, I must have my wits about me! *Something* is going to happen, Luigi, and I am not at all sure what it is.'

'Anything I can do, Monsieur—'

Poirot made a sign. Luigi slipped discreetly away. Stephen Carter was returning to the table.

'We are still deserted, Mr Carter,' said Poirot.

'Oh—er—quite,' said the other.

'You know Mr Barton Russell well?'

'Yes, known him a good while.'

'His sister-in-law, little Miss Weatherby, is very charming.'

'Yes, pretty girl.'

'You know her well, too?'

'Quite.'

'Oh, quite, quite,' said Poirot.

Carter stared at him.

The music stopped and the others returned. Barton Russell said to a waiter:

'Another bottle of champagne—quickly.'

Then he raised his glass.

'See here, folks. I'm going to ask you to drink a toast. To tell you the truth, there's an idea back of this little party tonight. As you know, I'd ordered a table for six. There were only five of us. That gave us an empty place. Then, by a very strange coincidence, M. Hercule Poirot happened to pass by and I asked him to join our party.

'You don't know yet what an apt coincidence that was. You see that empty seat tonight represents a lady—the lady in whose memory this party is being given. This party, ladies and gentlemen, is being held in memory of my dear wife—Iris—who died exactly four years ago on this very date!'

There was a startled movement round the table. Barton Russell, his face quietly impassive, raised his glass.

127

'I'll ask you to drink to her memory. *Iris!*'

'Iris?' said Poirot sharply.

He looked at the flowers. Barton Russell caught his glance and gently nodded his head.

There were little murmurs round the table.

'Iris—Iris...'

Everyone looked startled and uncomfortable.

Barton Russell went on, speaking with his slow monotonous American intonation, each word coming out weightily.

'It may seem odd to you all that I should celebrate the anniversary of a death in this way—by a supper party in a fashionable restaurant. But I have a reason—yes, I have a reason. For M. Poirot's benefit, I'll explain.'

He turned his head towards Poirot.

'Four years ago tonight, M. Poirot, there was a supper party held in New York. At it were my wife and myself, Mr Stephen Carter who was attached to the Embassy in Washington, Mr Anthony Chapell who had been a guest in our house for some weeks, and Señora Valdez who was at that time enchanting New York City with her dancing. Little Pauline here'—he patted her shoulder—'was only sixteen but she came to the supper party as a special treat. You remember, Pauline?'

'I remember—yes.' Her voice shook a little.

'M. Poirot, on that night a tragedy happened. There was a roll of drums and the

128

cabaret started. The lights went down—all but a spotlight in the middle of the floor. When the lights went up again, M. Poirot, my wife was seen to have fallen forward on the table. She was dead—stone dead. There was potassium cyanide found in the dregs of her wine-glass, and the remains of the packet was discovered in her handbag.'

'She had committed suicide?' said Poirot.

'That was the accepted verdict ... It broke me up, M. Poirot. There was, perhaps, a possible reason for such an action—the police thought so. I accepted their decision.'

He pounded suddenly on the table.

'But I was not satisfied ... No, for four years I've been thinking and brooding—and I'm not satisfied: I don't believe Iris killed herself. I believe, M. Poirot, that she was murdered—by one of those people at the table.'

'Look here, sir—'

Tony Chapell half sprung to his feet.

'Be quiet, Tony,' said Russell. 'I haven't finished. One of them did it—I'm sure of that now. Someone who, under cover of the darkness, slipped the half emptied packet of cyanide into her handbag. I think I know which of them it was. I mean to know the truth—'

Lola's voice rose sharply.

'You are mad—crazee—who would have harmed her? No, you are mad. Me, I will not stay—'

129

She broke off. There was a roll of drums.

Barton Russell said:

'The cabaret. Afterwards we will go on with this. Stay where you are, all of you. I've got to go and speak to the dance band. Little arrangement I've made with them.'

He got up and left the table.

'Extraordinary business,' commented Carter. 'Man's mad.'

'He ees crazee, yes,' said Lola.

The lights were lowered.

'For two pins I'd clear out,' said Tony.

'No!' Pauline spoke sharply. Then she murmured, 'Oh, dear—oh, dear—'

'What is it, Mademoiselle?' murmured Poirot.

She answered almost in a whisper. 'It's horrible! It's just like it was that night—'

'Sh! Sh!' said several people.

Poirot lowered his voice.

'A little word in your ear.' He whispered, then patted her shoulder. 'All will be well,' he assured her.

'My God, listen,' cried Lola.

'What is it, Señora?'

'*It's the same tune*—the same song that they played that night in New York. Barton Russell must have fixed it. I don't like this.'

'Courage—courage—'

There was a fresh hush.

A girl walked out into the middle of the floor, a coal black girl with rolling eyeballs and white glistening teeth. She began to sing in a deep hoarse voice—a voice that was curiously moving.

I've forgotten you
I never think of you
The way you walked
The way you talked
The things you used to say
I've forgotten you
I never think of you
I couldn't say
For sure today
Whether your eyes were blue or grey
I've forgotten you
I never think of you.

I'm through
Thinking of you
I tell you I'm through
Thinking of you...
You ... you ... you ...

The sobbing tune, the deep golden negro voice had a powerful effect. It hypnotized—cast a spell. Even the waiters felt it. The whole room stared at her, hypnotized by the thick cloying emotion she distilled.

A waiter passed softly round the table filling up glasses, murmuring 'champagne' in an undertone but all attention was on the one glowing spot of light—the black woman whose ancestors came from Africa, singing in her deep voice:

> I've forgotten you
> I never think of you
> Oh, what a lie
> I shall think of you, think of you, think of you
>
> Till I die...

The applause broke out frenziedly. The lights went up. Barton Russell came back and slipped into his seat.

'She's great, that girl—' cried Tony.

But his words were cut short by a low cry from Lola.

'Look—look...'

And then they all saw. Pauline Weatherby dropped forward on to the table.

Lola cried:

'She's dead—just like Iris—like Iris in New York.'

Poirot sprang from his seat, signing to the others to keep back. He bent over the huddled form, very gently lifted a limp hand and felt for a pulse.

His face was white and stern. The others watched him. They were paralyzed, held in a trance.

Slowly, Poirot nodded his head.

'Yes, she is dead—*la pauvre petite*. And I

132

sitting by her! Ah! but this time the murderer shall not escape.'

Barton Russell, his face grey, muttered:

'Just like Iris ... She saw something—Pauline saw something that night—Only she wasn't sure—she told me she wasn't sure ... We must get the police ... Oh, God, little Pauline.'

Poirot said:

'Where is her glass?' He raised it to his nose. 'Yes, I can smell the cyanide. A smell of bitter almonds ... the same method, the same poison...'

He picked up her handbag.

'Let us look in her handbag.'

Barton Russell cried out:

'You don't believe this is suicide, too? Not on your life.'

'Wait,' Poirot commanded. 'No, there is nothing here. The lights went up, you see, too quickly, the murderer had not time. Therefore, the poison is still on him.'

'Or her,' said Carter.

He was looking at Lola Valdez.

She spat out:

'What do you mean—what do you say? That I killed her—eet is not true—not true—why should I do such a thing!'

'You had rather a fancy for Barton Russell yourself in New York. That's the gossip I heard. Argentine beauties are notoriously jealous.'

'That ees a pack of lies. And I do not come from the Argentine. I come from Peru. Ah—I spit upon you. I—' She relapsed into Spanish.

'I demand silence,' cried Poirot. 'It is for me to speak.'

Barton Russell said heavily:

'Everyone must be searched.'

Poirot said calmly:

'*Non, non*, it is not necessary.'

'What d'you mean, not necessary?'

'I, Hercule Poirot, know. I see with the eyes of the mind. And I will speak! M. Carter, *will you show us the packet in your breast pocket?*'

'There's nothing in my pocket. What the hell—'

'Tony, my good friend, if you will be so obliging.'

Carter cried out:

'Damn you—'

Tony flipped the packet neatly out before Carter could defend himself.

'There you are, M. Poirot, just as you said!'

'It's a damned lie,' cried Carter.

Poirot picked up the packet, read the label.

'Cyanide of potassium. The case is complete.'

Barton Russell's voice came thickly.

'Carter! I always thought so. Iris was in love with you. She wanted to go away with you. You didn't want a scandal for the sake of your precious career so you poisoned her. You'll hang for this, you dirty dog.'

'Silence!' Poirot's voice rang out, firm and authoritative. 'This is not finished yet. I, Hercule Poirot, have something to say. My friend here, Tony Chapell, he says to me when I arrive, that I have come in search of crime. That, it is partly true. There *was* crime in my mind—but it was to prevent a crime that I came. And I have prevented it. The murderer, he planned well—but Hercule Poirot he was one move ahead. He had to think fast, and to whisper quickly in Mademoiselle's ear when the lights went down. She is very quick and clever, Mademoiselle Pauline, she played her part well. Mademoiselle, will you be so kind as to show us that you are not dead after all?'

Pauline sat up. She gave an unsteady laugh.

'Resurrection of Pauline,' she said.

'Pauline—darling.'

'Tony!'

'My sweet.'

'Angel.'

Barton Russell gasped.

'I—I don't understand . . .'

'I will help you to understand, Mr Barton Russell. Your plan has miscarried.'

'My plan?'

'Yes, your plan. Who was the only man who had an *alibi* during the darkness. The man who left the table—you, Mr Barton Russell. But you returned to it under cover of the darkness, circling round it, with a champagne bottle, filling up glasses, putting cyanide in Pauline's

135

glass and dropping the half empty packet in Carter's pocket as you bent over him to remove a glass. Oh, yes, it is easy to play the part of a waiter in darkness when the attention of everyone is elsewhere. That was the real reason for your party tonight. The safest place to commit a murder is in the middle of a crowd.'

'What the—why the hell should I want to kill Pauline?'

'It might be, perhaps, a question of money. Your wife left you guardian to her sister. You mentioned that fact tonight. Pauline is twenty. At twenty-one or on her marriage you would have to render an account of your stewardship. I suggest that you could not do that. You have speculated with it. I do not know, Mr Barton Russell, whether you killed your wife in the same way, or whether her suicide suggested the idea of this crime to you, but I do know that tonight you have been guilty of attempted murder. It rests with Miss Pauline whether you are prosecuted for that.'

'No,' said Pauline. 'He can get out of my sight and out of this country. I don't want a scandal.'

'You had better go quickly, Mr Barton Russell, and I advise you to be careful in future.'

Barton Russell got up, his face working.

'To hell with you, you interfering little Belgian jackanapes.'

He strode out angrily.

Pauline sighed.

'M. Poirot, you've been wonderful...'

'You, Mademoiselle, you have been the marvellous one. To pour away the champagne, to act the dead body so prettily.'

'Ugh,' she shivered, 'you give me the creeps.'

He said gently:

'It was you who telephoned me, was it not?'

'Yes.'

'Why?'

'I don't know. I was worried and—frightened without knowing quite why I was frightened. Barton told me he was having this party to commemorate Iris' death. I realized he had some scheme on—but he wouldn't tell me what it was. He looked so—so queer and so excited that I felt something terrible might happen—only of course I never dreamed that he meant to—to get rid of *me*.'

'And so, Mademoiselle?'

'I'd heard people talking about you. I thought if I could only get you here perhaps it would stop anything happening. I thought that being a—a foreigner—if I rang up and pretended to be in danger and—and made it sound mysterious—'

'You thought the melodrama, it would attract me? That is what puzzled me. The message itself—definitely it was what you call "bogus"—it did not ring true. But the fear in the voice—that was real. Then I came—and you denied very categorically having sent me a

137

message.'

'I had to. Besides, I didn't want you to know it was me.'

'Ah, but I was fairly sure of that! Not at first. But I soon realized that the only two people who could know about the yellow irises on the table were you or Mr Barton Russell.'

Pauline nodded.

'I heard him ordering them to be put on the table,' she explained. 'That, and his ordering a table for six when I knew only five were coming, made me suspect—'

She stopped, biting her lip.

'What did you suspect, Mademoiselle?'

She said slowly:

'I was afraid—of something happening—to Mr Carter.'

Stephen Carter cleared his throat. Unhurriedly but quite decisively he rose from the table.

'Er—h'm—I have to—er—thank you, Mr Poirot. I owe you a great deal. You'll excuse me, I'm sure, if I leave you. Tonight's happenings have been rather upsetting.'

Looking after his retreating figure, Pauline said violently:

'I hate him. I've always thought it was—because of him that Iris killed herself. Oh, it's all so hateful...'

Poirot said gently:

'Forget, Mademoiselle ... forget ... Let the past go ... Think only of the present...'

138

Pauline murmured, 'Yes—you're right...'

Poirot turned to Lola Valdez.

'Señora, as the evening advances I become more brave. If you would dance with me now—'

'Oh, yes, indeed. You are!—you are ze cat's whiskers, M. Poirot. I inseest on dancing with you.'

'You are too kind, Señora.'

Tony and Pauline were left. They leant towards each other across the table.

'Darling Pauline.'

'Oh, Tony, I've been such a nasty spiteful spitfiring little cat to you all day. Can you ever forgive me?'

'Angel! This is Our Tune again. Let's dance.'

They danced off, smiling at each other and humming softly:

There's nothing like Love for making you
    miserable
There's nothing like Love for making you
    blue
Depressed
Possessed
Sentimental
Temperamental
There's nothing like Love
For getting you down.

There's nothing like Love for driving you
    crazy

There's nothing like Love for making you
    mad
Abusive
Allusive
Suicidal
Homicidal
There's nothing like Love
There's nothing like Love ...

TRENT AND THE FOOL-PROOF LIFT

E. C. BENTLEY

Walking all the way down Park Lane, along Knightsbridge, and down Sloane Street brings us to Cadogan Place, the home of journalist, artist and amateur detective Philip Trent whom H. R. F. Keating has referred to as 'the first of the ungreat detectives—the human ones'. The first appearance of the detective was, curiously, in Trent's Last Case, *published in 1913, but the book which was evidently a satire on detective fiction in general was such a success that the public were soon demanding more cases about the friendly, tactful and quietly humorous man of many talents. Trent is a tall, gangly figure, concerned and fallible, but respected both for his artistic talents and his skill as a journalist, and more often than not he is sent to investigate a case by his Fleet Street employers, the* Record. *Similarly, stories about him have also become widely admired—the critic Charles Shibuk called* Trent's Last Case, *'one of the ten best mystery novels of all time', while Dorothy L. Sayers admitted that her detective, Lord Peter Wimsey, owed a number of his characteristics and attitudes towards crime to Trent.*

Edmund Clerihew Bentley (1875–1956) was born in Shepherd's Bush, and qualified as a

141

lawyer, but instead chose to work as a journalist on the Daily Telegraph, *where he remained for over twenty years. Bentley confessed that he set out quite deliberately to write his first book as an exposure of what he saw as the 'sterility and artificiality of the contemporary detective story'. Initially he could find no one willing to publish his manuscript—his original title,* Philip Gasket's Last Case *may well not have enhanced his chances!—and it took the instincts of an American editor who happened to be visiting London to suggest that a new name for the sleuth and a new title for the book might make all the difference. It did.* The New York Times *at once called the story, 'one of the few classics of detective fiction', and its later success caused another critic, John Carter, to hail Bentley as 'the father of the contemporary detective story'. In the years which followed it was also filmed no less than three times: in 1920 starring Gregory Scott as Trent; then with Raymond Griffith in 1929 and once more in 1953 with Michael Wilding as a rather more attractive sleuth than his predecessors. In the following story, all three elements of Trent's persona are featured—the artist, the reporter and the curious amateur detective—as he endeavours to solve a particularly baffling crime in a most unusual location.*

*   *   *

142

One of the commonest forms of fatal accident in the life of the town is falling down a lift shaft. Every coroner of large urban experience has dealt with cases by the score, whether due to short-sight, negligence, faulty construction, or defective safety mechanism. And there is another possibility.

One perfect day in June M. Armand Binet-Gailly, who held an important agency in the wine trade, left his office in Jermyn Street rather earlier than usual, and strolled homewards through the Parks to his bachelor flat at 42 Rigby Street. This was a tall old house, 'converted' from the errors of its pre-Victorian youth. There were five flats, and M. Binet-Gailly's was the second above the ground level. About 5.30—so went his statement to the police—he entered by the front door which always stood open during the daytime, and went to the lift at the end of the hall. The lift was not at the ground floor, as he could see through the lattice gate, and he pressed the button which should bring it down. But nothing happened.

M. Binet-Gailly was very much annoyed. A portly man, he did not relish the prospect of climbing two flights of stairs on a warm day when he had paid for lift service. He aimlessly seized and shook the handle of the lattice gate. To his amazement, the gate slid aside as if the lift were in place. It should, of course, have been impossible to move it unless the lift were there. The whole system was out of order, he thought. He put his head into the shaft and looked upwards. There was the lift, so far as he could judge, at the top floor. Then, as he drew back his head, his eye was caught by something at the bottom of the shallow well in which the lift-shaft ended. There was a strong electric ceiling lamp always alight at this dark end of the hall, and it showed M. Binet-Gailly quite enough.

Like most of his countrymen, he had served in arms, and things of this kind did not upset him. Plump though he was, he began to clamber down into the well; then he bethought himself. Certainly there could be no life in that crumpled bundle of humanity. The thing to do was to leave it untouched until the arrival of the police. M. Binet-Gailly went to the door communicating with the basement and bellowed downstairs for Pimblett, the caretaker. 42 Rigby Street, though distant by little more than the breadth of Oxford Street from the elegance of Mayfair, did not rise to the luxury of a uniformed porter, and neither Pimblett nor his wife was usually to be seen after the morning job of cleaning the hall and staircase was done.

Pimblett, who also had served in arms, and had seen more dirty work than had M. Binet-Gailly, took in the situation at a glance. Wasting no words, he strode to the hall telephone and rang up the police station. Both men then mounted the stairs to find which gate it was through which the unknown—for the face of the corpse could not be seen—had plunged to his death. On the floor immediately above M. Binet-Gailly's they found the gate drawn back. On this floor was the flat occupied by Mr Anthony Villiers Maxwell—a young man of sporting tastes—and his valet. M. Binet-Gailly proposed ringing the bell of the flat to make inquiries, but Pimblett remarked that the police would prefer to have all that left to them.

*　　　*　　　*

An hour later M. Binet-Gailly, sipping a glass of Campari in his own rooms, discussed with his servant, by name Aristide, what he had just learnt of this mysterious affair. The dead man had turned out to be his own landlord, Mr Stephen Havelock Hermon, who had bought the house a few years before, and had installed his nephew, Anthony Maxwell, in the flat above-stairs on its falling vacant soon afterwards. There had been some slight lack of sympathy between M. Binet-Gailly and Mr Hermon, owing to the fact that Mr Hermon had among his eccentricities a passionate hatred of liquor in every form, and when he purchased the place had not concealed his chagrin on finding that one of the sitting tenants was engaged in the wine trade, which

145

Mr Hermon preferred to call the drink-traffic.

No one in the building had seen Mr Hermon enter it that afternoon. No one had seen him at all before the finding of his body. No one had known of his intention to come to the house. Mr Clayton Haggett, the famous surgeon, who had the top flat, had not been at home; his housekeeper had heard no ring. Anthony Maxwell also had been out, and his valet had had the afternoon 'off'. Aristide could vouch for it, as he had already informed the police that no one had called at M. Binet-Gailly's. Mr Lucian Corderoy, the eminent dress designer, and his wife had both been at his shop in Malyon Street, and their 'daily' servant was never in the place after twelve noon. As for Sir George Stower, the Keeper of Phoenician Antiquities at the British Museum, he was enjoying a hard-earned holiday at Margate, and his flat on the ground floor had been shut up for some days past.

'But naturally,' remarked Aristide, fingering a swarthy chin, 'the old gentleman wished to call upon his nephew.'

'It is very probable,' M. Binet-Gailly agreed. 'He was devoted to that young animal, and they say he had no other relative living. The nephew will be his heir, no doubt, and he will make the money roll a little faster than the uncle ever did.'

'Ah! when one is young,' observed Aristide sentimentally.

'And when one is a waster by nature,' M. Binet-Gailly added. 'Well, Aristide, it is time for me to dress.'

*   *   *

Philip Trent, in his first outline of the case for the readers of the *Record*, had given these facts about the other tenants of the building. 'It is naturally assumed [he wrote] that Mr Hermon had called, as he often did, to see his nephew, to whom he is said to have been much attached. His ringing at the door had been resultless, and he had turned away to go down by the way he had come. He had opened the gate, believing the lift to be in position there—and stepped out into emptiness. He was known to be extremely short-sighted. His neck, so says the police surgeon, was broken, and there were other injuries that must have been immediately fatal. When his body was found he had been dead not more than an hour.

'This is very simple, but it leaves all the important questions unanswered.

'Why was not the lift where he expected it to be? He had only just left it; and according to the information gathered by the police there had been no one leaving or entering any of the flats since the early afternoon, when Mr Clayton Haggett and Mr Maxwell went out.

'Why was it at the top floor?

'How was it that he had been able to open

147

the gate, which should have been locked automatically the moment the lift moved from that floor?

'Why was the gate on the ground floor unlocked? Why indeed? Conceivably the mechanism of the upstairs gate had gone wrong, so that Mr Hermon could open it; but the gate at the bottom could not be opened by a dead man.

'Why were all the other gates in working order—the top gate, where the lift was, unlocked; the other two locked?

'On this very vital point I have had some conversation with the expert who was sent to investigate by the firm which built and installed the lift. The mechanism, he told me, was tested by the makers at monthly intervals, and had been in perfect order at the last examination, ten days before. The system was as nearly fool-proof as it could be. "But," he added, "it isn't tool-proof. Any engineer could see with half an eye that both those locks had been forced."

'Here are the elements of a very sinister mystery. Some one who was not Mr Hermon forced the ground-floor gate. Presumably he forced the other. The only persons known to have been in the house from three o'clock onwards were the caretaker in the basement, the French manservant in M. Binet-Gailly's flat, and the housekeeper in Mr Haggett's. Did some one enter the house before Mr Hermon; or did some one accompany him? To this point the inquiries of the police are being directed—so far, I believe, without result.

'If Mr Hermon was a victim of violence, it is hard to think that any feeling of ill-will could have been at work. It is true that he was a man of strong opinions, often violently expressed in public controversy—the hard knocks exchanged between him and his tenant, Mr Clayton Haggett, in their dispute over vivisection last year will be remembered. But he was always a fair and even a chivalrous fighter, on the friendliest footing with opponents to whom he was personally known. His nature was kindly and generous, his great wealth was largely devoted to works of benevolence; the hospital endowments made by him as memorials to his late wife are but a part of his service to humanity.'

Trent did not try to intrude on the sorrow of Anthony Maxwell, but he had from the young man's valet, Joseph Weaver, some material information. He learnt that the nephew felt his loss very deeply indeed; that he did not look like the same man. He had, Weaver said, a feeling heart. A little wild he might have been—young gentlemen would be young gentlemen—but he had what they call a nice nature. He owed everything to Mr Hermon, who had been a father to him after his parents died when he was a child. Naturally he was very much upset.

Trent reflected privately on the deceitfulness

of appearances; for he knew Anthony Maxwell by sight, and would not have said that either his eye, his mouth, or his bearing proclaimed the niceness of his nature. Perhaps Weaver was being loyal to his employer. He did not look particularly loyal; but then he did not look anything to speak of. He had the expressionlessness of his calling. His quiet voice, neat clothes, and sleek black hair suggested nothing but discretion. Trent asked a question.

Mr Hermon, Weaver said, came up fairly often on business from his place in Surrey, and when he did so, always visited his nephew. Sometimes he came on purpose to see him. No; Mr Maxwell had not been expecting him on the day of the accident; he had given no notice that he was coming. If he had done so, Mr Maxwell would naturally have been at home. Weaver thought it unlikely that Mr Hermon had been intending to call on any of the other tenants. He did do so from time to time, to talk about some matters of repairs or other landlord's business; but that would always be by appointment, and not during the working day. All the tenants, Weaver pointed out, were busy men, with the exception of Mr Maxwell; they would seldom be at home until the evening.

Yes; Mr Hermon attended personally to the management of all his house property in the West End. There was a good deal of it, and it gave him occupation. No; he was not what they call a hard landlord; quite the contrary, Weaver would say. Mr Hermon liked to do things for people, being a very generous man, as Weaver had good reason to know.

'You mean that he was generous to you,' Trent suggested. 'A present for you when he called here—that sort of thing?'

'Mr Hermon always behaved like a gentleman,' Weaver said demurely. 'But I meant more than that, sir. You see, I was two years in his service before I came to Mr Maxwell; that is how I came to know so much about his habits, and to appreciate his kindness. Then when Mr Hermon went on a tour round the world, he suggested I should go to Mr Maxwell, who was not satisfied with the valet he had then; and I have remained in his service since then—about nine months ago it would be.

*   *   *

When Trent went to talk it over with his friend Chief-Inspector Bligh, he found that officer cheerfully interested in what he described as a very nice case.

'There's nothing easy,' he said, 'about it so far. Of course, it's a murder—that's certain. You have heard what the lift company's man says. And, of course, it was meant to look as if it might be an accident.'

'Then how about the ground-floor gate

being forced as well as the other? That doesn't look like an accident.'

'Well, what does it look like?' Mr Bligh wanted to know.

'It looks to me as it looks to you, I suppose. When the old man had been pushed into the lift-shaft, the murderer realized that something had gone wrong with his plan. Hermon had had something on him that might give the murderer away if it was found on the body. The only thing for him to do was to run downstairs, prise open the bottom gate, and take what he wanted off the body. If Pimblett or anybody appeared while he was doing so, he could say he had seen the old man open the gate and fall down the shaft, and had rushed down and forced the gate to see if he was still alive.'

The inspector nodded. 'Yes; that's the idea. And he did get what he wanted, presumably; and nobody did see him. Of course, it's the sort of place where nobody is about most of the time, and the man who did the job knew that.'

'Well, how about the people who live here? Are they all above suspicion?'

'There is no such thing,' Mr Bligh declared, 'as being above suspicion—not if I do the suspecting. And it just happens that most of them haven't an alibi. The Museum man has, of course; his flat was shut up, and is still. And the Corderoys were at their dress shop till after six. But the Frenchman was alone when he came in and reported having found the body;

152

and his story of how he found it, and what time he entered the house, is quite unsupported. Maxwell says he lunched at his flat, went out immediately afterwards, and spent all the afternoon at Lord's watching Lancashire take a licking from Middlesex; then went to his club with some other bright boys, had drinks, and came home to dress for dinner. But Lord's is a place you can dodge out of and return to later, and it's no distance for a car to Rigby Street. Then there's Clayton Haggett, the surgeon. He had lunch in his flat too, after a morning at the hospital; went down to his car at two-thirty, had an operation at a nursing-home and another at a private house; finished by four-fifteen, had a cup of tea, and then spent two hours driving about down Richmond way— just to take the air, and nobody with him all that time, which is a pity.'

'He didn't like Hermon,' Trent remarked. 'He was very bitter in that tussle they had over vivisection.'

'Yes, and he's got a naughty temper when he's crossed. Loses his self-control. He had to resign from the Hunter Club for knocking a man down in the smoking-room. Nobody would have anything to do with him if he wasn't such a wizard with the knife.'

'And what about the servants in the building? Do they come into the picture at all?'

'All I can tell you is that none of their stories can be checked. Pimblett says he was in the basement all the afternoon until the Frenchman shouted for him; his wife was away calling on her sister in Highbury. The French manservant and Haggett's housekeeper say they never opened the doors of their flats until the police looked them up after the finding of the body. Maxwell's man says he had the afternoon off, went out after his master had gone, and sat through the cinema programme at the Byzantine, getting back a little before Anthony did. Well, what good's that? Like the other three, he can't prove anything at all about where he was for some hours before the police were called in.'

'Any of them ever been in trouble?'

'Nothing known against any of them. Ex-Sergeant Pimblett—excellent record. Mrs Hargreaves, the housekeeper—ditto. Weaver used to be employed at Harding's the big barber shop in Duke Street, where old Hermon used to go when he was in town. He always had Weaver to attend to him, and at last he took him on as his valet. Afterwards—'

'Yes, he told me; he was switched on to Anthony. Perfectly respectable. And the French domestic?'

'All I know about Aristide Recot is that he has a wooden face and side-whiskers, and doesn't mind being seen in an apron. What I'm told by his master is that he has been with him for some years, and given every satisfaction. But what's the use? We had to consider the

154

servants, of course; but what motive could any of them have had? It's a different thing when you come to their employers. Haggett, for instance.'

Trent looked the inspector in the eyes. 'You were talking about motive,' he said gently. 'Is Haggett's resentment really the strongest you can think of? I don't like being teased.'

'All right; I was coming to it,' Mr Bligh responded with a faint grin. 'Yes, I suppose the expectation of coming into the greater part of a very large fortune might operate as a motive. That is what Maxwell will do, according to our information. Unless something happens to him. His uncle made him a very generous allowance, and he lived rent free, and Weaver's wages were paid by the old man. Maxwell ought to have been grateful, and perhaps he was; but there you are—he's a vicious young brute, and always in debt; and though Hermon wasn't strong, he might have lived to any old age. Now then! Will that do for you?'

'Something of the sort had crossed my mind,' Trent admitted. 'Certainly it will do— until something better comes along.'

Mr Bligh raised an impressive finger. 'And now,' he said, 'I'll tell you something that hadn't crossed your mind. It's information received. If it's right, the coroner will hear it at a later stage, but at present we would rather the murderer didn't know about it. You remember I mentioned that Clayton Haggett left his flat

155

at two-thirty that afternoon. Well, he had more to tell us than that. He went down by the lift, he said. It's rather a slow-motion lift. As it passed down by the floor below—Anthony's floor— Haggett heard some words spoken. He could see as he passed that the door of the flat was just being opened from inside, and as it opened he heard a loud bullying voice call out, "You do what I say, and look sharp about it. If you get on the wrong side of me, you know what to expect." That is as near as Haggett can go to the actual words he heard—I asked him to be particular.'

Trent stared at the inspector with kindling eyes. 'You do like saving up the best bit to the last, don't you? And you had this—this!— simply handed to you. On a plate.'

'With parsley round it,' added Mr Bligh unashamed.

'I have heard you use that phrase before,' Trent said thoughtfully. 'It meant, I think, that you were rather mistrustful of good things that came so easily. But now, what about this remarkable addition to the record? Did Haggett recognize the voice? Did he see anybody?'

'No. Haggett says it might have been Maxwell he heard talking; but he only knows Maxwell by sight, has never spoken to him, and has no idea what his voice would sound like if it was raised. And, of course, it might have been anybody else in the world. Then I

156

asked him what class of voice it was—like a curate's, or a dustman's, or what. All he could tell me was that it was not a coarse voice, and not a refined one; just middling. Very useful! But that isn't all. As the lift got to the bottom he heard a door above slam violently, which he assumed to be the one he had just seen being opened; and as he was getting into his car, Maxwell came out of the street door, with his hat on, looking furiously angry and very red in the face, and walked away rapidly.

Trent considered this. 'So that is Haggett's information. And what does Maxwell say about it?'

'He hasn't been asked—yet. He is being given a little more time to make mistakes. But, of course, it may all be a lie. Yes, you may look surprised; but Haggett isn't out of it yet, as I told you. There's another piece of news I've got for you which certainly isn't a lie. When Jackson did the post mortem he found something that wants a lot of explaining.'

'What! Another thing you are keeping dark?'

'For the present. He noticed that the finger nails of the right hand looked as if they had been scratching hard at something, and there was a very faint odour that he couldn't place; so he took some scrapings from the nails to be analyzed. They found some tiny scraps of human skin; also traces of some things with hydrocarbo scientific names that don't seem to

157

tell you much, and one thing that I have heard
of quite often before.'

'Yes. What?'

'Chloroform.'

*   *   *

Thinking it over in his studio, Trent could
make no more of this at first than Mr Bligh and
he had made between them. If there had been a
struggle, and if chloroform had been used, it
did seem to point to the one resident in the
house who might be presumed to know all
about chloroform and what could be done with
it. And Haggett was known to be violent
tempered and a good hater, as well as a very
able and successful professional man—not an
unknown combination of qualities. But Trent
found it hard to believe in such a character
expressing its dislike in murder done by tricky
and treacherous means. A quarrel; yes. An
assault; possibly. An assault with a fatal result,
legally a murder; such things did happen. But a
planned and cold-blooded crime, with the
murderer scheming to avoid detection by
means of a trumped-up tale—Trent did not see
it. In his experience, trained faculties, high
responsibility, and professional distinction did
not go with dirty actions and circumstantial
lying.

But if Haggett's story of what he had heard
and seen was true, how could it be fitted to the

known facts? Maxwell's own statement about the time at which he had left the building agreed with Haggett's. Weaver's statement was that he had, as was natural, gone out a little later. Both of them had said nothing of this loud-voiced unknown who had used threatening language in Maxwell's flat. It might have been Maxwell himself. Could it have been Hermon? But Hermon had been fond, even foolishly fond, of his nephew. Unless—and here opened a new vista of ugliness—both Maxwell and his servant had been concealing the truth on that point, building up the fiction of a generous benefactor whom for worlds Maxwell would not have injured. There might be purpose enough in their doing so. The inspector had not thought of that; at least (Trent reflected with a wry smile) he had not mentioned it. Hermon's visit, by the way, had been a surprise visit according to Weaver.

Trent, at this point in his meditations, rose and began to pace the studio. Soon he went across to the model's dressing-room and examined his appearance in the mirror there. His hair had been cut fairly recently, but another trimming would not upset the balance of nature, he thought. Within the hour he was one of a dozen sheeted forms, sitting in a strange chair before a tall mirror, and had met the attendant's opening comment on the warmth of the day with the due rejoinder that it looked like rain later on.

Trent, like many other men, found his thoughts the clearer for being written down, and would often prepare for the drafting of a dispatch that could be published by a private memorandum, including all that could not. That evening he sat at his bureau, and did not rise until the account of what he had discovered, and the conclusions drawn, was complete in black and white.

'Starting with the belief that Haggett's story was true [he wrote], I had to make out who the person in Maxwell's flat was who gave some order, in offensive words, coupled with a vague threat; and who the person ordered about and threatened was. As Bligh said, it might have been any one who used those words; some one who had not as yet come into view in the case. But it was as well to consider first those who were known to have been in the place; and one of these was Hermon. But the accounts we had of Hermon made this seem unlikely; and they were not only the accounts given by Maxwell and his valet. Hermon's general reputation was that of a man who would be the last in the world to bully and threaten. As for the others who had been in the other flats, there was no visible shadow of a reason for suspecting any one of them.

'There remained Maxwell and his valet.

'Maxwell might be capable of bullying and threatening. He is not a nice young man. Could

160

he have been the speaker, and either Hermon or Weaver the man spoken to?

'Well, is it likely? Maxwell is not a lunatic. No man in his senses would talk like that to his rich uncle whose fortune he expected to inherit; nor to his valet unless he was prepared for the man leaving him on the spot, and for being obliged to do his own valeting and cooking and housework until he could get another servant. Unless, of course, he had got either of them under his thumb in some way. Has Hermon, or Weaver, a guilty past, known to Maxwell?

'I had got as far as this when a new point occurred to me. Weaver, when I saw him, had told me that Maxwell had not been expecting his uncle's visit. As this looked very much like a plain lie, I thought some attention paid to Weaver might be worth the trouble; and so I went and had my hair cut at Harding's.

'The man who cut it was as ready for conversation as barbers usually are. I spoke of the fatal accident to Mr Hermon, and the barber, who may have been reading my own remarks on the subject, said that it was a funny sort of accident, giving his reasons for that view. Then I mentioned that I knew Mr Hermon's former valet had once had a job at Harding's. The man remembered both of them very well. He only wished he had the chance of bettering himself as Weaver had done. He had not known that Weaver had become Mr Maxwell's valet, but he had known that

Weaver had done very well for himself. Besides that, Weaver had come into a bit of money of his own; he had mentioned it confidential. He was quite the gentleman now, especially in the last six months. He had taken to having his hair done at Harding's once a fortnight, probably just to show off a bit among his old pals. Gold wrist-watch, diamond tie-pin, quite the swell. Liked to do himself well, too, in his time off; and why not if you could run to it? Sometimes he would have my barber and other friends from Harding's to meet him after hours, and would stand drinks like a lord; and you could always see he had had a few beforehand.

'So far, my visit to Harding's had yielded more than I had any right to expect. But this was not all. My man came at length to that stage of the proceedings at which it is usual for the barber to hint delicately that the condition of one's scalp is not all that could be wished, and that this could be remedied by the use of some sort of hair-wash. With a flash of inspiration I asked what Weaver was in the habit of buying for himself. The best hair tonic there is, said my barber with enthusiasm; Harding's own preparation, Capillax—just the thing for me; and I would understand that Weaver knew, as a hairdresser, how excellent it was. I thought, when I was told the price of it, that Weaver also knew how impressively costly it was. I was shown a bottle of Capillax; a green fluted bottle, with NOT TO BE TAKEN stamped in the glass. Why, I asked my barber, should I be forbidden to take Capillax if I should choose to buy Capillax?

'He turned the bottle over, and showed me on the back a tiny pasted label. It read:

> This preparation, containing among other valuable ingredients a small amount of Chloroform, is, in accordance with the Pharmacy Act, hereby labelled POISON.

'I ordered a bottle, of course. I thought my barber had earned his commission on the sale. And I asked him if he could tell me why chloroform should be used in a tonic for the hair, because I had thought it was for putting people to sleep. He said yes, but that was only the vapour of chloroform; in solution it acted as a stimulant to the skin, and had cleansing properties.

'My reconstruction of this crime is that Weaver planned the murder of Hermon. He had found out something that Maxwell did not dare have known about himself; he put the screw on him and bled him for every shilling he could raise. A servant who knows too much about his employer is a figure common enough in the odorous annals of blackmail. Weaver had "come into money" indeed! Probably he got rid of a lot of it by betting. Anyhow, the more he got, the more he wanted. He had tasted easy money; he could not do without it; and there was no more in sight. But he knew that Maxwell, when his uncle died, would be a rich man. Weaver thought it over; and he formed a plan, to be carried out the first time that opportunity offered.

'On the morning of Hermon's death Maxwell heard, by letter or telephone, that his uncle intended to call that afternoon. Weaver's tale, that the old man had given no notice of his coming, was hardly credible. It was the height of summer, and it was utterly unlikely that Maxwell would be staying indoors that afternoon unless he was expecting a visitor. Hermon would certainly have let him know he was coming. This was what Weaver had been waiting for. After lunch he told Maxwell to leave the flat, go somewhere where he could mix with friends, and stay away until dinner-time. I do not believe Maxwell knew what was intended, because Haggett's story makes it plain that he protested against this. He did not see why he should deliberately absent himself when his uncle had asked him to be at home; why should he affront the old man? Weaver then went to the door of the flat, and as he opened it he raised his voice in the bullying words that Haggett caught as the lift went down. Maxwell, in a furious temper, did as he was told.

'When Hermon arrived, coming up by the lift, Weaver opened the door to him. He

164

framed some lie to account for Maxwell's absence, and asked him to come in, perhaps for a rest and a cup of tea. Hermon did so; and while he was alone in the sitting-room, Weaver slipped out, took the lift to the floor above, and forced the lift gate on Maxwell's floor. When the old man went, Weaver saw him to the lift, opened the gate, and thrust him into the empty shaft. He knew better than most people how bad Hermon's sight was, and how little strength he had for a struggle. And here the plan went wrong. Hermon realized at the last instant that the lift was not there, and grabbed at Weaver as he felt the push given him. His right hand clutched Weaver's hair, tearing some of it out as he fell to his death, and lacerating the man's scalp.

'Weaver had seen instantly that if hair was found in the dead man's hand there would be an end of the theory that he had met with an accident. The police would be looking for a man with black hair and a scratched head; and they would not have far to look. There was only one thing for it. Weaver ran down to the ground floor, forced the gate there, stepped into the well, and carefully removed the hair he found in the dead man's grasp. There was nothing else he could do. He must simply stick to the story he had already made up, and trust to luck. After all, as far as he knew, there had been no witness whatever to anything that had passed.'

It was late by the time Trent had finished his memorandum. He read and re-read it, then slipped it into an envelope, addressed it to Mr Bligh at Scotland Yard, went out and registered it at the district post office.

*   *   *

Trent was at work in his studio next morning when the telephone bell called him.

Mr Bligh, not an effusive man by nature, said that Trent's report had reached him. 'There's no doubt but what you're right,' he went on. 'It's a pity, though, that we shall never hear what it was Weaver knew about Maxwell. It might very well have been a job for us.'

'Well, you called him a vicious young brute,' Trent said. 'With my morbid imagination and your fund of horrid experience, we ought to be able to guess a few of the things that it might have been. But why do you say you will never know? If you bring the murder home to Weaver, he will probably give Maxwell away, having no further use for his secret. It would be just like him.'

'Weaver won't do that.' There was a note of grimness in the inspector's voice. 'At eight fifteen last night Weaver was on his way down Coventry Street. He had been drinking, and couldn't walk straight. A dozen people saw him stumble off the kerb and into the road, right under a passing bus. He was killed instantly. His injuries—'

'Thanks, I don't want to hear about his injuries.' Trent wiped his brow. 'They were fatal—that's enough for me.'

'Yes, but there were some that weren't fatal. On the head, concealed by the hair, there were four deep scratches, not completely healed, and the signs of some hair having been torn out by the roots. I thought you'd like to know.'

THE CAVE OF ALI BABA

DOROTHY L. SAYERS

Appropriately, by walking across Belgravia, over Grosvenor Place and round Hyde Park Corner, we are soon at the doorway of the next of London's celebrated detectives—the man who was said to have been inspired by Philip Trent— the aristocratic Lord Peter Wimsey. Another of the immortals of the genre, Wimsey lives at 110 Piccadilly (a flat believed by members of the Dorothy L. Sayers Society to be on the site of the Park Lane Hotel), with his 'gentleman's gentleman', Bunter, who was his sergeant during the First World War. The younger son of the 15th Duke of Denver, Wimsey has an eclectic variety of hobbies including rare books, history, fine wines, music and cricket, but above all a passion for criminology which has made him, according to certain experts, the leading amateur detective in the capital. His aristocratic bearing fostered at Eton and Oxford is re-emphasized by his dandified appearance, man-about-town manners, and monocle. Among his associates are Inspector Charles Parker from Scotland Yard, and Harriet Vane, a mystery writer, with whom he fell in love and finally married after a tortuous courtship. The first of his cases, Whose Body?, *appeared in 1923, and*

169

it was not until fifty years later that his final adventure, 'Tallboys' was published. Lord Peter has appeared on the stage, on radio and in films and television, played by such skilled actors as Peter Haddon (in the first movie, The Silent Passenger, *in 1935), Robert Montgomery, Edward Petherbridge and Ian Carmichael who remains most viewers' ideal impersonation. H. R. F. Keating has called Wimsey, 'a person one can thoroughly believe in, like, and even love as many women readers do, or hate, as some male readers do'.*

Dorothy Leigh Sayers (1893–1957) never made any bones about the fact that she created Lord Peter to make money. Fascinated by religious literature and a dedicated poet, she had to work in an advertising agency to earn her living and it was there that the idea for her detective sprang into her mind and subsequently made her fortune. Unashamedly as she admitted her motives for writing crime fiction, Dorothy also attempted to make her stories literary as well as exciting and is consequently regarded as a trend-setter in this particular aspect of the history of the detective story. In the thirties she revealed her wide knowledge of the genre by editing three landmark anthologies of crime fiction for her publisher, Victor Gollancz, which are still held up today as models of their kind— not to mention being much prized by collectors. 'The Adventurous Exploit of The Cave of Ali Baba' (to give this tale its original title) is a fascinating Wimsey exploit in which disguise and deception are required to unmask another of London's master criminals...

*   *   *

In the front room of a grim and narrow house in Lambeth a man sat eating kippers and glancing through the *Morning Post*. He was smallish and spare, with brown hair rather too regularly waved and a strong, brown beard, cut to a point. His double-breasted suit of navy-blue and his socks, tie, and handkerchief, all scrupulously matched, were a trifle more point-device than the best taste approves, and his boots were slightly too bright a brown. He did not look a gentleman, not even a gentleman's gentleman, yet there was something about his appearance which suggested that he was accustomed to the manner of life in good families. The breakfast-table, which he had set with his own hands, was arrayed with the attention to detail which is exacted of good class servants. His action, as he walked over to a little side-table and carved himself a plate of ham, was the action of a superior butler; yet he was not old enough to be a retired butler; a footman, perhaps, who had come into a legacy.

He finished the ham with good appetite, and, as he sipped his coffee, read through attentively a paragraph which he had already

171

noticed and put aside for consideration.

'LORD PETER WIMSEY'S WILL
BEQUEST TO VALET
£10,000 TO CHARITIES

'The will of Lord Peter Wimsey, who was killed last December while shooting big game in Tanganyika, was proved yesterday at £500,000. A sum of £10,000 was left to various charities, including [here followed a list of bequests]. To his valet, Mervyn Bunter, was left an annuity of £500 and the lease of the testator's flat in Piccadilly. [Then followed a number of personal bequests.] The remainder of the estate, including the valuable collection of books and pictures at 110a Piccadilly, was left to the testator's mother, the Dowager Duchess of Denver.

*　　　*　　　*

'Lord Peter Wimsey was thirty-seven at the time of his death. He was the younger brother of the present Duke of Denver, who is the wealthiest peer in the United Kingdom. Lord Peter was distinguished as a criminologist and took an active part in the solution of several famous mysteries. He was a well-known book collector and man-about-town.'

*　　　*　　　*

The man gave a sigh of relief.

'No doubt about that,' he said aloud. 'People don't give their money away if they're going to come back again. The blighter's dead and buried right enough. I'm free.'

He finished his coffee, cleared the table, and washed up the crockery, took his bowler hat from the hall-stand, and went out.

A bus took him to Bermondsey. He alighted, and plunged into a network of gloomy streets, arriving after a quarter of an hour's walk at a seedy-looking public-house in a low quarter. He entered and called for a double whisky.

The house had only just opened, but a number of customers, who had apparently been waiting on the doorstep for this desirable event, were already clustered about the bar. The man who might have been a footman reached for his glass, and in doing so jostled the elbow of a flash person in a check suit and regrettable tie.

'Here!' expostulated the flash person, 'what d'yer mean by it? We don't want your sort here. Get out!'

He emphasized his remarks with a few highly coloured words, and a violent push in the chest.

'Bar's free to everybody, isn't it?' said the other, returning the shove with interest.

'Now then!' said the barmaid, 'none o' that. The gentleman didn't do it intentional, Mr Jukes.'

'Didn't he?' said Mr Jukes. 'Well, I *did*.'

'And you ought to be ashamed of yourself,' retorted the young lady, with a toss of the head. 'I'll have no quarrelling in my bar—not this time in the morning.'

'It was quite an accident,' said the man from Lambeth. 'I'm not one to make a disturbance, having always been used to the best houses. But if any gentleman *wants* to make trouble—'

'All right, all right,' said Mr Jukes, more pacifically. 'I'm not keen to give you a new face. Not but what any alteration wouldn't be for the better. Mind your manners another time, that's all. What'll you have?'

'No, no,' protested the other, 'this one must be on me. Sorry I pushed you. I didn't mean it. But I didn't like to be taken up so short.'

'Say no more about it,' said Mr Jukes generously. 'I'm standing this. Another double whisky, miss, and one of the usual. Come over here where there isn't so much of a crowd, or you'll be getting yourself into trouble again.'

He led the way to a small table in the corner of the room.

'That's all right,' said Mr Jukes. 'Very nicely done. I don't think there's any danger here, but you can't be too careful. Now, what about it, Rogers? Have you made up your mind to come in with us?'

'Yes,' said Rogers, with a glance over his shoulder, 'yes, I have. That is, mind you, if everything seems all right. I'm not looking for

174

trouble, and I don't want to get let in for any dangerous games. I don't mind giving you information, but it's understood as I take no active part in whatever goes on. Is that straight?'

'You wouldn't be allowed to take an active part if you wanted to,' said Mr Jukes. 'Why, you poor fish, Number One wouldn't have anybody but experts on his jobs. All you have to do is to let us know where the stuff is and how to get it. The Society does the rest. It's some organization, I can tell you. You won't even know who's doing it, or how it's done. You won't know anybody, and nobody will know you—accept Number One, of course. He knows everybody.'

'And you,' said Rogers.

'And me, of course. But I shall be transferred to another district. We shan't meet again after today, except at the general meetings, and then we shall all be masked.'

'Go on!' said Rogers incredulously.

'Fact. You'll be taken to Number One— he'll see you, but you won't see him. Then, if he thinks you're any good, you'll be put on the roll, and after that you'll be told where to make your reports to. There is a divisional meeting called once a fortnight, and every three months there's a general meeting and share-out. Each member is called up by number and has his whack handed over to him. That's all.'

'Well, but suppose two members are put on

the same job together?'

'If it's a daylight job, they'll be so disguised their mothers wouldn't know 'em. But it's mostly night work.'

'I see. But, look here—what's to prevent somebody following me home and giving me away to the police?'

'Nothing, of course. Only I wouldn't advise him to try it, that's all. The last man who had that bright idea was fished out of the river down Rotherhithe way, before he had time to get his precious report in. Number One knows everybody, you see.'

'Oh!—and who is this Number One?'

'There's lots of people would give a good bit to know that.'

'Does nobody know?'

'Nobody. He's a fair marvel, is Number One. He's a gentleman, I can tell you that, and a pretty high-up one, from his ways. *And* he's got eyes all round his head. *And* he's got an arm as long as from here to Australia. *But* nobody knows anything about him, unless it's Number Two, and I'm not even sure about her.'

'There are women in it, then?'

'You can bet your boots there are. You can't do a job without 'em nowadays. But that needn't worry you. The women are safe enough. They don't want to come to a sticky end, no more than you and me.'

'But, look here, Jukes—how about the money? It's a big risk to take. Is it worth it?'

'Worth it?' Jukes leant across the little marble-topped table and whispered.

'Coo!' gasped Rogers. 'And how much of that would I get, now?'

'You'd share and share alike with the rest, whether you'd been in that particular job or not. There's fifty members, and you'd get one-fiftieth, same as Number One and same as me.'

'Really? No kidding?'

'See that wet, see that dry!' Jukes laughed. 'Say, can you beat it? There's never been anything like it. It's the biggest thing ever been known. He's a great man, is Number One.'

'And do you pull off many jobs?'

'Many? Listen. You remember the Carruthers necklace, and the Gorleston Bank robbery? And the Faversham burglary? And the big Rubens that disappeared from the National Gallery? And the Frensham pearls? All done by the Society. And never one of them cleared up.'

Rogers licked his lips.

'But now, look here,' he said cautiously. 'Supposing I was a spy as you might say, and supposing I was to go straight off and tell the police about what you've been saying?'

'Ah!' said Jukes, 'suppose you did, eh? Well, supposing something nasty didn't happen to you on the way there—which I wouldn't answer for, mind—'

'Do you mean to say you've got me watched?'

177

'You can bet your sweet life we have. Yes. Well, *supposing* nothing happened on the way there, and you was to bring the slops to this pub, looking for yours truly—'

'Yes?'

'You wouldn't find me, that's all. I should have gone to Number Five.'

'Who's Number Five?'

'Ah! I don't know. But he's the man that makes you a new face while you wait. Plastic surgery, they call it. And new finger-prints. New everything. We go in for up-to-date methods in our show.'

Rogers whistled.

'Well, how about it?' asked Jukes, eyeing his acquaintance over the rim of his tumbler.

'Look here—you've told me a lot of things. Shall I be safe if I say "no"?'

'Oh, yes—if you behave yourself and don't make trouble for us.'

'H'm, I see. And if I say "yes"?'

'Then you'll be a rich man in less than no time, with money in your pocket to live like a gentleman. And nothing to do for it, except to tell us what you know about the houses you've been to when you were in service. It's money for jam if you act straight by the Society.'

Rogers was silent, thinking it over.

'I'll do it!' he said at last.

'Good for you, Miss! The same again, please. Here's to it, Rogers! I knew you were one of the right sort the minute I set eyes on you. Here's to money for jam, and take care of Number One! Talking of Number One, you'd better come round and see him tonight. No time like the present.'

'Right you are. Where'll I come to? Here?'

'Nix. No more of this little pub for us. It's a pity, because it's nice and comfortable, but it can't be helped. Now, what you've got to do is this. At ten o'clock tonight exactly, you walk north across Lambeth Bridge' (Rogers winced at this intimation that his abode was known), 'and you'll see a yellow taxi standing there, with the driver doing something to his engine. You'll say to him, "Is your bus fit to go?" and he'll say, "Depends where you want to go to." And you'll say, "Take me to Number One, London." There's a shop called that, by the way, but he won't take you there. You won't know where he's taking you, because the taxi-windows will be covered up, but you mustn't mind that. It's the rule for the first visit. Afterwards, when you're regularly one of us, you'll be told the name of the place. And when you get there, do as you're told and speak the truth, because, if you don't, Number One will deal with you. See?'

'I see.'

'Are you game? You're not afraid?'

'Of course I'm not afraid.'

'Good man! Well, we'd better be moving now. And I'll say good-bye, because we shan't see each other again. Good-bye—and good

179

luck!'

'Good-bye.'

They passed through the swing-doors, and out into the mean and dirty street.

*　　*　　*

The two years subsequent to the enrolment of the ex-footman Rogers in a crook society were marked by a number of startling and successful raids on the houses of distinguished people. There was the theft of the great diamond tiara from the Dowager Duchess of Denver; the burglary at the flat formerly occupied by the late Lord Peter Wimsey, resulting in the disappearance of £7,000 worth of silver and gold plate; the burglary at the country mansion of Theodore Winthrop, the millionaire—which, incidentally, exposed that thriving gentleman as a confirmed Society blackmailer and caused a reverberating scandal in Mayfair; and the snatching of the famous eight-string necklace of pearls from the neck of the Marchioness of Dinglewood during the singing of the Jewel Song in *Faust* at Covent Garden. It is true that the pearls turned out to be imitation, the original string having been pawned by the noble lady under circumstances highly painful to the Marquis, but the coup was nevertheless a sensational one.

On a Saturday afternoon in January, Rogers was sitting in his room in Lambeth, when a slight noise at the front door caught his ear. He sprang up almost before it had ceased, dashed through the small hallway, and flung the door open. The street was deserted. Nevertheless, as he turned back to the sitting-room, he saw an envelope lying on the hat-stand. It was addressed briefly to 'Number Twenty-one'. Accustomed by this time to the somewhat dramatic methods used by the Society to deliver its correspondence, he merely shrugged his shoulders, and opened the note.

It was written in cipher, and, when transcribed, ran thus:

> 'Number Twenty-one—An Extra-ordinary General Meeting will be held tonight at the house of Number One at 11.30. You will be absent at your peril. The word is FINALITY.'

Rogers stood for a little time considering this. Then he made his way to a room at the back of the house, in which there was a tall safe, built into the wall. He manipulated the combination and walked into the safe, which ran back for some distance, forming, indeed, a small strong-room. He pulled out a drawer marked 'Correspondence', and added the paper he had just received to the contents.

After a few moments he emerged, re-set the lock to a new combination, and returned to the sitting-room.

'Finality,' he said. 'Yes—I think so.' He stretched out his hand to the telephone—then appeared to alter his mind.

He went upstairs to an attic, and thence climbed into a loft close under the roof. Crawling among the rafters, he made his way into the farthest corner; then carefully pressed a knot on the timber-work. A concealed trap-door swung open. He crept through it, and found himself in the corresponding loft of the next house. A soft cooing noise greeted him as he entered. Under the skylight stood three cages, each containing a carrier pigeon.

He glanced cautiously out of the skylight, which looked out upon a high blank wall at the back of some factory or other. There was nobody in the dim little courtyard, and no window within sight. He drew his head in again, and, taking a small fragment of thin paper from his pocket-book, wrote a few letters and numbers upon it. Going to the nearest cage, he took out the pigeon and attached the message to its wing. Then he carefully set the bird on the window-ledge. It hesitated a moment, shifted its pink feet a few times, lifted its wings, and was gone. He saw it tower up into the already darkening sky over the factory roof and vanish into the distance.

He glanced at his watch and returned downstairs. An hour later he released the second pigeon, and in another hour the third. Then he sat down to wait.

At half-past nine he went up to the attic again. It was dark, but a few frosty stars were shining, and a cold air blew through the open window. Something pale gleamed faintly on the floor. He picked it up—it was warm and feathery. The answer had come.

He ruffled the soft plumes and found the paper. Before reading it, he fed the pigeon and put it into one of the cages. As he was about to fasten the door, he checked himself.

'If anything happens to me,' he said, 'there's no need for you to starve to death, my child.'

He pushed the window a little wider open and went downstairs again. The paper in his hand bore only the two letters, 'OK'. It seemed to have been written hurriedly, for there was a long smear of ink in the upper left-hand corner. He noted this with a smile, put the paper in the fire, and, going out into the kitchen, prepared and ate a hearty meal of eggs and corned beef from a new tin. He ate it without bread, though there was a loaf on the shelf near at hand, and washed it down with water from the tap, which he let run for some time before venturing to drink it. Even then he carefully wiped the tap, both inside and outside, before drinking.

When he had finished, he took a revolver from a locked drawer, inspecting the mechanism with attention to see that it was in working order, and loaded it with new cartridges from an unbroken packet. Then he sat down to wait again.

At a quarter before eleven, he rose and went out into the street. He walked briskly, keeping well away from the wall, till he came out into a well-lighted thoroughfare. Here he took a bus, securing the corner seat next to the conductor, from which he could see everybody who got on and off. A succession of buses eventually brought him to a respectable residential quarter of Hampstead. Here he alighted and, still keeping well away from the walls, made his way up to the Heath.

The night was moonless, but not altogether black, and, as he crossed a deserted part of the Heath, he observed one or two other dark forms closing in upon him from various directions. He paused in the shelter of a large tree, and adjusted to his face a black velvet mask, which covered him from brow to chin. At its base the number 21 was clearly embroidered in white thread.

At length a slight dip in the ground disclosed one of those agreeable villas which stand, somewhat isolated, among the rural surroundings of the Heath. One of the windows was lighted. As he made his way to the door, other dark figures, masked like himself, pressed forward and surrounded him. He counted six of them.

The foremost man knocked on the door of the solitary house. After a moment, it was opened slightly. The man advanced his head to the opening; there was a murmur, and the door opened wide. The man stepped in, and the door was shut.

When three of the men had entered, Rogers found himself to be the next in turn. He knocked, three times loudly, then twice faintly. The door opened to the extent of two or three inches, and an ear was presented to the chink. Rogers whispered, 'Finality.' The ear was withdrawn, the door opened, and he passed in.

Without any further word of greeting, Number Twenty-one passed into a small room on the left, which was furnished like an office, with a desk, a safe, and a couple of chairs. At the desk sat a massive man in evening dress, with a ledger before him. The new arrival shut the door carefully after him; it clicked to, on a spring lock. Advancing to the desk, he announced, 'Number Twenty-one, sir,' and stood respectfully waiting. The big man looked up, showing the number 1 startlingly white on his velvet mask. His eyes, of a curious hard blue, scanned Rogers attentively. At a sign from him, Rogers removed his mask. Having verified his identity with care, the President said, 'Very well, Number Twenty-one,' and made an entry in the ledger. The voice was hard and metallic, like his eyes. The close scrutiny from behind the immovable black mask seemed to make Rogers uneasy; he shifted his feet, and his eyes fell. Number One made a sign of dismissal, and Rogers, with a faint sigh as though of relief, replaced his mask and left the room. As he came out, the next comer passed in in his place.

The room in which the Society met was a large one, made by knocking the two largest of the first-floor rooms into one. It was furnished in the standardised taste of twentieth-century suburbia and brilliantly lighted. A gramophone in one corner blared out a jazz tune, to which about ten couples of masked men and women were dancing, some in evening dress and others in tweeds and jumpers.

In one corner of the room was an American bar. Rogers went up and asked the masked man in charge for a double whisky. He consumed it slowly, leaning on the bar. The room filled. Presently somebody moved across to the gramophone and stopped it. He looked round. Number One had appeared on the threshold. A tall woman in black stood beside him. The mask, embroidered with a white 2, covered hair and face completely; only her fine bearing and her white arms and bosom and the dark eyes shining through the eye-slits proclaimed her a woman of power and physical attraction.

'Ladies and gentlemen.' Number One was standing at the upper end of the room. The woman sat beside him; her eyes were cast down and betrayed nothing, but her hands were clenched on the arms of the chair and her whole figure seemed tensely aware.

'Ladies and gentlemen. Our numbers are two short tonight.' The masks moved; eyes were turned, seeking and counting. 'I need not inform you of the disastrous failure of our plan for securing the plans of the Court-Windlesham helicopter. Our courageous and devoted comrades, Number Fifteen and Number Forty-eight, were betrayed and taken by the police.'

An uneasy murmur arose among the company.

'It may have occurred to some of you that even the well-known steadfastness of these comrades might give way under examination. There is no cause for alarm. The usual orders have been issued, and I have this evening received the report that their tongues have been effectually silenced. You will, I am sure, be glad to know that these two brave men have been spared the ordeal of so great a temptation to dishonour, and that they will not be called upon to face a public trial and the rigours of a long imprisonment.'

A hiss of intaken breath moved across the assembled members like the wind over a barley-field.

'Their dependants will be discreetly compensated in the usual manner. I call upon Numbers Twelve and Thirty-four to undertake this agreeable task. They will attend me in my office for their instructions after the meeting. Will the Numbers I have named kindly signify

187

that they are able and willing to perform this duty?'

Two hands were raised in salute. The President continued, looking at his watch:

'Ladies and gentlemen, please take your partners for the next dance.'

The gramophone struck up again. Rogers turned to a girl near him in a red dress. She nodded, and they slipped into the movement of a fox-trot. The couples gyrated solemnly and in silence. Their shadows were flung against the blinds as they turned and stepped to and fro.

'What has happened?' breathed the girl in a whisper, scarcely moving her lips. 'I'm frightened, aren't you? I feel as if something awful was going to happen.'

'It does take one a bit short, the President's way of doing things,' agreed Roger, 'but it's safer like that.'

'Those poor men—'

A dancer, turning and following on their heels, touched Rogers on the shoulder.

'No talking, please,' he said. His eyes gleamed sternly; he twirled his partner into the middle of the crowd and was gone. The girl shuddered.

The gramophone stopped. There was a burst of clapping. The dancers again clustered before the President's seat.

'Ladies and gentlemen. You may wonder why this extraordinary meeting has been called. The reason is a serious one. The failure of our recent attempt was no accident. The police were not on the premises that night by chance. We have a traitor among us.'

Partners who had been standing close together fell distrustfully apart. Each member seemed to shrink, as a snail shrinks from the touch of a finger.

'You will remember the disappointing outcome of the Dinglewood affair,' went on the President, in his harsh voice. 'You may recall other smaller matters which have not turned out satisfactorily. All these troubles have been traced to their origin. I am happy to say that our minds can now be easy. The offender has been discovered and will be removed. There will be no more mistakes. The misguided member who introduced the traitor to our Society will be placed in a position where his lack of caution will have no further ill-effects. There is no cause for alarm.'

Every eye roved about the company, searching for the traitor and his unfortunate sponsor. Somewhere beneath the black masks a face must have turned white; somewhere under the stifling velvet there must have been a brow sweating, not with the heat of the dance. But the masks hid everything.

'Ladies and gentlemen, please take your partners for the next dance.'

The gramophone struck into an old and half-forgotten tune: 'There ain't nobody loves me'. The girl in red was claimed by a tall mask

189

in evening dress. A hand laid on Rogers's arm made him start. A small, plump woman in a green jumper slipped a cold hand into his. The dance went on.

When it stopped, amid the usual applause, everyone stood, detached, stiffened in expectation. The President's voice was raised again.

'Ladies and gentlemen, please behave naturally. This is a dance, not a public meeting.'

Rogers led his partner to a chair and fetched her an ice. As he stooped over her, he noticed the hurried rise and fall of her bosom.

'Ladies and gentlemen.' The endless interval was over. 'You will no doubt wish to be immediately relieved from suspense. I will name the persons involved. Number Thirty-seven!'

A man sprang up with a fearful, strangled cry.

'Silence!'

The wretch choked and gasped.

'I never—I swear I never—I'm innocent.'

'Silence. You have failed in discretion. You will be dealt with. If you have anything to say in defence of your folly, I will hear it later. Sit down.'

Number Thirty-seven sank down upon a chair. He pushed his handkerchief under the mask to wipe his face. Two tall men closed in upon him. The rest fell back, feeling the recoil

190

of humanity from one stricken by mortal disease.

The gramophone struck up.

'Ladies and gentlemen, I will now name the traitor. Number Twenty-one, stand forward.'

Rogers stepped forward. The concentrated fear and loathing of forty-eight pairs of eyes burned upon him. The miserable Jukes set up a fresh wail.

'Oh, my God! Oh, my God!'

'Silence! Number Twenty-one, take off your mask.'

The traitor pulled the thick covering from his face. The intense hatred of the eyes devoured him.

'Number Thirty-seven, this man was introduced here by you, under the name of Joseph Rogers, formerly second footman in the service of the Duke of Denver, dismissed for pilfering. Did you take steps to verify that statement?'

'I did—I did! As God's my witness, it was all straight. I had him identified by two of the servants. I made enquiries. The tale was straight—I'll swear it was.'

The President consulted a paper before him, then he looked at his watch again.

'Ladies and gentlemen, please take your partners...'

Number Twenty-one, his arms twisted behind him and bound, and his wrists handcuffed, stood motionless, while the dance of doom circled about him. The clapping, as it ended, sounded like the clapping of the men and women who sat, thirsty-lipped beneath the guillotine.

'Number Twenty-one, your name has been given as Joseph Rogers, footman, dismissed for theft. Is that your real name?'

'No.'

'What is your name?'

'Peter Death Bredon Wimsey.'

'We thought you were dead.'

'Naturally. You were intended to think so.'

'What has become of the genuine Joseph Rogers?'

'He died abroad. I took his place. I may say that no real blame attaches to your people for not having realized who I was. I not only took Rogers's place; I *was* Rogers. Even when I was alone, I walked like Rogers, I sat like Rogers, I read Rogers's books, and wore Rogers's clothes. In the end, I almost thought Rogers's thoughts. The only way to keep up a successful impersonation is never to relax.'

'I see. The robbery of your own flat was arranged?'

'Obviously.'

'The robbery of the Dowager Duchess, your mother, was connived at by you?'

'It was. It was a very ugly tiara—no real loss to anybody with decent taste. May I smoke, by the way?'

'You may not. Ladies and gentlemen...'

The dance was like the mechanical jigging of puppets. Limbs jerked, feet faltered. The prisoner watched with an air of critical detachment.

'Numbers Fifteen, Twenty-two, and Forty-nine. You have watched the prisoner. Has he made any attempts to communicate with anybody?'

'None.' Number Twenty-two was the spokesman. 'His letters and parcels have been opened, his telephone tapped, and his movements followed. His water-pipes have been under observation for Morse signals.'

'You are sure of what you say?'

'Absolutely.'

'Prisoner, have you been alone in this adventure? Speak the truth, or things will be made somewhat more unpleasant for you than they might otherwise be.'

'I have been alone. I have taken no unnecessary risks.'

'It may be so. It will, however, be as well that steps should be taken to silence the man at Scotland Yard—what is his name?—Parker. Also the prisoner's manservant, Mervyn Bunter, and possibly also his mother and sister. The brother is a stupid oaf, and not, I think, likely to have been taken into the prisoner's confidence. A precautionary watch will, I think, meet the necessities of his case.'

The prisoner appeared, for the first time, to be moved.

193

'Sir, I assure you that my mother and sister know nothing which could possibly bring danger on the Society.'

'You should have thought of their situation earlier. Ladies and gentlemen, please take—'

'No—no!' Flesh and blood could endure the mockery no longer. 'No! Finish with him. Get it over. Break up the meeting. It's dangerous. The police—'

'Silence!'

The President glanced round at the crowd. It had a dangerous look about it. He gave way. 'Very well. Take the prisoner away and silence him. He will receive Number four treatment. And be sure you explain it to him carefully first.'

'Ah!'

The eyes expressed a wolfish satisfaction. Strong hands gripped Wimsey's arms.

'One moment—for God's sake let me die decently.'

'You should have thought this over earlier. Take him away. Ladies and gentlemen, be satisfied—he will not die quickly.'

'Stop! Wait!' cried Wimsey desperately. 'I have something to say. I don't ask for life—only for a quick death. I—I have something to sell.'

'To sell?'

'Yes.'

'We make no bargains with traitors.'

'No—but listen! Do you think I have not

194

thought of this? I am not so mad. I have left a letter.'

'Ah! now it is coming. A letter. To whom?'

'To the police. If I do not return tomorrow—'

'Well?'

'The letter will be opened.'

'Sir,' broke in Number Fifteen. 'This is bluff. The prisoner has not sent any letter. He has been strictly watched for many months.'

'Ah! but listen. I left the letter before I came to Lambeth.'

'Then it can contain no information of value.'

'Oh, but it does.'

'What?'

'The combination of my safe.'

'Indeed? Has this man's safe been searched?'

'Yes, sir.'

'What did it contain?'

'No information of importance, sir. An outline of our organisation—the name of this house—nothing that cannot be altered and covered before morning.'

Wimsey smiled. 'Did you investigate the inner compartment of the safe?'

There was a pause.

'You hear what he says,' snapped the President sharply. 'Did you find this inner compartment?'

'There was no inner compartment, sir. He is trying to bluff.'

'I hate to contradict you,' said Wimsey, with an effort at his ordinary pleasant tone, 'but I really think you must have overlooked the inner compartment.'

'Well,' said the President, 'and what do you say is in this inner compartment, if it does exist?'

'The names of every member of this Society, with their addresses, photographs, and finger-prints.'

'What?'

The eyes round him now were ugly with fear. Wimsey kept his face steadily turned towards the President.

'How do you say you have contrived to get this information?'

'Well, I have been doing a little detective work on my own, you know.'

'But you have been watched.'

'True. The finger-prints of my watchers adorn the first page of the collection.'

'This statement can be proved?'

'Certainly. I will prove it. The name of Number Fifty, for example—'

'Stop!'

A fierce muttering arose. The President silenced it with a gesture.

'If you mention names here, you will certainly have no hope of mercy. There is a fifth treatment—kept specially for people who mention names. Bring the prisoner to my office. Keep the dance going.'

The President took an automatic from his hip-pocket and faced his tightly fettered prisoner across the desk.

'Now speak!' he said.

'I should put that thing away, if I were you,' said Wimsey contemptuously. 'It would be a much pleasanter form of death than treatment Number five, and I might be tempted to ask for it.'

'Ingenious,' said the President, 'but a little too ingenious. Now, be quick; tell me what you know.'

'Will you spare me if I tell you?'

'I make no promises. Be quick.'

Wimsey shrugged his bound and aching shoulders.

'Certainly. I will tell you what I know. Stop me when you have heard enough.'

He leaned forward and spoke low. Overhead the noise of the gramophone and the shuffling of feet bore witness that the dance was going on. Stray passers-by crossing the Heath noted that the people in the lonely house were making a night of it again.

*   *   *

'Well,' said Wimsey, 'am I to go on?'

From beneath the mask the President's voice sounded as though he were grimly smiling.

'My lord,' he said, 'your story fills me with regret that you are not, in fact, a member of our

197

Society. Wit, courage, and industry are valuable to an association like ours. I fear I cannot persuade you? No—I supposed not.'

He touched a bell on his desk.

'Ask the members kindly to proceed to the supper-room,' he said to the mask who entered.

The 'supper-room' was on the ground-floor, shuttered and curtained. Down its centre ran a long, bare table, with chairs set about it.

'A Barmecide feast, I see,' said Wimsey pleasantly. It was the first time he had seen this room. At the far end, a trap-door in the floor gaped ominously.

The President took the head of the table.

'Ladies and gentlemen,' he began, as usual—and the foolish courtesy had never sounded so sinister—'I will not conceal from you the seriousness of the situation. The prisoner has recited to me more than twenty names and addresses which were thought to be unknown, except to their owners and to me. There has been great carelessness'—his voice rang harshly—'which will have to be looked into. Finger-prints have been obtained—he has shown me the photographs of some of them. How our investigators came to overlook the inner door of this safe is a matter which calls for enquiry.'

'Don't blame them,' put in Wimsey. 'It was meant to be overlooked, you know. I made it like that on purpose.'

198

The President went on, without seeming to notice the interruption.

'The prisoner informs me that the book with the names and addresses is to be found in this inner compartment, together with certain letters and papers stolen from the houses of members, and numerous objects bearing authentic finger-prints. I believe him to be telling the truth. He offers the combination of the safe in exchange for a quick death. I think the offer should be accepted. What is your opinion, ladies and gentlemen?'

'The combination is known already,' said Number Twenty-two.

'Imbecile! This man has told us, and has proved to me, that he is Lord Peter Wimsey. Do you think he will have forgotten to alter the combination? And then there is the secret of the inner door. If he disappears tonight and the police enter his house—'

'I say,' said a woman's rich voice, 'that the promise should be given and the information used—and quickly. Time is getting short.'

A murmur of agreement went round the table.

'You hear,' said the President, addressing Wimsey. 'The Society offers you the privilege of a quick death in return for the combination of the safe and the secret of the inner door.'

'I have your word for it?'

'You have.'

'Thank you. And my mother and sister?'

'If you in your turn will give us your word— you are a man of honour—that these women know nothing that could harm us, they shall be spared.'

'Thank you, sir. You may rest assured, upon my honour, that they know nothing. I should not think of burdening any woman with such dangerous secrets—particularly those who are dear to me.'

'Very well. It is agreed—yes?'

The murmur of assent was given, though with less readiness than before.

'Then I am willing to give you the information you want. The word of the combination is UNRELIABILITY.'

'And the inner door?'

'In anticipation of the visit of the police—the inner door—which might have presented difficulties—is open.'

'Good! You understand that if the police interfere with our messenger—'

'That would not help me, would it?'

'It is a risk,' said the President thoughtfully, 'but a risk which I think we must take. Carry the prisoner down to the cellar. He can amuse himself by contemplating apparatus Number five. In the meantime, Numbers Twelve and Forty-six—'

'No, no!'

A sullen mutter of dissent arose and swelled threateningly.

'No,' said a tall man with a voice like treacle.

200

'No—why should any members be put in possession of this evidence? We have found one traitor among us tonight and more than one fool. How are we to know that Numbers Twelve and Forty-six are not fools and traitors also?'

The two men turned savagely upon the speaker, but a girl's voice struck into the discussion, high and agitated.

'Hear, hear! That's right, I say. How about us? We ain't going to have our names read by somebody we don't know nothing about. I've had enough of this. They might sell the 'ole lot of us to the narks.'

'I agree,' said another member. 'Nobody ought to be trusted, nobody at all.'

The President shrugged his shoulders.

'Then what, ladies and gentlemen, do you suggest?'

There was a pause. Then the same girl shrilled out again:

'I say Mr President oughter go himself. He's the only one as knows all the names. It won't be no cop to him. Why should we take all the risk and trouble and him sit at home and collar the money? Let him go himself, that's what I say.'

A long rustle of approbation went round the table.

'I second that motion,' said a stout man who wore a bunch of gold seals at his fob. Wimsey smiled as he looked at the seals; it was that trifling vanity which had led him directly to the name and address of the stout man, and he felt a certain affection for the trinkets on that account.

The President looked round.

'It is the wish of the meeting, then, that I should go?' he said, in an ominous voice.

Forty-five hands were raised in approbation. Only the woman known as Number Two remained motionless and silent, her strong white hands clenched on the arm of the chair.

The President rolled his eyes slowly round the threatening ring till they rested upon her.

'Am I to take it that this vote is unanimous?' he enquired.

The woman raised her head.

'Don't go,' she gasped faintly.

'You hear,' said the President, in a faintly derisive tone. 'This lady says, don't go.'

'I submit that what Number Two says is neither here nor there,' said the man with the treacly voice. 'Our own ladies might not like us to be going, if they were in madam's privileged position.' His voice was an insult.

'Hear, hear!' cried another man. 'This is a democratic society, this is. We don't want no privileged classes.'

'Very well,' said the President. 'You hear, Number Two. The feeling of the meeting is against you. Have you any reasons to put forward in favour of your opinion?'

'A hundred. The President is the head and

soul of our Society. If anything should happen to him—where should we be? You'—she swept the company magnificently with her eyes—'you have all blundered. We have your carelessness to thank for all this. Do you think we should be safe for five minutes if the President were not here to repair your follies?'

'Something in that,' said a man who had not hitherto spoken.

'Pardon my suggesting,' said Wimsey maliciously, 'that, as the lady appears to be in a position peculiarly favourable for the reception of the President's confidences, the contents of my modest volume will probably be no news to her. Why should not Number Two go herself?'

'Because I say she must not,' said the President sternly, checking the quick reply that rose to his companion's lips. 'If it is the will of the meeting, I will go. Give me the key of the house.'

One of the men extracted it from Wimsey's jacket-pocket and handed it over.

'Is the house watched?' he demanded of Wimsey.

'No.'

'That is the truth?'

'It is the truth.'

The President turned at the door.

'If I have not returned in two hours' time,' he said, 'act for the best to save yourselves, and do what you like with the prisoner. Number Two will give orders in my absence.'

He left the room. Number Two rose from her seat with a gesture of command.

'Ladies and gentlemen. Supper is now considered over. Start the dancing again.'

*   *   *

Down in the cellar the time passed slowly, in the contemplation of apparatus Number five. The miserable Jukes, alternately wailing and raving, at length shrieked himself into exhaustion. The four members guarding the prisoners whispered together from time to time.

'An hour and a half since the President left,' said one.

Wimsey glanced up. Then he returned to his examination of the room. There were many curious things in it, which he wanted to memorize.

Presently the trap-door was flung open. 'Bring him up!' cried a voice. Wimsey rose immediately, and his face was rather pale.

The members of the gang were again seated round the table. Number Two occupied the President's chair, and her eyes fastened on Wimsey's face with a tigerish fury, but when she spoke it was with a self-control which roused his admiration.

'The President has been two hours gone,' she said. 'What has happened to him? Traitor twice over—what has happened to him?'

'How should I know?' said Wimsey. 'Perhaps he has looked after Number One and gone while the going was good!'

She sprang up with a little cry of rage, and came close to him.

'Beast! liar!' she said, and struck him on the mouth. 'You know he would never do that. He is faithful to his friends. What have you done with him? Speak—or I will make you speak. You two, there—bring the irons. He *shall* speak!'

'I can only form a guess, madame,' replied Wimsey, 'and I shall not guess any the better for being stimulated with hot irons, like Pantaloon at the circus. Calm yourself, and I will tell you what I think. I think—indeed, I greatly fear—that Monsieur le Président in his hurry to examine the interesting exhibits in my safe may, quite inadvertently, no doubt, have let the door of the inner compartment close behind him. In which case—'

He raised his eyebrows, his shoulders being too sore for shrugging, and gazed at her with a limpid and innocent regret.

'What do you mean?'

Wimsey glanced round the circle. 'I think,' he said, 'I had better begin from the beginning by explaining to you the mechanism of my safe. It is rather a nice safe,' he added plaintively. 'I invented the idea myself—not the principle of its working, of course; that is a matter for scientists—but just the idea of the thing.

'The combination I gave you is perfectly correct as far as it goes. It is a three-alphabet thirteen-letter lock by Bunn & Fishett—a very good one of its kind. It opens the outer door, leading into the ordinary strong-room, where I keep my cash and my Froth Blower's cuff-links and all that. But there is an inner compartment with two doors, which open in a quite different manner. The outermost of these two inner doors is merely a thin steel skin, painted to look like the back of the safe and fitting closely, so as not to betray any join. It lies in the same plane as the wall of the room, you understand, so that if you were to measure the outside and the inside of the safe you would discover no discrepancy. It opens outwards with an ordinary key, and, as I truly assured the President, it was left open when I quitted my flat.'

'Do you think,' said the woman sneeringly, 'that the President is so simple as to be caught in a so obvious trap? He will have wedged open that inner door undoubtedly.'

'Undoubtedly, madame. But the sole purpose of that outer inner door, if I may so express myself, is to appear to be the only inner door. But hidden behind the hinge of that door is another door, a sliding panel, set so closely in the thickness of the wall that you would hardly see it unless you knew it was there. This door was also left open. Our revered Number One had nothing to do but to walk straight through into the inner compartment of the safe, which, by the way, is built into the chimney of the old basement kitchen, which runs up the house at that point. I hope I make myself clear?'

'Yes, yes—get on. Make your story short.'

Wimsey bowed, and, speaking with even greater deliberation than ever, resumed:

'Now, this interesting list of the Society's activities, which I have had the honour of compiling, is written in a very large book— bigger, even, than Monsieur le Président's ledger which he uses downstairs. (I trust, by the way, madame, that you have borne in mind the necessity of putting that ledger in a safe place. Apart from the risk of investigation by some officious policeman, it would be inadvisable that any junior member of the Society should get hold of it. The feeling of the meeting would, I fancy, be opposed to such an occurrence.)'

'It is secure,' she answered hastily. '*Mon dieu!* Get on with your story.'

'Thank you—you have relieved my mind. Very good. This big book lies on a steel shelf at the back of the inner compartment. Just a moment. I have not described this inner compartment to you. It is six feet high, three feet wide, and three feet deep. One can stand up in it quite comfortably, unless one is very tall. It suits me nicely—as you may see, I am not more than five feet eight and a half. The President has the advantage of me in height; he might be a little cramped, but there would be room for him to squat if he grew tired of standing. By the way, I don't know if you know it, but you have tied me up rather tightly.'

'I would have you tied till your bones were locked together. Beat him, you! He is trying to gain time.'

'If you beat me,' said Wimsey, 'I'm damned if I'll speak at all. Control yourself, madame; it does not do to move hastily when your king is in check.'

'Get on!' she cried again, stamping with rage.

'Where was I? Ah! the inner compartment. As I say, it is a little snug—the more so that it is not ventilated in any way. Did I mention that the book lay on a steel shelf?'

'You did.'

'Yes. The steel shelf is balanced on a very delicate concealed spring. When the weight of the book—a heavy one, as I said—is lifted, the shelf rises almost imperceptibly. In rising it makes an electrical contact. Imagine to yourself, madame; our revered President steps in—propping the false door open behind him—he sees the book—quickly he snatches it up. To make sure that it is the right one, he opens it—he studies the pages. He looks about for the other objects I have mentioned, which bear the marks of fingerprints. And silently, but very, very quickly—you can imagine it, can you not?—the secret panel, released by the rising of the shelf, leaps across like a panther behind him. Rather a trite simile, but apt, don't you think?'

'My God! oh, my God!' Her hand went up as though to tear the choking mask from her face. 'You—you devil—devil! What is the word that opens the inner door? Quick! I will have it torn out of you—the word!'

'It is not a hard word to remember, madame—though it has been forgotten before now. Do you recollect, when you were a child, being told the tale of *Ali Baba and the Forty Thieves*? When I had that door made, my mind reverted, with rather a pretty touch of sentimentality, in my opinion, to the happy hours of my childhood. The words that open the door are—"Open Sesame".'

'Ah! How long can a man live in this devil's trap of yours?'

'Oh,' said Wimsey cheerfully, 'I should think he might hold out a few hours if he kept cool and didn't use up the available oxygen by shouting and hammering. If we went there at once, I dare say we should find him fairly all right.'

'I shall go myself. Take this man and—do your worst with him. Don't finish him till I come back. I want to see him die!'

'One moment,' said Wimsey, unmoved by this amiable wish. 'I think you had better take me with you.'

'Why—why?'

'Because, you see, I'm the only person who can open the door.'

'But you have given me the word. Was that a lie?'

'No—the word's all right. But, you see, it's one of these new-style electric doors. In fact, it's really the very latest thing in doors. I'm rather proud of it. It opens to the words "Open Sesame" all right—*but to my voice only.*'

'Your voice? I will choke your voice with my own hands. What do you mean—your voice only?'

'Just what I say. Don't clutch my throat like that, or you may alter my voice so that the door won't recognize it. That's better. It's apt to be rather pernickety about voices. It got stuck up for a week once, when I had a cold and could only implore it in a hoarse whisper. Even in the ordinary way, I sometimes have to try several times before I hit on the exact right intonation.'

She turned and appealed to a short, thick-set man standing beside her.

'Is this true? Is it possible?'

'Perfectly, ma'am, I'm afraid,' said the man civilly. From his voice Wimsey took him to be a superior workman of some kind—probably an engineer.

'Is it an electrical device? Do you understand it?'

'Yes, ma'am. It will have a microphone arrangement somewhere, which converts the sound into a series of vibrations controlling an

210

electric needle. When the needle has traced the correct pattern, the circuit is completed and the door opens. The same thing can be done by light vibrations equally easily.'

'Couldn't you open it with tools?'

'In time, yes, ma'am. But only by smashing the mechanism, which is probably well protected.'

'You may take that for granted,' interjected Wimsey reassuringly.

She put her hands to her head.

'I'm afraid we're done in,' said the engineer, with a kind of respect in his tone for a good job of work.

'No—wait! Somebody must know—the workmen who made this thing?'

'In Germany,' said Wimsey briefly.

'Or—yes, yes, I have it—a gramophone. This—this—*he*—shall be made to say the word for us. Quick—how can it be done?'

'Not possible, ma'am. Where should we get the apparatus at half-past three on a Sunday morning? The poor gentleman would be dead long before...'

There was a silence, during which the sounds of the awakening day came through the shuttered windows. A motor-horn sounded distantly.

'I give in,' she said. 'We must let him go. Take the ropes off him. You will free him, won't you?' she went on, turning piteously to Wimsey. 'Devil as you are, you are not such a devil as that! You will go straight back and save him!'

'Let him go, nothing!' broke in one of the men. 'He doesn't go to peach to the police, my lady, don't you think it. The President's done in, that's all, and we'd all better make tracks while we can. It's all up, boys. Chuck this fellow down the cellar and fasten him in, so he can't make a row and wake the place up. I'm going to destroy the ledgers. You can see it done if you don't trust me. And you, Thirty, you know where the switch is. Give us a quarter of an hour to clear, and then you can blow the place to glory.'

'No! You can't go—you can't leave him to die—your President—your leader—my—I won't let it happen. Set this devil free. Help me, one of you, with the ropes—'

'None of that, now,' said the man who had spoken before. He caught her by the wrists, and she twisted, shrieking, in his arms, biting and struggling to get free.

'Think, think,' said the man with the treacly voice. 'It's getting on to morning. It'll be light in an hour or two. The police may be here any minute.'

'The police!' She seemed to control herself by a violent effort. 'Yes, yes, you are right. We must not imperil the safety of all for the sake of one man. *He* himself would not wish it. That is so. We will put this carrion in the cellar where it cannot harm us, and depart, every one to his

212

own place, while there is time.'

'And the other prisoner?'

'He? Poor fool—he can do no harm. He knows nothing. Let him go,' she answered contemptuously.

In a few minutes' time Wimsey found himself bundled unceremoniously into the depths of the cellar. He was a little puzzled. That they should refuse to let him go, even at the price of Number One's life, he could understand. He had taken the risk with his eyes open. But that they should leave him as a witness against them seemed incredible.

The men who had taken him down strapped his ankles together and departed, switching the lights out as they went.

'Hi! Kamerad!' said Wimsey. 'It's a bit lonely sitting here. You might leave the light on.'

'It's all right, my friend,' was the reply. 'You will not be in the dark long. They have set the time-fuse.'

The other man laughed with rich enjoyment, and they went out together. So that was it. He was to be blown up with the house. In that case the President would certainly be dead before he was extricated. This worried Wimsey; he would rather have been able to bring the big crook to justice. After all, Scotland Yard had been waiting six years to break up this gang.

He waited, straining his ears. It seemed to him that he heard footsteps over his head. The

213

gang had all crept out by this time…

There was certainly a creak. The trap-door had opened; he felt, rather than heard, somebody creeping into the cellar.

'Hush!' said a voice in his ear. Soft hands passed over his face, and went fumbling about his body. There came the cold touch of steel on his wrists. The ropes slackened and dropped off. A key clicked in the handcuffs. The strap about his ankles was unbuckled.

'Quick! quick! they have set the time-switch. The house is mined. Follow me as fast as you can. I stole back—I said I had left my jewellery. It was true. I left it on purpose. *He* must be saved—only you can do it. Make haste!'

Wimsey, staggering with pain, as the blood rushed back into his bound and numbed arms, crawled after her into the room above. A moment, and she had flung back the shutters and thrown the window open.

'Now go! Release him! You promise?'

'I promise. And I warn you, madame, that this house is surrounded. When my safe-door closed it gave a signal which sent my servant to Scotland Yard. Your friends are all taken—'

'Ah! But you go—never mind me—quick! The time is almost up.'

'Come away from this!'

He caught her by the arm, and they went running and stumbling across the little garden. An electric torch shone suddenly in the bushes.

'That you, Parker?' cried Wimsey. 'Get your

214

fellows away. Quick! the house is going up in a minute.'

The garden seemed suddenly full of shouting, hurrying men. Wimsey, floundering in the darkness, was brought up violently against the wall. He made a leap at the coping, caught it, and hoisted himself up. His hands groped for the woman; he swung her up beside him. They jumped; everyone was jumping; the woman caught her foot and fell with a gasping cry. Wimsey tried to stop himself, tripped over a stone, and came down headlong. Then, with a flash and a roar, the night went up in fire.

*   *   *

Wimsey picked himself painfully out from among the débris of the garden wall. A faint moaning near him proclaimed that his companion was still alive. A lantern was turned suddenly upon them.

'Here you are!' said a cheerful voice. 'Are you all right, old thing? Good lord! what a hairy monster!'

'All right,' said Wimsey. 'Only a bit winded. Is the lady safe? H'm—arm broken, apparently—otherwise sound. What's happened?'

'About half a dozen of 'em got blown up; the rest we've bagged.' Wimsey became aware of a circle of dark forms in the wintry dawn. 'Good Lord, what a day! What a come-back for a

215

public character! You old stinker—to let us go on for two years thinking you were dead! I bought a bit of black for an arm-band. I did, really. Did anybody know, besides Bunter?'

'Only my mother and sister. I put it in a secret trust—you know, the thing you send to executors and people. We shall have an awful time with the lawyers, I'm afraid, proving I'm me. Hullo! Is that friend Sugg?'

'Yes, my lord,' said Inspector Sugg, grinning and nearly weeping with excitement. 'Damned glad to see your lordship again. Fine piece of work, your lordship. They're all wanting to shake hands with you, sir.'

'Oh, Lord! I wish I could get washed and shaved first. Awfully glad to see you all again, after two years' exile in Lambeth. Been a good little show, hasn't it?'

'Is he safe?'

Wimsey started at the agonized cry.

'Good Lord!' he cried. 'I forgot the gentleman in the safe. Here, fetch a car, quickly. I've got the great big top Moriarty of the whole bunch quietly asphyxiating at home. Here—hop in, and put the lady in too. I promised we'd get back and save him— though' (he finished the sentence in Parker's ear) 'there may be murder charges too, and I wouldn't give much for his chance at the Old Bailey. Whack her up. He can't last much longer shut up there. He's the bloke you've been wanting, the man at the back of the

216

Morrison case and the Hope-Wilmington case, and hundreds of others.'

*   *   *

The cold morning had turned the streets grey when they drew up before the door of the house in Lambeth. Wimsey took the woman by the arm and helped her out. The mask was off now, and showed her face, haggard and desperate, and white with fear and pain.

'Russian, eh?' whispered Parker in Wimsey's ear.

'Something of the sort. Damn! the front door's blown shut, and the blighter's got the key with him in the safe. Hop through the window, will you?'

Parker bundled obligingly in, and in a few seconds threw open the door to them. The house seemed very still. Wimsey led the way to the back room, where the strong-room stood. The outer door and the second door stood propped open with chairs. The inner door faced them like a blank green wall.

'Only hope he hasn't upset the adjustment with thumping at it,' muttered Wimsey. The anxious hand on his arm clutched feverishly. He pulled himself together, forcing his tone to one of cheerful commonplace.

'Come on, old thing,' he said, addressing himself conversationally to the door. 'Show us your paces. Open Sesame, confound you.

217

Open Sesame!'

The green door slid suddenly away into the wall. The woman sprang forward and caught in her arms the humped and senseless thing that rolled out from the safe. Its clothes were torn to ribbons, and its battered hands dripped blood.

'It's all right,' said Wimsey, 'it's all right! He'll live—to stand his trial.'

THE BORDER-LINE CASE

MARGERY ALLINGHAM

Further along Piccadilly—not far from famous Piccadilly Circus—in a little cul-de-sac called Bottle Street lives another of the city's aristocratic detectives, Albert Campion, with his indefatigable Cockney manservant, Magersfontein Lugg. Art collector, wine connoisseur and clubman, Campion was a confirmed bachelor for a considerable portion of his career until he met Lady Amanda Fitton, an energetic and shrewd young woman with a passion for mechanics and engineering. Much of the detective's early life is shrouded in mystery—certainly his noble birth and given name of 'Rudolph' are hardly mentioned along with his occupation until he returned from intelligence work during the Second World War and moved into a bachelor flat at 17a Bottle Street, which is located above a police station. His valet, Lugg, is a reformed burglar who brings to Campion's aid an insider's knowledge of the criminal mind plus unswerving devotion. The detective himself has a well-developed skill at seeming a bit stupid in order to fool his criminal adversaries and is an expert at disguise—having solved one early case in drag! Following his debut in The Crime at Black

Dudley (1929), *Campion ages gradually in the later stories, becoming less frenetic and more serious, his fair hair turning a distinguished white and the eyes behind his large horn-rimmed glasses appearing more perceptive and sympathetic to the victims of crime. His cases have ranged from international criminal conspiracies to helping young society girls in trouble. He is even described in one adventure as having all the hall-marks of a 'universal uncle'. Campion's most constant associate among the forces of law and order is Inspector Stanislaus Oates.*

Margery Allingham (1904–1966) was born in London into a family of writers and published her first book, a novel about smuggling, when she was still a teenager. After her marriage to another author, Philip Youngman Carter in 1927, she began to produce the series of novels about Albert Campion which would make her famous—writing either at the couple's flat in Great Russell Street or their retreat at Tolleshunt d'Arcy, a remote hamlet on the Essex coast. The first of her books to be filmed was Tiger in the Smoke *(1956), an action-packed adventure about a manhunt in the London underworld with Donald Sinden; and in 1988* Campion *was adapted for BBC television starring Peter Davison, Brian Glover as Lugg and Andrew Burt as Inspector Oates. In 'The Border-line Case' (published in 1969) Campion finds himself in a sticky situation both literally and figuratively when, one hot summer night, he is drawn into a case of a London gangland killing . . .*

* * *

It was so hot in London that night that we slept with the wide skylight in our city studio open and let the soot-blacks fall in on us willingly, so long as they brought with them a single stirring breath to move the stifling air. Heat hung on the dark horizons and beneath our particular bowl of sky the city fidgeted, breathless and uncomfortable.

The early editions of the evening papers carried the story of the murder. I read it when they came along about three o'clock on the following afternoon. My mind took in the details lazily, for my eyelids were sticky and the printed words seemed remote and unrelated to reality.

It was a straightforward little incident, or so I thought it, and when I had read the guarded half-column I threw the paper over to Albert Campion, who had drifted in to lunch and stayed to sit quietly in a corner, blinking behind his spectacles, existing merely, in the sweltering day.

The newspapers called the murder the 'Coal Court Shooting Case', and the facts were simple.

At one o'clock in the morning, when

221

Vacation Street, N.E., had been a deserted lane of odoriferous heat, a policeman on the beat had seen a man stumble and fall to the pavement. The intense discomfort of the night being uppermost in his mind, he had not unnaturally diagnosed a case of ordinary collapse and, after loosening the stranger's collar, had summoned the ambulance.

When the authorities arrived, however, the man was pronounced to be dead and the body was taken to the mortuary, where it was discovered that death had been due to a bullet wound neatly placed between the shoulder-blades. The bullet had made a small blue hole and, after perforating the left lung, had furrowed the heart itself, finally coming to rest in the body structure of the chest.

Since this was so, and the fact that the police constable had heard no untoward sound, it had been reasonable to believe that the shot had been fired at some little distance from a gun with a silencer.

Mr Campion was only politely interested. The afternoon certainly was hot and the story, as it then appeared, was hardly original or exciting. He sat on the floor reading it patiently, his long thin legs stretched out in front of him.

'Someone died at any rate,' he remarked at last and added after a pause: 'Poor chap! Out of the frying-pan ... Dear me, I suppose it's the locality which predisposes one to think of that.

Ever seen Vacation Street, Margery?'

I did not answer him. I was thinking how odd it was that a general irritant like the heat should make the dozens of situations arising all round one in the great city seem suddenly almost personal. I found I was desperately sorry for the man who had been shot, whoever he was.

It was Stanislaus Oates who told us the real story behind the half-column in the evening paper. He came in just after four, looking for Campion. He was a Detective-Inspector in those days and had just begun to develop the habit of chatting over his problems with the pale young man in the horn-rimmed spectacles. Theirs was an odd relationship. It was certainly not a case of the clever amateur and the humble policeman: rather the irritable and pugnacious policeman taking it out on the inoffensive, friendly representative of the general public.

On this occasion Oates was rattled.

'It's a case right down your street,' he said briefly to Campion as he sat down. 'Seems to be impossible, for one thing.'

He explained after a while, having salved his conscience by pointing out that he had no business to discuss the case and excusing himself most illogically on grounds of the heat.

'It's "low-class" crime,' he went on briskly. 'Practically gang-shooting. And probably quite uninteresting to all of you who like

223

romance in your crimes. However, it's got me right down on two counts: the first because the man who shot the fellow who died couldn't possibly have done so, and second because I was wrong about the girl. They're so true to type, these girls, that you can't even rely on the proverbial exception.'

He sighed as if the discovery had really grieved him.

We heard the story of Josephine as we sat round in the paralysingly hot studio and, although I never saw the girl then or afterwards, I shall not forget the scene; the three of us listening, breathing rather heavily, while the Inspector talked.

She had been Donovan's girl, so Oates said, and he painted a picture of her for us: slender and flat-chested, with black hair and eyes like a Russian madonna's in a transparent face. She wore blouses, he said, with lace on them and gold ornaments, little chains and crosses and frail brooches whose security was reinforced by gilt safety-pins. She was only twenty, Oates said, and added enigmatically that he would have betted on her, but that it served him right and showed him there was no fool like an old one.

He went on to talk about Donovan, who, it seemed, was thirty-five and had spent ten years of his life in goal. The Inspector did not seem to think any the less of him for that. The fact seemed to put the man in a definite category in his mind and that was all.

'Robbery with violence and the R.O. boys,' he said with a wave of his hand and smiled contentedly as though he had made everything clear. 'She was sixteen when he found her and he's given her hell ever since.'

While he still held our interest he mentioned Johnny Gilchick. Johnny Gilchick was the man who was dead.

Oates, who was never more sentimental than was strictly reasonable in the circumstances, let himself go about Josephine and Johnny Gilchick. It was love, he said—love, sudden, painful and ludicrous; and he admitted that he liked to see it.

'I had an aunt once who used to talk about the Real Thing,' he explained, 'and embarrassingly silly the old lady sounded, but after seeing those two youngsters meet and flame and go on until they were a single fiery entity—youngsters who were pretty ordinary tawdry material without it—I find myself sympathizing with her if not condoning the phrase.'

He hesitated and his smooth grey face cracked into a deprecating smile.

'Well, we were both wrong, anyway,' he murmured, 'my aunt and I. Josephine let her Johnny down just as you'd expect her to and after he had got what was coming to him and was lying in the mortuary he was born to lie in she upped and perjured her immortal soul to

225

swear his murderer an alibi. Not that her testimony is of much value as evidence. That's beside the point. The fact remains that she's certainly done her best. You may think me sentimental, but it depresses me. I thought that girl was genuine and my judgement was out.'

Mr Campion stirred.

'Could we have the details?' he asked politely. 'We've only seen the evening paper. It wasn't very helpful.'

Oates glared at him balefully.

'Frankly, the facts are exasperating,' he said. 'There's a little catch in them somewhere. It must be something so simple that I missed it altogether. That's really why I've come to look for you. I thought you might care to come along and take a glance at the place. What about it?'

There was no general movement. It was too hot to stir. Finally the Inspector took up a piece of chalk and sketched a rough diagram on the bare boards of the model's throne.

'This is Vacation Street,' he said, edging the chalk along a crack. 'It's the best part of a mile long. Up this end, here by the chair, it's nearly all wholesale houses. This sandbin I'm sketching in now marks the boundary of two police divisions. Well, here, ten yards to the left, is the entrance to Coal Court, which is a cul-de-sac composed of two blank backs of warehouse buildings and a café at the far end. The café is open all night. It serves the printers from the two big presses farther down the road. That's its legitimate trade. But it is also a sort of unofficial headquarters for Donovan's mob. Josephine sits at the desk downstairs and keeps an eye on the door. God knows what hours she keeps. She always seems to be there.'

He paused and there came into my mind a recollection of the breathless night through which we had all passed, and I could imagine the girl sitting there in the stuffy shop with her thin chest and her great black eyes.

The Inspector was still speaking.

'Now,' he said, 'there's an upstairs room in the café. It's on the second floor. That's where our friend Donovan spent most of his evening. I expect he had a good few friends with him and we shall locate them all in time.'

He bent over the diagram.

'Johnny Gilchick died here,' he said, drawing a circle about a foot beyond the square which indicated the sandbin. 'Although the bobby was right down the road, he saw him pause under the lamp post, stagger and fall. He called the Constable from the other division and they got the ambulance. All that is plain sailing. There's just one difficulty. Where was Donovan when he fired the shot? There were two policemen in the street at the time, remember. At the moment of the actual shooting one of them, the Never Street man, was making a round of a warehouse yard, but the other, the Phyllis Court chap, was there on

227

the spot, not forty yards away, and it was he who actually saw Johnny Gilchick fall, although he heard no shot. Now I tell you, Campion, there's not an ounce of cover in the whole of that street. How did Donovan get out of the café, where did he stand to shoot Johnny neatly through the back, and how did he get back again without being seen? The side walls of the cul-de-sac are solid concrete backs of warehouses, there is no way round from the back of the café, nor could he possibly have gone over the roofs. The warehouses tower over the café like liners over a tug. Had he come out down the road one or other of the bobbies must have been certain to have seen him. How did he do it?'

'Perhaps Donovan didn't do it,' I ventured and received a pitying glance for my temerity.

'That's the one fact,' said the Inspector heavily. 'That's the one thing I do know. I know Donovan. He's one of the few English mob boys who carry guns. He served five years with the gangs in New York and has the misfortune to take his liquor in bouts. After each bout he has a period of black depression, during which he may do anything. Johnny Gilchick used to be one of Donovan's mob and when Johnny fell for the girl he turned in the gang, which was adding insult to injury where Donovan was concerned.'

He paused and smiled.

'Donovan was bound to get Johnny in the
228

end,' he said. 'It was never anything but a question of time. The whole mob expected it. The neighbourhood was waiting for it. Donovan had said openly that the next time Johnny dropped into the café would be his final appearance there. Johnny called last night, was ordered out of the place by the terrified girl, and finally walked out of the cul-de-sac. He turned the corner and strolled down the road. Then he was shot by Donovan. There's no way round it, Campion. The doctors say that death was as near instantaneous as may be. Johnny Gilchick could not have walked three paces with the bullet in his back. As for the gun, that was pretty obviously Donovan's too. We haven't actually picked it up yet, but we know he had one of the type we are after. It's a clear case, a straightforward case, if only we knew where Donovan stood when he fired the shot.'

Mr Campion looked up. His eyes were thoughtful behind his spectacles.

'The girl gave Donovan an alibi?' he inquired.

Oates shrugged his shoulders. 'Rather,' he said. 'She was passionate about it. He was there the whole time, every minute of the time, never left the upper room once in the whole evening. I could kill her and she would not alter her story; she'd take her dying oath on it and so on. It didn't mean anything either way. Still, I was sorry to see her doing it, with her boy friend barely cold. She was sucking up to the mob, of course; probably had excellent reasons for doing so. Yet, as I say, I was sorry to hear her volunteering the alibi before she was asked.'

'Ah! she volunteered it, did she?' Campion was interested.

Oates nodded and his small eyes widened expressively.

'Forced it on us. Came roaring round to the police station with it. Threw it off her chest as if she were doing something fine. I'm not usually squeamish about that sort of thing, but it gave me a distinct sense of distaste, I don't mind telling you. Frankly, I gave her a piece of my mind. Told her to go and look at the body, for one thing.'

'Not kind of you,' observed Mr Campion mildly. 'And what did she do?'

'Oh, blubbered herself sick, like the rest of 'em.' Oates was still disgruntled. 'Still, that's not of interest. What girls like Josephine do or don't do doesn't really matter. She was saving her own skin. If she hadn't been so enthusiastic about it I'd have forgiven her. It's Donovan who is important. Where was Donovan when he fired?'

The shrill chatter of the telephone answered him and he glanced at me apologetically.

'I'm afraid that's mine,' he said. 'You don't mind, do you? I left the number with the Sergeant.'

He took off the receiver and as he bent his

head to listen his face changed. We watched him with an interest it was far too hot to dissemble.

'Oh,' he said flatly after a long pause. 'Really? Well, it doesn't matter either way, does it? ... Still, what did she do it for? ... What? ... I suppose so ... Yes? ... Really?'

He seemed suddenly astounded as his informant at the other end of the wire evidently came out with a second piece of information more important than the first.

'You can't be certain ... you are? ... What?'

The faraway voice explained busily. We could hear its steady drone. Inspector Oates's exasperation grew.

'Oh, all right, all right,' he said at last. 'I'm crackers ... we're all crackers ... have it your own damned way.'

With which vulgar outburst he rang off.

'Alibi sustained?' inquired Mr Campion.

'Yes.' The Inspector grunted out the word. 'A couple of printers who were in the downstairs room swear he did not go through the shop all the evening. They're sound fellows. Make good witnesses. Yet Donovan shot Johnny. I'm certain of it. He shot him clean through the concrete angle of a piano warehouse as far as I can see.' He turned to Campion almost angrily. 'Explain that, can you?'

Mr Campion coughed. He seemed a little embarrassed.

231

'I say, you know,' he ventured, 'there are just two things that occur to me.'

'Then out with them, son.' The Inspector lit a cigarette and wiped his face. 'Out with them. I'm not proud.'

Mr Campion coughed again. 'Well, the—er—heat, for one thing, don't you know,' he said with profound uneasiness. 'The heat, and one of your concrete walls.'

The Inspector swore a little and apologized.

'If anyone could forget this heat he's welcome,' he said. 'What's the matter with the wall, too?'

Mr Campion bent over the diagram on the boards of the throne. He was very apologetic.

'Here is the angle of the warehouse,' he said, 'and here is the sandbin. Here to the left is the lamp post where Johnny Gilchick was found. Farther on to the left is the P.C. from Never Street examining a courtyard and temporarily off the scene, while to the right, on the other side of the entrance to Coal Court, is another constable, P.C. someone-or-other, of Phyllis Court. One is apt to—er—think of the problem as though it were contained in four solid walls, two concrete walls, two policemen.'

He hesitated and glanced timidly at the Inspector.

'When is a policeman not a concrete wall, Oates? In—er well, in just such heat ... do you think, or don't you?'

Oates was staring at him, his eyes narrowed.

232

'Damn it!' he said explosively. 'Damn it, Campion, I believe you're right. I knew it was something so simple that it was staring me in the face.'

They stood together looking down at the diagram. Oates stooped to put a chalk cross at the entrance to the cul-de-sac.

'It was *that* lamp post,' he said. 'Give me that telephone. Wait till I get hold of that fellow.'

While he was carrying on an excited conversation we demanded an explanation from Mr Campion and he gave it to us at last, mild and apologetic as usual.

'Well, you see,' he said, 'there's the sandbin. The sandbin marks the boundary of two police divisions. Policeman A, very hot and tired, sees a man collapse from the heat under a lamp post on his territory. The man is a little fellow and it occurs to Policeman A that it would be a simple matter to move him to the next lamp post on the other side of the sandbin, where he would automatically become the responsibility of Policeman B, who is even now approaching. Policeman A achieves the change and is bending over the prostrate figure when his colleague comes up. Since he knows nothing of the bullet wound, the entrance to the cul-de-sac, with its clear view to the café, second-floor room, has no significance in his mind. Today, when its full importance must have dawned upon him, he evidently thinks it best to hold his tongue.'

Oates came back from the phone triumphant.

'The first bobby went on leave this morning,' he said. 'He was an old hand. He must have spotted the chap was dead, took it for granted it was the heat, and didn't want to be held up here by the inquest. Funny I didn't see that in the beginning.'

We were all silent for some moments.

'Then—the girl?' I began at last.

The Inspector frowned and made a little grimace of regret.

'A pity about the girl,' he said. 'Of course it was probably an accident. Our man who saw it happen said he couldn't be sure.'

I stared at him and he explained, albeit a little hurriedly.

'Didn't I tell you? When my sergeant phoned about the alibi he told me. As Josephine crossed the road after visiting the mortuary this morning she stepped under a bus ... Oh yes, instantly.'

He shook his head. He seemed uncomfortable.

'She thought she was making a gesture when she came down to the station, don't you see? The mob must have told her to swear that no one had been in the upstairs room; that must have been their first story until they saw how the luck lay. So when she came beetling down to us she must have thought she was risking her life to give her Johnny's murderer away, while

234

instead of that she was simply giving the fellow an alibi ... Funny the way things happen, isn't it?'

He glanced at Campion affectionately.

'It's because you don't get your mind cluttered up with the human element that you see these things so quickly,' he said. 'You see everything in terms of A and B. It makes all the difference.'

Mr Campion, the most gentle of men, made no comment at all.

THE SANTA CLAUS CLUB

JULIAN SYMONS

A brisk walk of half a mile takes us down Lower Regent Street, then left along Pall Mall and into that great landmark of London, Trafalgar Square. Here, in the Soames Building with its view across the invariably busy square, is the small office of Francis Quarles who has been described by Suspense *magazine as 'the most gentlemanly private eye of them all'. Francis is a big man, bulky rather than fat, which in his cramped office tends to enhance his size even more. He is over six foot tall, and takes a pride in his appearance: favouring well-cut suits, silk shirts and colourful, patterned ties. He is never seen without a buttonhole (preferably a carnation) in his lapel. To some of the men of business and politics who consult him this makes Quarles seem a bit of a dandy, while the beautiful women from society and show business who seek his help find him sexually fascinating. He is, as his cases make clear, a highly deceptive character, much tougher than he initially looks and with a formidable brain that law-breakers tangle with at their cost. The first of Quarles' action-packed adventures, 'The Case of XX-2' appeared in* Ellery Queen's Mystery Magazine *in August 1952 and the first collection,* Francis*

237

Quarles Investigates, *was published in 1965.*

Julian Symons (1912–1994) was widely known as 'the crime writers' crime writer' and won most of the major awards in the genre including the Cartier Diamond Dagger Award from the Crime Writers' Association for a 'lifetime's achievement' in the field and several others from equally prestigious organizations like the Mystery Writers of America. Born in London, Julian worked as a secretary in an engineering company and as an advertising copywriter, before his friend George Orwell helped him to become a freelance book columnist and thereafter a biographer, poet and criminologist. As well as his various acclaimed non-fiction works such as A Reasonable Doubt *(1960),* A Pictorial History of Crime *(1966) and* Bloody Murder *(1972), he has written a number of books featuring Inspector Bland in which he started his attempt to blend the literary values of the conventional novel with the excitement of the thriller—an achievement that has reached fruition in some of his latest books like* Death's Darkest Face *(1990). Although Julian later stopped living in the city where he grew up, he was a very clubable man—he was, in fact, a founder member of the Crime Writers' Association as well as a past chairman—a fact which gives an added piquancy to this adventure of his gentlemanly private eye which first appeared in 1960.*

238

*   *   *

It is not often, in real life, that letters are written recording implacable hatred nursed over the years, or that private detectives are invited by peers to select dining clubs, or that murders occur at such dining clubs, or that they are solved on the spot by a process of deduction. The case of the Santa Claus Club provided an example of all these rarities.

The case began one day, a week before Christmas, when Francis Quarles went to see Lord Acrise. He was a rich man, Lord Acrise, and an important one, the chairman of this big building concern and director of that and the other insurance company, and consultant to the Government on half a dozen matters. He had been a harsh, intolerant man in his prime, and was still hard enough in his early seventies, Quarles guessed, as he looked at the beaky nose, jutting chin and stony blue eyes.

They sat in the study of Acrise's house just off the Brompton Road.

'Just tell me what you think of these,' Lord Acrise said.

These were three letters, badly typed on a machine with a worn ribbon. They were all signed with the name James Gliddon. The first two contained vague references to some wrong done to Gliddon by Acrise in the past. They were written in language that was wild but unmistakably threatening. *You have been a*

239

whited sepulchre for too long, but now your time has come ... You don't know what I'm going to do, now I've come back, but you won't be able to help wondering and worrying ... The mills of God grind slowly, but they're going to grind you into little bits for what you've done to me.

The third letter was more specific. *So the thief is going to play Santa Claus. That will be your last evening alive. I shall be there, Joe Acrise, and I shall watch with pleasure as you squirm in agony.*

Quarles looked at the envelopes. They were plain and cheap. The address was typed, and the word *Personal* was on top of each envelope.

'Who is James Gliddon?' he asked.

The stony eyes glared at him. 'I'm told you're to be trusted. Gliddon was a school friend of mine. We grew up together in the slums of Nottingham. We started a building company together. It did well for a time, then went bust. There was a lot of money missing. Gliddon kept the books. He got five years for fraud.'

'Have you heard from him since then? I see all these letters are recent.'

'He's written half a dozen letters, I suppose, over the years. The last one came—oh, seven years ago, I should think. From the Argentine.' Acrise stopped, then added abruptly, 'Snewin tried to find him for me, but he'd disappeared.'

'Snewin?'

'My secretary. Been with me twelve years.'

He pressed a bell. An obsequious, fattish man, whose appearance somehow put Quarles in mind of an enormous mouse, scurried in.

'Snewin—did we keep any of those old letters from Gliddon?'

'No, sir. You told me to destroy them.'

'The last ones came from the Argentine, right?'

'From Buenos Aires, to be exact, sir.'

Acrise nodded, and Snewin scurried out.

Quarles said, 'Who else knows this story about Gliddon?'

'Just my wife.'

'And what does this mean about you playing Santa Claus?'

'I'm this year's chairman of the Santa Claus Club. We hold our raffle and dinner next Monday.'

Then Quarles remembered. The Santa Claus Club had been formed by ten rich men. Each year they met, every one of them dressed up as Santa Claus, and held a raffle. The members took it in turn to provide the prize that was raffled—it might be a case of Napoleon brandy, a modest cottage with some exclusive salmon fishing rights attached to it, or a Constable painting. Each Santa Claus bought one ticket for the raffle, at a cost of one thousand guineas. The total of ten thousand guineas was given to a Christmas charity. After the raffle the assembled Santa Clauses, each accompanied by one guest, ate a traditional

English Christmas dinner.

The whole thing was a combination of various English characteristics: enjoyment of dressing up, a wish to help charities and the desire also that the help given should not go unrecorded.

'I want you to find Gliddon,' Lord Acrise said. 'Don't mistake me, Mr Quarles. I don't want to take action against him, I want to help him. I wasn't to blame, don't think I admit that, but it was hard that Jimmy Gliddon should go to jail. I'm a hard man, have been all my life, but I don't think my worst enemies would call me mean. Those who've helped me know that when I die they'll find they're not forgotten. Jimmy Gliddon must be an old man now. I'd like to set him up for the rest of his life.'

'To find him by next Monday is a tall order,' Quarles said. 'But I'll try.'

He was at the door when Acrise said, 'By the way, I'd like you to be my guest at the Club dinner on Monday night...'

* * *

There were two ways of trying to find Gliddon; by investigation of his career after leaving prison, and through the typewritten letters. Quarles took the job of tracing the past, leaving the letters to his secretary, Molly Player.

From Scotland Yard he found out that Gliddon had spent nearly four years in prison, from 1913 to late 1916. He had joined a Nottinghamshire regiment when he came out, and the records of this regiment showed that he had been demobilized in August, 1919, with the rank of Sergeant. In 1923 he had been given a sentence of three years for an attempt to smuggle diamonds. Thereafter all trace of him in Britain vanished.

Quarles made some expensive telephone calls to Buenos Aires, where the letters had come from seven years earlier. He learned that Gliddon had lived in that city from a time just after the second world war until 1955. He ran an import-export business, and was thought to have been living in other South American Republics during the war. His business was said to have been a cloak for smuggling, both of drugs and of suspected Nazis, whom he got out of Europe into the Argentine. In 1955 a newspaper had accused Gliddon of arranging the entry into the Argentine of a Nazi war criminal named Hermann Breit. Gliddon disappeared. A couple of weeks later a battered body was washed up just outside the city.

'It was identified as Señor Gliddon,' the liquid voice said over the telephone. 'But you know, Señor Quarles, in such matters the police are sometimes unhappy to close their files.'

'There was still some doubt?'

243

'Yes. Not very much, perhaps. But in these cases there is often a measure of doubt.'

Molly Player found out nothing useful about the paper and envelopes. They were of the sort that could be bought in a thousand stores and shops in London and elsewhere. She had no more luck with the typewriter.

Lord Acrise made no comment on Quarles' recital of failure. 'See you on Monday evening, seven-thirty, black tie,' he said, and barked with laughter. 'Your host will be Santa Claus.'

'I'd like to be there earlier.'

'Good idea. Any time you like. You know where it is? Robert the Devil Restaurant...'

The Robert the Devil Restaurant is situated inconspicuously in Mayfair. It is not a restaurant in the ordinary sense of the word, for there is no public dining-room, but simply several private rooms accommodating any number of guests from two to thirty. Perhaps the food is not quite the best in London, but it is certainly the most expensive.

It was here that Quarles arrived at half-past six, a big, suave man, rather too conspicuously elegant perhaps in a midnight-blue dinner jacket. He talked to Albert, the *maître d'hotel*, whom he had known for some years, took an unobtrusive look at the waiters, went into and admired the sparkling kitchens.

Albert observed his activities with tolerant amusement. 'You are here on some sort of business, Mr Quarles?'

244

'I am a guest, Albert. I am also a kind of bodyguard. Tell me, how many of your waiters have joined you in the past twelve months?'

'Perhaps half a dozen. They come, they go.'

'Is there anybody at all on your staff—waiters, kitchen staff, anybody—who has joined you in the past year, and who is over sixty years old?'

'No. There is not such a one.'

The first of the guests came just after a quarter-past seven. This was the brain surgeon Sir James Erdington, with a guest whom Quarles recognized as the Arctic explorer, Norman Endell. After that they came at intervals of a minute or two: a junior minister in the Government; one of the three most important men in the motor industry; a general elevated to the peerage to celebrate his retirement; a theatrical producer named Roddy Davis, who had successfully combined commerce and culture.

As they arrived, the hosts went into a special robing room to put on their Santa Claus clothes, while the guests drank sherry.

At seven-twenty-five Snewin scurried in, gasped, 'Excuse me, place names, got to put them out,' and went into the dining-room. Through the open door Quarles glimpsed a large oval table, gleaming with silver, bright with roses.

After Snewin came Lord Acrise, jutting-nosed and fearsome-eyed. 'Sorry to have kept you waiting,' he barked, and asked conspiratorially, 'Well?'

'No sign.'

'False alarm. Lot of nonsense. Got to dress up now.'

He went into the robing room with his box—each of the hosts had a similar box, labelled 'Santa Claus'—and came out again bewigged, bearded and robed. 'Better get the business over, and then we can enjoy ourselves. You can tell 'em to come in,' he said to Albert.

This referred to the photographers, who had been clustered outside, and now came into the room specially provided for holding the raffle. In the centre of the room was a table, and on the table stood this year's prize, two exquisite T'ang horses. On the other side of the table were ten chairs arranged in a semi-circle, and on these sat the Santa Clauses. Their guests stood inconspicuously at the side.

The raffle was conducted with the utmost seriousness. Each Santa Claus had a numbered slip. These slips were put into a tombola, and Acrise put in his hand and drew out one of them. Flash bulbs exploded.

'The number drawn is eight,' Acrise announced, and Roddy Davis waved the counterfoil in his hand.

'Isn't that *wonderful*? It's my ticket.' He went over to the horses, picked up one. 'I'm bound to say that they couldn't have gone to *anybody* who'd have appreciated them more.'

Quarles, standing near the general, whose face was as red as his robe, heard him mutter something uncomplimentary. Charity, he reflected, was not universal, even in a gathering of Santa Clauses. Then there were more flashes, the photographers disappeared, and Quarles' views about the nature of charity were reinforced when, as they were about to go into the dining-room, Sir James Erdington said, 'Forgotten something, haven't you, Acrise?'

With what seemed dangerous quietness Acrise answered, 'Have I? I don't think so.'

'It's customary for the Club and guests to sing "Noel" before we go in to dinner.'

'You didn't come to last year's dinner. It was agreed then that we should give it up. Carols after dinner, much better.'

'I must say I thought that was just for last year, because we were late,' Roddy Davis fluted.

'Suggest we put it to the vote,' Erdington said sharply.

Half a dozen of the Santas now stood looking at each other with subdued hostility. Then suddenly the Arctic explorer, Endell, began to sing 'Noel, Noel' in a rich bass. There was the faintest flicker of hesitation, and then the guests and their hosts joined in. The situation was saved.

At dinner Quarles found himself with Acrise on one side of him and Roddy Davis on the other. Endell sat at Acrise's other side, and beyond him was Erdington. Turtle soup was followed by grilled sole, and then three great turkeys were brought in. The helpings of turkey were enormous. With the soup they drank a light, dry sherry, with the sole Chassagne Montrachet, with the turkey an Aloxe Corton.

'And who are *you*?' Roddy Davis peered at Quarles' card and said, 'Of course, I know your name.'

'I am a criminologist.' This sounded better, Quarles thought, than 'private detective'.

'I remember your monograph on criminal calligraphy. Quite fascinating.'

So Davis *did* know who he was. It would be easy, Quarles thought, to underrate the intelligence of this man.

'These beards really do get in the way rather,' Davis said. 'But there, one must suffer for tradition. Have you known Acrise long?'

'Not very. I'm greatly privileged to be here.'

Quarles had been watching, as closely as he could, the pouring of the wine, the serving of the food. He had seen nothing suspicious. Now, to get away from Davis' questions, he turned to his host.

'Damned awkward business before dinner,' Acrise said. 'Might have been, at least. Can't let well alone, Erdington.' He picked up his turkey leg, attacked it with Elizabethan gusto, wiped his mouth and fingers with his napkin. 'Like this wine?'

'It's excellent.'

'Chose it myself. They've got some good Burgundies here.' Acrise's speech was slightly slurred, and it seemed to Quarles that he was rapidly getting drunk.

'Do you have any speeches?'

'No speeches. Just sing carols. But I've got a little surprise for 'em.'

'What sort of surprise?'

'Very much in the spirit of Christmas, and a good joke too. But if I told you, it wouldn't be a surprise, would it?'

There was a general cry of pleasure as Albert himself brought in the great plum pudding, topped with holly and blazing with brandy.

'That's the most wonderful pudding I've ever seen in my life,' Endell said. 'Are we really going to eat it?'

'Of course,' Acrise said irritably. He stood up, swaying a little, and picked up the knife beside the pudding.

'I don't like to be critical, but our Chairman is really not cutting the pudding very well,' Roddy Davis whispered to Quarles. And indeed, it was more of a stab than a cut that Acrise made at the pudding. Albert took over, and cut it quickly and efficiently. Bowls of brandy butter were circulated.

Quarles leaned towards Acrise. 'Are you all right?'

'Of course I'm all right.'

The slurring was very noticeable now. Acrise

ate no pudding, but he drank some more wine, and dabbed at his lips. When the pudding was finished, he got slowly to his feet again and toasted the Queen. Cigars were lighted. Acrise was not smoking. He whispered something to the waiter, who nodded and left the room. Acrise got up again, leaning heavily on the table.

'A little surprise,' he said. 'In the spirit of Christmas.'

Quarles had thought that he was beyond being surprised by the activities of the Santa Claus Club, but he was astonished at the sight of the three figures who entered the room.

They were led by Snewin, somehow more mouselike than ever, wearing a long, white smock and a red nightcap with a tassel. He was followed by an older man dressed in a kind of grey sackcloth, with a face so white that it might have been covered in plaster of Paris. This man carried chains, which he shook. At the rear came a young-middle-aged lady who seemed to be completely hung with tinsel.

'I am Scrooge,' said Snewin.

'I am Marley,' wailed grey sackcloth, clanking his chains vigorously.

'And I,' said the young-middle-aged lady, with abominable sprightliness, 'am the ghost of Christmas past.'

There was a ripple of laughter.

'We have come,' said Snewin in a thin, mouse voice, 'to perform for you our own interpretation of *A Christmas Carol* . . . Oh, sir, what's the matter?'

Lord Acrise stood up in his robes, tore off his wig, pulled at his beard, tried to say something. Then he clutched at the side of his chair and fell sideways, so that he leaned heavily against Endell and slipped slowly to the floor.

There ensued a minute of confused, important activity. Endell made some sort of exclamation and rose from his chair, slightly obstructing Quarles. Erdington was first beside the body, holding the wrist in his hand, listening for the heart. Then they were all crowding round. Snewin, at Quarles' left shoulder, was babbling something, and at his right were Roddy Davis and Endell.

'Stand back,' Erdington snapped. He stayed on his knees for another few moments, looking curiously at Acrise's puffed, distorted face, bluish around the mouth. Then he stood up.

'He's dead.'

There was a murmur of surprise and horror, and now they all drew back, as men do instinctively from the presence of death.

'Heart attack?' somebody said.

Quarles moved to his side. 'I'm a private detective, Sir James. Lord Acrise feared an attempt on his life, and asked me to come along here.'

'You seem to have done well so far,' Erdington said drily.

'May I look at the body?'

'If you wish.'

As Quarles bent down, he caught the smell of bitter almonds. 'There's a smell like prussic acid, but the way he died precludes cyanide, I think. He seemed to become very drunk during dinner, and his speech was blurred. Does that suggest anything to you?'

'I'm a brain surgeon, not a physician.' Erdington stared at the floor. 'Nitro benzene?'

'That's what I thought. We shall have to notify the police.'

Quarles went to the door and spoke to a disturbed Albert. Then he returned to the room and clapped his hands.

'Gentlemen. My name is Francis Quarles, and I am a private detective. Lord Acrise asked me to come here tonight because he had received a threat that this would be his last evening alive. The threat said, "I shall be there, and I shall watch with pleasure as you squirm in agony." Lord Acrise has been poisoned. It seems certain that the man who made the threat is in this room.'

'Gliddon,' a voice said. Snewin had divested himself of the white smock and red nightcap, and now appeared as his customary respectable self.

'Yes. This letter, and others he had received, were signed with the name of James Gliddon, a man who bore a grudge against Lord Acrise which went back nearly half a century.

252

Gliddon became a professional smuggler and crook. He would now be in his late sixties.'

'But dammit man, this Gliddon's not here.' That was the General, who took off his wig and beard. 'Lot of tomfoolery.'

In a shamefaced way the other members of the Santa Claus Club removed their facial trappings. Marley took off his chains and the lady discarded her cloak of tinsel.

Quarles said, 'Isn't he here? But Lord Acrise is dead.'

Snewin coughed. 'Excuse me, sir, but would it be possible for my colleagues from our local dramatic society to retire?'

'Everybody must stay in this room until the police arrive,' Quarles said grimly. 'The problem, as you will all realize, is how the poison was administered. All of us ate the same food, drank the same wine. I sat next to Lord Acrise, and I watched as closely as possible to make sure of this. After dinner some of you smoked cigars or cigarettes, but not Lord Acrise.'

'Just a moment.' It was Roddy Davis who spoke. 'This sounds fantastic, but wasn't it Sherlock Holmes who said that when you'd eliminated all other possibilities, even a fantastic one must be right? Supposing poison in powder form was put on to Acrise's food? Through the pepper pots, say...'

Erdington was shaking his head, but Quarles unscrewed both salt and pepper pots and

253

tasted their contents. 'Salt and pepper,' he said briefly. 'Hello, what's this?'

'It's Acrise's napkin,' Endell said. 'What's remarkable about that?'

'It's a napkin, but not the one Acrise used. He wiped his mouth half a dozen times on his napkin, and wiped his greasy fingers on it too, when he'd gnawed a turkey bone. He must certainly have left grease marks on it. But look at this napkin.'

He held it up, and they saw that it was spotless. Quarles said softly, 'The murderer's mistake.'

Quarles turned to Erdington. 'Sir James and I agree that the poison used was probably nitro benzene. This is deadly as a liquid, but it is also poisonous as a vapour—isn't that so?'

Erdington nodded. 'You'll remember the case of the unfortunate young man who used shoe polish containing nitro benzene on damp shoes, put them on and wore them, and was killed by the fumes.'

'Yes. Somebody made sure that Lord Acrise had a napkin that had been soaked in nitro benzene but was dry enough to use. The same person substituted the proper napkin, the one belonging to the restaurant, after Acrise was dead.'

'That means the napkin must still be here,' Davis said.

'It does.'

'Then I vote that we submit to a search!'

254

'That won't be necessary,' Quarles said. 'Only one person here fulfils all the qualifications of the murderer.'

'James Gliddon?'

'No. Gliddon is almost certainly dead, as I found out when I made enquiries about him. But the murderer is somebody who knew about Acrise's relationship with Gliddon, and tried to be clever by writing those letters to lead us along a wrong track.' He paused. 'Then the murderer is somebody who had the opportunity of coming in here before dinner, and who knew exactly where Acrise would be sitting.'

There was a dead silence in the room.

Quarles said, 'He removed any possible suspicion from himself, as he thought, by being absent from the dinner table, but he arranged to come in afterwards to exchange the napkins. He probably put the poisoned napkin into the clothes he discarded. As for motive, long-standing hatred might be enough, but he is also somebody who knew that he would benefit handsomely when Acrise died . . . stop him, will you?'

But the General, with a tackle reminiscent of the days when he had been the best wing three-quarter in the country, had already brought to the floor Lord Acrise's secretary, Snewin.

THE INCAUTIOUS BURGLAR

JOHN DICKSON CARR

Moving on from Trafalgar Square brings us to Charing Cross Station and, just behind it, the stylish group of buildings which make up Adelphi Terrace. Here, at number 1, the gargantuan private detective, Dr Gideon Fell, has his office; and if he is not busy on a case, he will alternately be found discoursing on his love of good beer and tobacco or else telling jokes which he is constantly surprised make other people laugh. Fell, with his three chins, drooping moustache, and rumbling voice, bears a striking resemblance to the great English writer G. K. Chesterton, and like him, wears a huge cape and glasses perched on the end of his nose. His obvious eccentricity is underlined by the fact that he much prefers tackling cases where there is some hint of the supernatural involved, and he will happily travel hundreds of miles to prove that there is a rational explanation for the events after all. As Dorothy L. Sayers has observed, 'Dr Fell always arrives in time to dispel the ghosts with a fat chuckle and a blast of common sense.' Once met, he is never forgotten either, and there are a number of grateful clients who have been heard to say that they think of him as a mixture of Father Christmas and Old King Cole! The doctor's appreciation of good beer is another incentive for him to travel, making him something of a forerunner in the campaign for real ales...

John Dickson Carr (1906–1977), who has been called the master of the 'impossible crime' story, was another American whose inspiration to write detective fiction came, initially, when he was still a youngster and read G. K. Chesterton's stories of Father Brown and then, more specifically, when he settled in London with his English wife. When Carr made the decision to devise a detective of his own he made no secret of the fact that his man was modelled on Chesterton, 'in the hope I was creating a character everybody would like.' In 23 novels, beginning with Hag's Nook *(1933), and dozens of short stories, John not only made Fell likeable but wholly memorable, too. (Sadly, John Dickson Carr was actually invited to join the London Detection Club in 1936 when G. K. Chesterton was its president, but just before they were due to meet—and doubtless discuss their doppelgänger, Dr Fell—the older man was struck down with his fatal illness.) In the story of 'The Incautious Burglar', the superweight sleuth is found once again running down a good pint of beer at the same time as he is hunting down a criminal.*

*   *   *

Two guests, who were not staying the night at

Cranleigh Court, left at shortly past eleven o'clock. Marcus Hunt saw them to the front door. Then he returned to the dining-room, where the poker-chips were now stacked into neat piles of white, red, and blue.

'Another game?' suggested Rolfe.

'No good,' said Derek Henderson. His tone, as usual, was weary. 'Not with just the three of us.'

Their host stood by the sideboard and watched them. The long, low house, overlooking the Weald of Kent, was so quiet that their voices rose with startling loudness. The dining-room, large and panelled, was softly lighted by electric wall-candles which brought out the sombre colours of the paintings. It is not often that anybody sees, in one room of an otherwise commonplace country house, two Rembrandts and a Van Dyck. There was a kind of defiance about those paintings.

To Arthur Rolfe—the art dealer—they represented enough money to make him shiver. To Derek Henderson—the art critic— they represented a problem. What they represented to Marcus Hunt was not apparent.

Hunt stood by the sideboard, his fists on his hips, smiling. He was a middle-sized, stocky man, with a full face and a high complexion. Equip him with a tuft of chin-whisker, and he would have looked like a Dutch burgher for a Dutch brush. His shirt-front bulged out untidily. He watched with ironical amusement while Henderson picked up a pack of cards in long fingers, cut them into piles, and shuffled with a sharp flick of each thumb which made the cards melt together like a conjuring trick.

Henderson yawned.

'My boy,' said Hunt, 'you surprise me.'

'That's what I try to do,' answered Henderson, still wearily. He looked up. 'But why do you say so, particularly?'

Henderson was young, he was long, he was lean, he was immaculate; and he wore a beard. It was a reddish beard, which moved some people to hilarity. But he wore it with an air of complete naturalness.

'I'm surprised,' said Hunt, 'that you enjoy anything so bourgeois—so plebeian—as poker.'

'I enjoy reading people's characters,' said Henderson. 'Poker's the best way to do it, you know.'

Hunt's eyes narrowed. 'Oh? Can you read my character, for instance?'

'With pleasure,' said Henderson. Absently he dealt himself a poker-hand, face up. It contained a pair of fives, and the last card was the ace of spades. Henderson remained staring at it for a few seconds before he glanced up again.

'And I can tell you,' he went on, 'that you surprise me. Do you mind if I'm frank? I had always thought of you as the Colossus of

Business; the smasher; the plunger; the fellow who took the long chances. Now, you're not like that at all.'

Marcus Hunt laughed. But Henderson was undisturbed.

'You're tricky, but you're cautious. I doubt if you ever took a long chance in your life. Another surprise'—he dealt himself a new hand—'is Mr Rolfe here. He's the man who, given the proper circumstances, would take the long chances.'

Arthur Rolfe considered this. He looked startled, but rather flattered. Though in height and build not unlike Hunt, there was nothing untidy about him. He had a square, dark face, with thin shells of eyeglasses, and a worried forehead.

'I doubt that,' he declared, very serious about this. Then he smiled. 'A person who took long chances in my business would find himself in the soup.' He glanced round the room. 'Anyhow, I'd be too cautious to have three pictures, with an aggregate value of thirty thousand pounds, hanging in an unprotected downstairs room with french windows giving on a terrace.' An almost frenzied note came into his voice. 'Great Scot! Suppose a burglar—'

'Damn!' said Henderson unexpectedly.

Even Hunt jumped.

Ever since the poker-party, an uneasy atmosphere had been growing. Hunt had picked up an apple from a silver fruit-bowl on the sideboard. He was beginning to pare it with a fruit-knife, a sharp wafer-thin blade which glittered in the light of the wall-lamps.

'You nearly made me slice my thumb off,' he said, putting down the knife. 'What's the matter with you?'

'It's the ace of spades,' said Henderson, still languidly. 'That's the second time it's turned up in five minutes.'

Arthur Rolfe chose to be dense. 'Well? What about it?'

'I think our young friend is being psychic,' said Hunt, good-humoured again. 'Are you reading characters, or only telling fortunes?'

Henderson hesitated. His eyes moved to Hunt, and then to the wall over the sideboard where Rembrandt's 'Old Woman with Cap' stared back with the immobility and skin-colouring of a red Indian. Then Henderson looked towards the french windows opening on the terrace.

'None of my affair,' shrugged Henderson. 'It's your house and your collection and your responsibility. But this fellow Butler: what do you know about him?'

Marcus Hunt looked boisterously amused.

'Butler? He's a friend of my niece's. Harriet picked him up in London, and asked me to invite him down here. Nonsense! Butler's all right. What are you thinking, exactly?'

'Listen!' said Rolfe, holding up his hand.

*　　*　　*

The noise they heard, from the direction of the terrace, was not repeated. It was not repeated because the person who had made it, a very bewildered and uneasy young lady, had run lightly and swiftly to the far end, where she leaned against the balustrade.

Lewis Butler hesitated before going after her. The moonlight was so clear that one could see the mortar between the tiles which paved the terrace, and trace the design of the stone urns along the balustrade. Harriet Davis wore a white gown with long and filmy skirts, which she lifted clear of the ground as she ran.

Then she beckoned to him.

She was half-sitting, half-leaning against the rail. Her white arms were spread out, fingers gripping the stone. Dark hair and dark eyes became even more vivid by moonlight. He could see the rapid rise and fall of her breast; he could even trace the shadow of her eyelashes.

'That was a lie, anyhow,' she said.

'What was?'

'What my Uncle Marcus said. You heard him.' Harriet Davis's fingers tightened still more on the balustrade. But she nodded her head vehemently, with fierce accusation. 'About my knowing you. And inviting you here. I never saw you before this weekend. Either Uncle Marcus is going out of his mind, or ... will you answer me just one question?'

263

'If I can.'

'Very well. Are you by any chance a crook?'

She spoke with as much simplicity and directness as though she had asked him whether he might be a doctor or a lawyer. Lewis Butler was not unwise enough to laugh. She was in that mood where, to any woman, laughter is salt to a raw wound; she would probably have slapped his face.

'To be quite frank about it,' he said, 'I'm not. Will you tell me why you asked?'

'This house,' said Harriet, looking at the moon, 'used to be guarded with burglar alarms. If you as much as touched a window, the whole place started clanging like a fire-station. He had all the burglar alarms removed last week. Last week.' She took her hands off the balustrade, and pressed them together hard. 'The pictures used to be upstairs, in a locked room next to his bedroom. He had them moved downstairs—last week. It's almost as though my uncle *wanted* the house to be burgled.'

Butler knew that he must use great care here.

'Perhaps he does.' (Here she looked at Butler quickly, but did not comment.) 'For instance,' he went on idly, 'suppose one of his famous Rembrandts turned out to be a fake? It might be a relief not to have to show it to his expert friends.'

The girl shook her head.

'No,' she said. 'They're all genuine. You see,

264

I thought of that too.'

Now was the time to hit, and hit hard. To Lewis Butler, in his innocence, there seemed to be no particular problem. He took out his cigarette-case, and turned it over without opening it.

'Look here, Miss Davis, you're not going to like this. But I can tell you of cases in which people were rather anxious to have their property "stolen". If a picture is insured for more than its value, and then it is mysteriously "stolen" one night—'

'That might be all very well too,' answered Harriet, still calmly. 'Except that not one of those pictures has been insured.'

The cigarette-case, which was of polished metal, slipped through Butler's fingers and fell with a clatter on the tiles. It spilled cigarettes, just as it spilled and confused his theories. As he bent over to pick it up, he could hear a church clock across the Weald strike the half-hour after eleven.

'You're sure of that?'

'I'm perfectly sure. He hasn't insured any of his pictures for as much as a penny. He says it's a waste of money.'

'But—'

'Oh, I know! And I don't know why I'm talking to you like this. You're a stranger, aren't you?' She folded her arms, drawing her shoulders up as though she were cold. Uncertainty, fear, and plain nerves flicked at

265

her eyelids. 'But then Uncle Marcus is a stranger too. Do you know what I think? *I* think he's going mad.'

'Hardly as bad as that, is it?'

'Yes, go on,' the girl suddenly stormed at him. 'Say it: go on and say it. That's easy enough. But you don't see him when his eyes seem to get smaller, and all that genial-country-squire look goes out of his face. He's not a fake: he hates fakes, and goes out of his way to expose them. But, if he hasn't gone clear out of his mind, what's he up to? What can he be up to?'

In something over three hours they found out.

*   *   *

The burglar did not attack until half-past two in the morning. First he smoked several cigarettes in the shrubbery below the rear terrace. When he heard the church clock strike, he waited a few minutes more, and then slipped up the steps to the french windows of the dining-room.

A chilly wind stirred at the turn of the night, in the hour of suicides and bad dreams. It smoothed grass and trees with a faint rustling. When the man glanced over his shoulder, the last of the moonlight distorted his face: it showed less a face than the blob of a black cloth mask under a greasy cap pulled down over his ears.

He went to work on the middle window, with the contents of a folding tool-kit not so large as a motorist's. He fastened two short strips of adhesive tape to the glass just beside the catch. Then his glass cutter sliced out a small semi-circle inside the tape.

It was done not without noise: it crunched like a dentist's drill in a tooth, and the man stopped to listen.

There was no answering noise. No dog barked.

With the adhesive tape holding the glass so that it did not fall and smash, he slid his gloved hand through the opening and twisted the catch. The weight of his body deadened the creaking window when he pushed inside.

He knew exactly what he wanted. He put the tool-kit into his pocket, and drew out an electric torch. Its beam moved across to the sideboard; it touched gleaming silver, a bowl of fruit, and a wicked little knife thrust into an apple as though into someone's body; finally, it moved up the hag-face of the 'Old Woman with Cap.'

This was not a large picture, and the burglar lifted it down easily. He prised out glass and frame. Though he tried to roll up the canvas with great care, the brittle paint cracked across in small stars which wounded the hag's face. The burglar was so intent on this that he never noticed the presence of another person in the room.

He was an incautious burglar: he had no sixth sense which smelt murder.

Up on the second floor of the house, Lewis Butler was awakened by a muffled crash like that of metal objects falling.

He had not fallen into more than a half-doze all night. He knew with certainty what must be happening, though he had no idea of why, or how, or to whom.

Butler was out of bed, and into his slippers, as soon as he heard the first faint clatter from downstairs. His dressing-gown would, as usual, twist itself up like a rolled umbrella and defy all attempts to find the arm-holes whenever he wanted to hurry. But the little flashlight was ready in the pocket.

That noise seemed to have roused nobody else. With certain possibilities in his mind, he had never in his life moved so fast once he managed to get out of his bedroom. Not using his light, he was down two flights of deep-carpeted stairs without noise. In the lower hall he could feel a draught, which meant that a window or door had been opened somewhere. He made straight for the dining-room.

But he was too late.

Once the pencil-beam of Butler's flashlight had swept round, he switched on a whole blaze of lights. The burglar was still here, right enough. But the burglar was lying very still in front of the sideboard; and, to judge by the amount of blood on his sweater and trousers, he would never move again.

'That's done it,' Butler said aloud.

A silver service, including a tea-urn, had been toppled off the sideboard. Where the fruit-bowl had fallen, the dead man lay on his back among a litter of oranges, apples, and a squashed bunch of grapes. The mask still covered the burglar's face; his greasy cap was flattened still further on his ears; his gloved hands were thrown wide.

Fragments of smashed picture-glass lay round him, together with the empty frame, and the 'Old Woman with Cap' had been half crumpled up under his body. From the position of the most conspicuous bloodstains, one judged that he had been stabbed through the chest with the stained fruit-knife beside him.

'*What is it?*' said a voice almost at Butler's ear.

He could not have been more startled if the fruit-knife had pricked his ribs. He had seen nobody turning on lights in the hall, nor had he heard Harriet Davis approach. She was standing just behind him, wrapped in a Japanese kimono, with her dark hair round her shoulders. But, when he explained what had happened, she would not look into the dining-room; she backed away, shaking her head violently, like an urchin ready for flight.

'You had better wake up your uncle,' Butler

269

said briskly, with a confidence he did not feel. 'And the servants. I must use your telephone.' Then he looked her in the eyes. 'Yes, you're quite right. I think you've guessed it already. I'm a police-officer.'

She nodded.

'Yes. I guessed. Who are you? And is your name really Butler?'

'I'm a sergeant of the Criminal Investigation Department. And my name really is Butler. Your uncle brought me here.'

'Why?'

'I don't know. He hasn't got round to telling me.'

This girl's intelligence, even when overshadowed by fear, was direct and disconcerting. 'But, if he wouldn't say why he wanted a police-officer, how did they come to send you? He'd have to tell them, wouldn't he?'

Butler ignored it. 'I must see your uncle. Will you go upstairs and wake him, please?'

'I can't,' said Harriet. 'Uncle Marcus isn't in his room.'

'Isn't—?'

'No. I knocked at the door on my way down. He's gone.'

Butler took the stairs two treads at a time. Harriet had turned on all the lights on her way down, but nothing stirred in the bleak, over-decorated passages.

Marcus Hunt's bedroom was empty. His dinner-jacket had been hung up neatly on the back of a chair, shirt laid across the seat with collar and tie on top of it. Hunt's watch ticked loudly on the dressing-table. His money and keys were there too. But he had not gone to bed, for the bedspread was undisturbed.

The suspicion which came to Lewis Butler, listening to the thin insistent ticking of that watch in the drugged hour before dawn, was so fantastic that he could not credit it.

He started downstairs again, and on the way he met Arthur Rolfe blundering out of another bedroom down the hall. The art dealer's stocky body was wrapped in a flannel dressing-gown. He was not wearing his eyeglasses, which gave his face a bleary and rather caved-in expression. He planted himself in front of Butler, and refused to budge.

'Yes,' said Butler. 'You don't have to ask. It's a burglar!'

'I knew it,' said Rolfe calmly. 'Did he get anything?'

'No. He was murdered.'

For a moment Rolfe said nothing, but his hand crept into the breast of his dressing-gown as though he felt pain there.

'Murdered? You don't mean the *burglar* was murdered?'

'Yes.'

'But why? By an accomplice, you mean? Who is the burglar?'

'That,' snarled Lewis Butler, 'is what I intend to find out.'

In the lower hall he found Harriet Davis, who was now standing in the doorway of the dining-room and looking steadily at the body by the sideboard. Though her face hardly moved a muscle, her eyes brimmed over.

'You're going to take off the mask, aren't you?' she asked, without turning round.

Stepping with care to avoid squashed fruit and broken glass, Butler leaned over the dead man. He pushed back the peak of the greasy cap; he lifted the black cloth mask, which was clumsily held by an elastic band; and he found what he expected to find.

The burglar was Marcus Hunt—stabbed through the heart while attempting to rob his own house.

*　　*　　*

'You see, sir,' Butler explained to Dr Gideon Fell on the following afternoon, 'that's the trouble. However you look at it, the case makes no sense.'

Again he went over the facts.

'Why should the man burgle his own house and steal his own property? Every one of those paintings is valuable, and not a single one is insured! Consequently, why? Was the man a simple lunatic? What did he think he was doing?'

The village of Sutton Valence, straggling like a grey-white Italian town along the very peak of the Weald, was full of hot sunshine. In the apple orchard behind the white inn of the *Tabard*, Dr Gideon Fell sat at a garden table among wasps, with a pint tankard at his elbow. Dr Fell's vast bulk was clad in a white linen suit. His pink face smoked in the heat, and his wary lookout for wasps gave him a regrettably wall-eyed appearance as he pondered.

He said:

'Superintendent Hadley suggested that I might—harrumph—look in here. The local police are in charge, aren't they?'

'Yes. I'm merely standing by.'

'Hadley's exact words to me were, "It's so crazy that nobody but you will understand it." The man's flattery becomes more nauseating every day.' Dr Fell scowled. 'I say. Does anything else strike you as queer about this business?'

'Well, why should a man burgle his own house?'

'No, no, no!' growled Dr Fell. 'Don't be obsessed with that point. Don't become hypnotized by it. For instance'—a wasp hovered near his tankard, and he distended his cheeks and blew it away with one vast puff like Father Neptune—'for instance, the young lady seems to have raised an interesting question. If Marcus Hunt wouldn't say why he wanted a detective in the house, why did the C.I.D. consent to send you?'

Butler shrugged his shoulders.

'Because,' he said, 'Chief Inspector Ames thought Hunt was up to funny business, and meant to stop it.'

'What sort of funny business?'

'A faked burglary to steal his own pictures for the insurance. It looked like the old, old game of appealing to the police to divert suspicion. In other words, sir, exactly what this appeared to be: until I learned (and today proved) that not one of those damned pictures has ever been insured for a penny.'

Butler hesitated.

'It can't have been a practical joke,' he went on. 'Look at the elaborateness of it! Hunt put on old clothes from which all tailors' tabs and laundry marks were removed. He put on gloves and a mask. He got hold of a torch and an up-to-date kit of burglar's tools. He went out of the house by the back door; we found it open later. He smoked a few cigarettes in the shrubbery below the terrace; we found his footprints in the soft earth. He cut a pane of glass ... but I've told you all that.'

'And then,' mused Dr Fell, 'somebody killed him.'

'Yes. The last and worst "why". Why should anybody have killed him?'

'H'm. Clues?'

'Negative.' Butler took out his notebook. 'According to the police surgeon, he died of a direct heart-wound from a blade (presumably that fruit-knife) so thin that the wound was difficult to find. There were a number of his fingerprints, but nobody else's. We did find one odd thing, though. A number of pieces in the silver service off the sideboard were scratched in a queer way. It looked almost as though, instead of being swept off the sideboard in a struggle, they had been piled up on top of each other like a tower; and then pushed—'

Butler paused, for Dr Fell was shaking his big head back and forth with an expression of gargantuan distress.

'Well, well, well,' he was saying; 'well, well, well. And you call that negative evidence?'

'Isn't it? It doesn't explain why a man burgles his own house.'

'Look here,' said the doctor mildly. 'I should like to ask you just one question. What is the most important point in this affair? One moment! I did not say the most interesting; I said the most important. Surely it is the fact that a man has been murdered?'

'Yes, sir. Naturally.'

'I mention the fact'—the doctor was apologetic—'because it seems in danger of being overlooked. It hardly interests you. You are concerned only with Hunt's senseless masquerade. You don't mind a throat being cut; but you can't stand a leg being pulled. Why not try working at it from the other side, and asking who killed Hunt?'

Butler was silent for a long time.

'The servants are out of it,' he said at length.

'They sleep in another wing on the top floor; and for some reason,' he hesitated, 'somebody locked them in last night.' His doubts, even his dreads, were beginning to take form. 'There was a fine blow-up over that when the house was roused. Of course, the murderer could have been an outsider.'

'You know it wasn't,' said Dr Fell. 'Would you mind taking me to Cranleigh Court?'

*　　*　　*

They came out on the terrace in the hottest part of the afternoon.

Dr Fell sat down on a wicker settee, with a dispirited Harriet beside him. Derek Henderson, in flannels, perched his long figure on the balustrade. Arthur Rolfe alone wore a dark suit and seemed out of place. For the pale green and brown of the Kentish lands, which rarely acquired harsh colour, now blazed. No air stirred, no leaf moved, in that brilliant thickness of heat; and down in the garden, towards their left, the water of the swimming-pool sparkled with hot, hard light. Butler felt it like a weight on his eyelids.

Derek Henderson's beard was at once languid and yet aggressive.

'It's no good,' he said. 'Don't keep on asking me why Hunt should have burgled his own house. But I'll give you a tip.'

'Which is?' inquired Dr Fell.

'Whatever the reason was,' returned Henderson, sticking out his neck, 'it was a good reason. Hunt was much too canny and cautious ever to do anything without a good reason. I told him so last night.'

Dr Fell spoke sharply. 'Cautious? Why do you say that?'

'Well, for instance. I take three cards on the draw. Hunt takes one. I bet; he sees me and raises. I cover that, and raise again. Hunt drops out. In other words, it's fairly certain he's filled his hand, but not so certain I'm holding much more than a pair. Yet Hunt drops out. So with my three sevens I bluff him out of his straight. He played a dozen hands last night just like that.'

Henderson began to chuckle. Seeing the expression on Harriet's face, he checked himself and became preternaturally solemn.

'But then, of course,' Henderson added, 'he had a lot on his mind last night.'

Nobody could fail to notice the change of tone.

'So? And what did he have on his mind?'

'Exposing somebody he had always trusted,' replied Henderson coolly. 'That's why I didn't like it when the ace of spades turned up so often.'

'You'd better explain that,' said Harriet, after a pause. 'I don't know what you're hinting at, but you'd better explain that. He told you he intended to expose somebody he had always trusted?'

'No. Like myself, he hinted at it.'

It was the stolid Rolfe who stormed into the conversation then. Rolfe had the air of a man determined to hold hard to reason, but finding it difficult.

'Listen to me,' snapped Rolfe. 'I have heard a great deal, at one time or another, about Mr Hunt's liking for exposing people. Very well!' He slid one hand into the breast of his coat, in a characteristic gesture. 'But where in the name of sanity does that leave us? He wants to expose someone. And, to do that, he puts on outlandish clothes and masquerades as a burglar. Is that sensible? I tell you, the man was mad! There's no other explanation.'

'There are five other explanations,' said Dr Fell.

Derek Henderson slowly got up from his seat on the balustrade, but he sat down again at a savage gesture from Rolfe.

Nobody spoke.

'I will not, however,' pursued Dr Fell, 'waste your time with four of them. We are concerned with only one explanation: the real one.'

'And you know the real one?' asked Henderson sharply.

'I rather think so.'

'Since when?'

'Since I had the opportunity of looking at all of you,' answered Dr Fell.

He settled back massively in the wicker

settee, so that its frame creaked and cracked like a ship's bulkhead in a heavy sea. His vast chin was out-thrust, and he nodded absently as though to emphasize some point that was quite clear in his own mind.

'I've already had a word with the local inspector,' he went on suddenly. 'He will be here in a few minutes. And, at my suggestion, he will have a request for all of you. I sincerely hope nobody will refuse.'

'Request?' said Henderson. 'What request?'

'It's a very hot day,' said Dr Fell, blinking towards the swimming-pool. 'He's going to suggest that you all go in for a swim.'

Harriet uttered a kind of despairing mutter, and turned as though appealing to Lewis Butler.

'That,' continued Dr Fell, 'will be the politest way of drawing attention to the murderer. In the meantime, let me call your attention to one point in the evidence which seems to have been generally overlooked. Mr Henderson, do you know anything about direct heart-wounds made by a steel blade as thin as a wafer?'

'Like Hunt's wound? No. What about them?'

'There's practically no exterior bleeding,' answered Dr Fell.

'But—!' Harriet was beginning, when Butler stopped her.

'The police surgeon, in fact, called attention

to that wound which was so "difficult to find". The victim dies almost at once; and the edges of the wound compress. But in that case,' argued Dr Fell, 'how did the late Mr Hunt come to have so much blood on his sweater, and even splashed on his trousers?'

'Well?'

'He didn't,' answered Dr Fell simply. 'Mr Hunt's blood never got on his clothes at all.'

'I can't stand this,' said Harriet, jumping to her feet. 'I—I'm sorry, but have you gone mad yourself? Are you telling us we didn't see him lying by that sideboard, with blood on him?'

'Oh, yes. You saw that.'

'Let him go on,' said Henderson, who was rather white round the nostrils. 'Let him rave.'

'It is, I admit, a fine point,' said Dr Fell. 'But it answers your question, repeated to the point of nausea, as to why the eminently sensible Mr Hunt chose to dress up in burglar's clothes and play burglar. The answer is short and simple. He didn't.'

*　　　*　　　*

'It must be plain to everybody,' Dr Fell went on, opening his eyes wide, 'that Mr Hunt was deliberately setting a trap for someone—the real burglar.

'He believed that a certain person might try to steal one or several of his pictures. He probably knew that this person had tried similar games before, in other country houses: that is, an inside job which was carefully planned to look like an outside job. So he made things easy for his thief, in order to trap him, with a police-officer in the house.

'The burglar, a sad fool, fell for it. This thief, a guest in the house, waited until well past two o'clock in the morning. He then put on his old clothes, mask, gloves, and the rest of it. He let himself out by the back door. He went through all the motions we have erroneously been attributing to Marcus Hunt. Then the trap snapped. Just as he was rolling up the Rembrandt, he heard a noise. He swung his light round. And he saw Marcus Hunt, in pyjamas and dressing-gown, looking at him.

'Yes, there was a fight. Hunt flew at him. The thief snatched up a fruit-knife and fought back. In that struggle, Marcus Hunt forced his opponent's hand back. The fruit-knife gashed the thief's chest, inflicting a superficial but badly bleeding gash. It sent the thief over the edge of insanity. He wrenched Marcus Hunt's wrist half off, caught up the knife, and stabbed Hunt to the heart.

'Then, in a quiet house, with a little beam of light streaming out from the torch on the sideboard, the murderer sees something that will hang him. He sees the blood from his own superficial wound seeping down his clothes.

'How is he to get rid of those clothes? He cannot destroy them, or get them away from

281

the house. Inevitably the house will be searched, and they will be found. Without the blood-stains, they would seem ordinary clothes in his wardrobe. But with the blood-stains—'

'There is only one thing he can do.'

Harriet Davis was standing behind the wicker settee, shading her eyes against the glare of the sun. Her hand did not tremble when she said:

'He changed clothes with my uncle.'

'That's it,' growled Dr Fell. 'That's the whole sad story. The murderer dressed the body in his own clothes, making a puncture with the knife in sweater, shirt, and undervest. He then slipped on Mr Hunt's pyjamas and dressing-gown, which at a pinch he could always claim as his own. Hunt's wound had bled hardly at all. His dressing-gown, I think, had come open in the fight so that all the thief had to trouble him was a tiny puncture in the jacket of the pyjamas.

'But, once he had done this, he had to hypnotize you all into the belief that there would have been no time for a change of clothes. He had to make it seem that the fight occurred just *then*. He had to rouse the house. So he brought down echoing thunders by pushing over a pile of silver, and slipped upstairs.'

Dr Fell paused.

'The burglar could never have been Marcus
282

Hunt, you know,' he added. 'We learn that Hunt's fingerprints were all over the place. Yet the murdered man was wearing gloves.'

There was a swishing of feet in the grass below the terrace, and a tread of heavy boots coming up the terrace steps. The local Inspector of police, buttoned up and steaming in his uniform, was followed by two constables.

Dr Fell turned round a face of satisfaction.

'Ah!' he said, breathing deeply. 'They've come to see about that swimming-party, I imagine. It is easy to patch up a flesh-wound with lint and cotton, or even a handkerchief. But such a wound will become infernally conspicuous in anyone who is forced to climb into bathing-trunks.'

'But it couldn't have been—' cried Harriet. Her eyes moved round. Her fingers tightened on Lewis Butler's arm, an instinctive gesture which he was to remember long afterwards, when he knew her even better.

'Exactly,' agreed the doctor, wheezing with pleasure. 'It could not have been a long, thin, gangling fellow like Mr Henderson. It assuredly could not have been a small and slender girl like yourself.

'There is only one person who, as we know, is just about Marcus Hunt's height and build; who could have put his own clothes on Hunt without any suspicion. That is the same person who, though he managed to staunch the

283

wound in his chest, has been constantly running his hand inside the breast of his coat to make certain the bandage is secure. Just as Mr Rolfe is doing now.'

Arthur Rolfe sat very quiet, with his right hand still in the breast of his jacket. His face had grown smeary in the hot sunlight, but the eyes behind those thin shells of glasses remained inscrutable. He spoke only once, through dry lips, after they had cautioned him.

'I should have taken the young pup's warning,' he said. 'After all, he told me I would take long chances.'

THE BONES OF THE CASE

R. AUSTIN FREEMAN

Just as we began this tour in one of London's most lawless black spots, so it seems appropriate that it should end in the area which has come to epitomize law and order, The Temple. The last part of our walk, then, takes us along the Embankment to number 5A Kings Bench Walk in the Inner Temple Gardens. In this little island of tranquillity beside the Embankment can be found the chambers of Dr John Thorndyke who has been described by Chris Steinbrunner and Otto Penzler as 'the greatest medico-legal detective of all time'. Thorndyke is also the most handsome of all the London detectives: tall, slim, athletic and with a symmetrical face in the classic mould. He has superb eyesight, too, and extremely dexterous hands. The good doctor combines the professions of lawyer and forensic scientist and brings a painstaking attention to scientific and technical detail whenever he is tackling a case. He considers himself 'an investigator of crime' rather than a detective, and never travels anywhere without his inevitable green case full of miniature instruments and chemicals. Thorndyke is always more concerned with examining the minutiae of crime—the physical clues left at the scene—

rather than the people involved, and never allows personal emotions to cloud his judgement. His exceptional reasoning powers are augmented by a deep knowledge of such subjects as archaeology, anatomy, botany, ophthalmology and Egyptology. Dr Thorndyke receives invaluable aid on his cases from Nathaniel Polton, his laboratory assistant and butler, and Christopher Jervis, his faithful chronicler. Introduced to the public in 1907 in The Red Thumb Mark—*the first of 21 novels and 40 short stories—the fame of Thorndyke is such that he has since been the subject of several parodies and pastiches as well as being featured on television three times: first in 1964 played by the gentlemanly Peter Copley; in 1971 by the Shakespearean actor, John Neville; and the following years by Barrie Ingham, probably better known as the arms salesman, Hine.*

Richard Austin Freeman (1862–1943), who was born in Soho, was actually a practising surgeon and eye-and-throat specialist who was forced to give up medicine because of ill health and instead turned his knowledge and imagination to writing crime fiction. Apart from the unique Dr Thorndyke, he is also credited with inventing the 'inverted' detective story in The Singing Bone *(1912) in which the reader's interest is focused not on whether the criminal will be caught, but* how. *Freeman said he had the idea for Thorndyke when he was a student in the 1880's, but did not get down to committing the idea to paper until prompted by the success of his fellow physician Dr Arthur Conan Doyle with Sherlock Holmes. He was reluctant to agree that he had a model for his hero, but there is little doubt that he bears striking resemblances to Professor Alfred Taylor, the author of the definitive work,* Principles and Practices of Medical Jurisprudence *(1865), which was Freeman's 'bible' as a student. All of the Dr Thorndyke short stories which helped ensure his wider public fame in* Pearson's Magazine *have stood the test of time well, but there is perhaps no better case to finish with than 'The Bones of the Case' in which the investigator from the Temple finds himself involved in a murder case as grisly as any committed by Jack the Ripper—and thereby brings our tour of London After Midnight round full circle to a most suitable finale. The case will also be all the more welcome to admirers of Dr Thorndyke for it is one of only three short stories about him which were not collected in the mammoth volume,* The Best Dr Thorndyke Detective Stories, *published in 1973...*

Part I

Mr Percival Bland was a somewhat uncommon type of criminal. In the first place he really had an appreciable amount of common-sense. If he had only had a little more, he would not have been a criminal at all. As it was, he had just sufficient judgment to perceive that the consequences of unlawful acts accumulate as the acts are repeated; to realize that the criminal's position must, at length, become untenable; and to take what he considered fair precautions against the inevitable catastrophe.

But in spite of these estimable traits of character and the precautions aforesaid, Mr Bland found himself in rather a tight place and with a prospect of increasing tightness. The causes of this uncomfortable tension do not concern us, and may be dismissed with the remark, that, if one perseveringly distributes flash Bank of England notes among the money-changers of the Continent, there will come a day of reckoning when those notes are tendered to the exceedingly knowing old lady who lives in Threadneedle Street.

Mr Bland considered uneasily the approaching storm-cloud as he raked over the 'miscellaneous property' in the Sale-rooms of Messrs Plimpton. He was a confirmed frequenter of auctions, as was not unnatural; for the criminal is essentially a gambler. And criminal and auction-frequenter have one quality in common; each hopes to get something of value without paying the market price for it.

So Percival turned over the dusty oddments and his own difficulties at one and the same time. The vital questions were: When would the storm burst? And would it pass by the harbour of refuge that he had been at such pains to construct? Let us inspect that harbour of refuge.

A quiet flat in the pleasant neighbourhood of Battersea bore a name-plate inscribed, Mr Robert Lindsay; and the tenant was known to the porter and the charwoman who attended to the flat, as a fair-haired gentleman who was engaged in the book trade as a travelling agent, and was consequently a good deal away from home. Now Mr Robert Lindsay bore a distinct resemblance to Percival Bland; which was not surprising seeing that they were first cousins (or, at any rate, they said they were; and we may presume that they knew). But they were not very much alike. Mr Lindsay had flaxen, or rather sandy, hair; Mr Bland's hair was black. Mr Bland had a mole under his left eye; Mr Lindsay had no mole under his eye—but carried one in a small box in his waistcoat pocket.

At somewhat rare intervals the cousins called on one another; but they had the very worst of luck, for neither of them ever seemed to find the other at home. And what was even more odd was that whenever Mr Bland spent an evening at home in his lodgings over the oil shop in Bloomsbury, Mr Lindsay's flat was empty; and as sure as Mr Lindsay was at home in his flat so surely were Mr Bland's lodgings vacant for the time being. It was a queer coincidence, if anyone had noticed it; but nobody ever did.

However, if Percival saw little of his cousin, it was not a case of 'out of sight, out of mind'. On the contrary; so great was his solicitude for the latter's welfare that he not only had made a will constituting him his executor and sole legatee, but he had actually insured his life for no less a sum than three thousand pounds; and this will, together with the insurance policy, investment securities and other necessary documents, he had placed in the custody of a highly respectable solicitor. All of which did him great credit. It isn't every man who is willing to take so much trouble for a mere cousin.

Mr Bland continued his perambulations, pawing over the miscellaneous raffle from sheer force of habit, reflecting on the coming crisis in his own affairs, and on the provisions that he had made for his cousin Robert. As for the latter, they were excellent as far as they went, but they lacked definiteness and perfect completeness. There was the contingency of a 'stretch', for instance; say fourteen years penal servitude. The insurance policy did not cover that. And, meanwhile, what was to become of the estimable Robert?

He had bruised his thumb somewhat severely in a screw-cutting lathe, and had abstractedly turned the handle of a bird-organ until politely requested by an attendant to desist, when he came upon a series of boxes containing, according to the catalogue, 'a collection of surgical instruments the property of a lately deceased practitioner'. To judge by the appearance of the instruments, the practitioner must have commenced practice in his early youth and died at a very advanced age. They were an uncouth set of tools, of no value whatever excepting as testimonials to the amazing tenacity of life of our ancestors; but Percival fingered them over according to his wont, working the handle of a complicated brass syringe and ejecting a drop of greenish fluid on to the shirt-front of a dressy Hebrew (who requested him to 'point the dam thing at thomeone elth nectht time'), opening musty leather cases, clicking off spring scarifiers and feeling the edges of strange, crooked-bladed knives. Then he came upon a largish black box, which, when he raised the lid, breathed out an ancient and fish-like aroma and exhibited a collection of bones, yellow, greasy-looking and spotted in places with mildew. The catalogue described them as 'a complete set of human osteology'; but they were not an ordinary 'student's set', for the bones of the hands and feet, instead of being strung together on cat-gut, were united by their original ligaments and were of an unsavoury brown colour.

'I thay, misther,' expostulated the Hebrew, 'shut that bocth. Thmellth like a blooming inquetht.'

But the contents of the black box seemed to have a fascination for Percival. He looked in at those greasy remnants of mortality, at the brown and mouldy hands and feet and the skull that peeped forth eerily from the folds of a flannel wrapping; and they breathed out something more than that stale and musty odour. A suggestion—vague and general at first, but rapidly crystallizing into distinct shape—seemed to steal out of the black box into his consciousness; a suggestion that somehow seemed to connect itself with his estimable cousin Robert.

For upwards of a minute he stood motionless, as one immersed in reverie, the lid poised in his hand and a dreamy eye fixed on the half-uncovered skull. A stir in the room roused him. The sale was about to begin. The members of the knock-out and other habitués seated themselves on benches around a long, baize-covered table; the attendants took possession of the first lots and opened their catalogues as if about to sing an introductory chorus; and a gentleman with a waxed moustache and a striking resemblance to his late Majesty, the third Napoleon, having ascended to the rostrum bespoke the attention of the assembly by a premonitory tap with his hammer.

How odd are some of the effects of a guilty conscience! With what absurd self-consciousness do we read into the minds of others our own undeclared intentions, when those intentions are unlawful! Had Percival Bland wanted a set of human bones for any legitimate purpose—such as anatomical study—he would have bought it openly and unembarrassed. Now, he found himself earnestly debating whether he should not bid for some of the surgical instruments, just for the sake of appearances; and there being little time in which to make up his mind—for the deceased practitioner's effects came first in the catalogue—he was already the richer by a set of cupping-glasses, a tooth-key, and an instrument of unknown use and diabolical aspect, before the fateful lot was called.

At length the black box was laid on the table, an object of obscene mirth to the knockers-out, and the auctioneer read the entry:

'Lot seventeen; a complete set of human osteology. A very useful and valuable set of specimens, gentlemen.'

He looked round at the assembly majestically, oblivious of sundry inquiries as to the identity of the deceased and the verdict of the coroner's jury, and finally suggested five shillings.

'Six,' said Percival.

An attendant held the box open, and, chanting the mystic word 'Loddlemen!' (which, being interpreted, meant 'Lot, gentlemen'), thrust it under the rather bulbous nose of the smart Hebrew; who remarked that 'they 'ummed a bit too much to thoot him' and pushed it away.

'Going at six shillings,' said the auctioneer, reproachfully; and as nobody contradicted him, he smote the rostrum with his hammer and the box was delivered into the hands of Percival on the payment of that modest sum.

Having crammed the cupping-glasses, the tooth-key and the unknown instrument into the box, Percival obtained from one of the attendants a length of cord, with which he secured the lid. Then he carried his treasure out into the street, and, chartering a four-wheeler, directed the driver to proceed to Charing Cross Station. At the station he booked the box in the cloak-room (in the name of Simpson) and left it for a couple of hours; at the expiration of which he returned, and, employing a different porter, had it conveyed to a hansom, in which it was borne to his lodgings over the oil-shop in Bloomsbury. There he, himself, carried it, unobserved, up the stairs, and, depositing it in a large cupboard, locked the door and pocketed the key.

And thus was the curtain rung down on the first act.

The second act opened only a couple of days later, the office of call-boy—to pursue the metaphor to the bitter end—being discharged by a Belgian police official who emerged from the main entrance to the Bank of England. What should have led Percival Bland into so unsafe a neighbourhood it is difficult to imagine, unless it was that strange fascination that seems so frequently to lure the criminal to places associated with his crime. But there he was within a dozen paces of the entrance when the officer came forth, and mutual recognition was instantaneous. Almost equally instantaneous was the self-possessed Percival's decision to cross the road.

It is not a nice road to cross. The old-fashioned horse-driver would condescend to shout a warning to the indiscreet wayfarer. Not so the modern chauffeur, who looks stonily before him and leaves you to get out of the way of Juggernaut. He knows his 'exonerating' coroner's jury. At the moment, however, the procession of Juggernauts was at rest; but Percival had seen the presiding policeman turn to move away and he darted across the fronts of the vehicles even as they started. The foreign officer followed. But in that moment the whole procession had got in motion. A motor omnibus thundered past in front of him; another was bearing down on him relentlessly. He hesitated, and sprang back; and then a taxi-cab, darting out from behind, butted him heavily, sending him sprawling in the road, whence he scrambled as best he could back on to the pavement.

Percival, meanwhile, had swung himself lightly on to the footboard of the first omnibus just as it was gathering speed. A few seconds saw him safely across at the Mansion House, and in a few more, he was whirling down Queen Victoria Street. The danger was practically over, though he took the precaution to alight at St Paul's, and, crossing to Newgate Street, board another west-bound omnibus.

That night he sat in his lodgings turning over his late experience. It had been a narrow shave. That sort of thing mustn't happen again. In fact, seeing that the law was undoubtedly about to be set in motion, it was high time that certain little plans of his should be set in motion, too. Only, there was a difficulty; a serious difficulty. And as Percival thought round and round that difficulty his brows wrinkled and he hummed a soft refrain.

'Then is the time for disappearing.
Take a header—down you go—'

A tap at the door cut his song short. It was his landlady, Mrs Brattle; a civil woman, and particularly civil just now. For she had a little request to make.

'It was about Christmas Night, Mr Bland,' said Mrs Brattle. 'My husband and me thought of spending the evening with his brother at Hornsey, and we were going to let the maid go home to her mother's for the night, if it wouldn't put you out.'

'Wouldn't put me out in the least, Mrs Brattle,' said Percival.

'You needn't sit up for us, you see,' pursued Mrs Brattle, 'if you'd just leave the side door unbolted. We shan't be home before two or three, but we'll come in quiet not to disturb you.'

'You won't disturb me,' Percival replied with a genial laugh. 'I'm a sober man in general; but "Christmas comes but once a year." When once I'm tucked up in bed, I shall take a bit of waking on Christmas Night.'

Mrs Brattle smiled indulgently. 'And you won't feel lonely, all alone in the house?'

'Lonely!' exclaimed Percival. 'Lonely! With a roaring fire, a jolly book, a box of good cigars and a bottle of sound port—ah, and a second bottle if need be. Not I.'

Mrs Brattle shook her head. 'Ah,' said she, 'you bachelors! Well, well. It's a good thing to be independent,' and with this profound reflection she smiled herself out of the room and descended the stairs.

As her footsteps died away Percival sprang from his chair and began excitedly to pace the room. His eyes sparkled and his face was wreathed with smiles. Presently he halted before the fireplace, and, gazing into the embers, laughed aloud.

'Damn funny!' said he. 'Deuced rich! Neat! Very neat! Ha! Ha!' And here he resumed his interrupted song:

'When the sky above is clearing
297

When the sky above is clearing
Bob up serenely, bob up serenely,
Bob up serenely from below!'

Which may be regarded as closing the first scene of the second act.

During the few days that intervened before Christmas, Percival went abroad but little; and yet he was a busy man. He did a little surreptitious shopping, venturing out as far as Charing Cross Road; and his purchases were decidedly miscellaneous. A porridge saucepan, a second-hand copy of *Gray's Anatomy*, a rabbit skin, a large supply of glue and upwards of ten pounds of shin of beef seems a rather odd assortment; and it was a mercy that the weather was frosty, for otherwise Percival's bedroom, in which these delicacies were deposited under lock and key, would have yielded odorous traces of its wealth.

But it was in the long evenings that his industry was most conspicuous; and then it was that the big cupboard with the excellent lever lock, which he himself had fixed on, began to fill up with the fruits of his labours. In those evenings the porridge saucepan would simmer on the hob with a rich lading of good Scotch glue, the black box of the deceased practitioner would be hauled forth from its hiding-place, and the well-thumbed *Gray* laid open on the table.

It was an arduous business though; a stiffer

task than he had bargained for. The right and left bones were so confoundedly alike, and the bones that joined were so difficult to fit together. However, the plates in *Gray* were large and very clear, so it was only a question of taking enough trouble.

His method of work was simple and practical. Having fished a bone out of the box, he would compare it with the illustrations in the book until he had identified it beyond all doubt, when he would tie on it a paper label with its name and side—right or left. Then he would search for the adjoining bone, and, having fitted the two together, would secure them with a good daub of glue and lay them in the fender to dry. It was a crude and horrible method of articulation that would have made a museum curator shudder. But it seemed to answer Percival's purpose—whatever that may have been—for gradually the loose 'items' came together into recognizable members such as arms and legs, the vertebrae—which were, fortunately, strung in their order on a thick cord—were joined up into a solid backbone, and even the ribs, which were the toughest job of all, fixed on in some semblance of a thorax. It was a wretched performance. The bones were plastered with gouts of glue and yet would have broken apart at a touch. But, as we have said, Percival seemed satisfied, and as he was the only person concerned, there was nothing more to be said.

In due course, Christmas Day arrived. Percival dined with the Brattles at two, dozed after dinner, woke up for tea, and then, as Mrs Brattle, in purple and fine raiment, came in to remove the tea-tray, he spread out on the table the materials for the night's carouse. A quarter of an hour later, the side-door slammed, and, peering out of the window, he saw the shopkeeper and his wife hurrying away up the gas-lit street towards the nearest omnibus route.

Then Mr Percival Bland began his evening's entertainment; and a most remarkable entertainment it was, even for a solitary bachelor, left alone in a house on Christmas Night. First, he took off his clothing and dressed himself in a fresh suit. Then, from the cupboard, he brought forth the reconstituted 'set of osteology', and, laying the various members on the table, returned to the bedroom, whence he presently reappeared with a large, unsavoury parcel which he had disinterred from a trunk. The parcel, being opened, revealed his accumulated purchases in the matter of shin of beef.

With a large knife, providently sharpened beforehand, he cut the beef into large, thin slices which he proceeded to wrap around the various bones that formed the 'complete set'; whereby their nakedness was certainly mitigated though their attractiveness was by no means increased. Having thus 'clothed the dry bones', he gathered up the scraps of offal that were left, to be placed presently inside the trunk. It was an extraordinary proceeding, but the next was more extraordinary still.

Taking up the newly clothed members one by one, he began very carefully to insinuate them into the garments that he had recently shed. It was a ticklish business, for the glued joints were as brittle as glass. Very cautiously the legs were separately inducted, first into underclothing and then into trousers, the skeleton feet were fitted with the cast-off socks and delicately persuaded into the boots. The arms, in like manner, were gingerly pressed into their various sleeves and through the arm-holes of the waistcoat; and then came the most difficult task of all—to fit the garments on the trunk. For the skull and ribs, secured to the back-bone with mere spots of glue, were ready to drop off at a shake; and yet the garments had to be drawn over them with the arms enclosed in the sleeves. But Percival managed it at last by resting his 'restoration' in the big, padded arm-chair and easing the garments on inch by inch.

It now remained only to give the finishing touch; which was done by cutting the rabbit-skin to the requisite shape and affixing it to the skull with a thin coat of stiff glue; and when the skull had thus been finished with a sort of crude, makeshift wig, its appearance was so appalling as even to disturb the nerves of the matter-of-fact Percival. However, this was no occasion for cherishing sentiment. A skull in an extemporized wig or false scalp might be, and in fact was, a highly unpleasant object; but so was a Belgian police officer.

Having finished the 'restoration', Percival fetched the water-jug from his bedroom, and, descending to the shop, the door of which had been left unlocked, tried the taps of the various drums and barrels until he came to the one which contained methylated spirit; and from this he filled his jug and returned to the bedroom. Pouring the spirit out into the basin, he tucked a towel round his neck and filling his sponge with spirit, proceeded very vigorously to wash his hair and eyebrows and as, by degrees, the spirit in the basin grew dark and turbid, so did his hair and eyebrows grow lighter in colour until, after a final energetic rub with a towel, they had acquired a golden or sandy hue indistinguishable from that of the hair of his cousin Robert. Even the mole under his eye was susceptible to the changing conditions, for when he had wetted it thoroughly with spirit, he was able with the blade of a penknife, to peel it off as neatly as if it had been stuck on with spirit-gum. Having done which, he deposited it in a tiny box which he carried in his waistcoat pocket.

The proceedings which followed were unmistakable as to their object. First he carried the basin of spirit through into the sitting-room and deliberately poured its contents on to the floor by the arm-chair. Then, having returned the basin to the bedroom, he again went down to the shop, where he selected a couple of galvanised buckets from the stock, filled them with paraffin oil from one of the great drums and carried them upstairs. The oil from one bucket he poured over the arm-chair and its repulsive occupant; the other bucket he simply emptied on the carpet, and then went down to the shop for a fresh supply.

When this proceeding had been repeated once or twice the entire floor and all the furniture were saturated, and such a reek of paraffin filled the air of the room that Percival thought it wise to turn out the gas. Returning to the shop, he poured a bucketful of oil over the stack of bundles of firewood, another over the counter and floor and a third over the loose articles on the walls and hanging from the ceiling. Looking up at the latter he now perceived a number of greasy patches where the oil had soaked through from the floor above, and some of these were beginning to drip on to the shop floor.

He now made his final preparations. Taking a bundle of 'Wheel' firelighters, he made a small pile against the stack of firewood. In the midst of the firelighters he placed a ball of string saturated in paraffin; and in the central hole of the ball he stuck a half-dozen diminutive Christmas candles. This mine was now ready. Providing himself with a stock of firelighters, a few balls of paraffined string and a dozen or so of the little candles, he went upstairs to the sitting-room, which was immediately above the shop. Here, by the glow of the fire, he built up one or two piles of firelighters around and, partly under the arm-chair, placed the balls of string on the piles and stuck two or three bundles in each ball. Everything was now ready. Stepping into the bedroom, he took from the cupboard a spare overcoat, a new hat and a new umbrella—for he must leave his old hats, coat and umbrella in the hall. He put on the coat and hat, and, with the umbrella in his hand, returned to the sitting-room.

Opposite the arm-chair he stood awhile, irresolute, and a pang of horror shot through him. It was a terrible thing that he was going to do; a thing the consequences of which no one could foresee. He glanced furtively at the awful shape that sat huddled in the chair, its horrible head all awry and its rigid limbs sprawling in hideous grotesque deformity. It was but a dummy, a mere scarecrow; but yet, in the dim firelight, the grisly face under that horrid wig seemed to leer intelligently, to watch him with secret malice out of its shadowy eye-sockets, until he looked away with clammy skin and a shiver of half-superstitious terror.

But this would never do. The evening had run out, consumed by these engrossing labours; it was nearly eleven o'clock, and high time for him to be gone. For if the Brattles should return prematurely he was lost. Pulling himself together with an effort, he struck a match and lit the little candles one after the other. In a quarter of an hour or so, they would have burned down to the balls of string, and then—

He walked quickly out of the room; but, at the door, he paused for a moment to look back at the ghastly figure, seated rigidly in the chair with the lighted candles at its feet, like some foul fiend appeased by votive fires. The unsteady flames threw flickering shadows on its face that made it seem to mow and gibber and grin in mockery of all his care and caution. So he turned and tremblingly ran down the stairs—opening the staircase window as he went. Running into the shop, he lit the candles there and ran out again, shutting the door after him.

Secretly and guiltily he crept down the hall, and opening the door a few inches peered out. A blast of icy wind poured in with a light powdering of dry snow. He opened his umbrella, flung open the door, looked up and down the empty street, stepped out, closed the door softly and strode away over the whitening pavement.

Part II

It was one of the axioms of medico-legal practice laid down by my colleague, John Thorndyke, that the investigator should be constantly on his guard against the effect of suggestion. Not only must all prejudices and preconceptions be avoided, but when information is received from outside, the actual, undeniable facts must be carefully sifted from the inferences which usually accompany them. Of the necessity for this precaution our insurance practice furnished an excellent instance in the case of the fire at Mr Brattle's oil-shop.

The case was brought to our notice by Mr Stalker of the 'Griffin' Fire and Life Insurance Society a few days after Christmas. He dropped in, ostensibly to wish us a Happy New Year, but a discreet pause in the conversation on Thorndyke's part elicited a further purpose.

'Did you see the account of that fire in Bloomsbury?' Mr Stalker asked.

'The oil-shop? Yes. But I didn't note any details, excepting that a man was apparently burnt to death and that the affair happened on the twenty-fifth of December.'

'Yes, I know,' said Mr Stalker. 'It seems uncharitable, but one can't help looking a little askance at these quarter-day fires. And the date isn't the only doubtful feature in this one; the Divisional Officer of the Fire Brigade, who has looked over the ruins, tells me that there are some appearances suggesting that the fire broke out in two different places—the shop and the first-floor room over it. Mind you, he doesn't say that it actually did. The place is so thoroughly gutted that very little is to be learned from it; but that is his impression; and it occurred to me that if you were to take a look at the ruins, your radiographic eye might detect something that he had overlooked.'

'It isn't very likely,' said Thorndyke. 'Every man to his trade. The Divisional Officer looks at a burnt house with an expert eye, which I do not. My evidence would not carry much weight if you were contesting the claim.'

'Perhaps not,' replied Mr Stalker, 'and we are not anxious to contest the claim unless there is manifest fraud. Arson is a serious matter.'

'It is wilful murder in this case,' remarked Thorndyke.

'I know,' said Stalker. 'And that reminds me that the man who was burnt happens to have been insured in our office, too. So we stand a double loss.'

'How much?' asked Thorndyke.

'The dead man, Percival Bland, had insured his life for three thousand pounds.'

Thorndyke became thoughtful. The last statement had apparently made more impression on him than the former ones.

'If you want me to look into the case for

you,' said he, 'you had better let me have all the papers connected with it, including the proposal forms.'

Mr Stalker smiled. 'I thought you would say that—know you of old, you see—so I slipped the papers in my pocket before coming here.'

He laid the documents on the table and asked: 'Is there anything that you want to know about the case?'

'Yes,' replied Thorndyke. 'I want to know all that you can tell me.'

'Which is mighty little,' said Stalker; 'but such as it is, you shall have it.

'The oil-shop man's name is Brattle and the dead man, Bland, was his lodger. Bland appears to have been a perfectly steady, sober man in general; but it seems that he had announced his intention of spending a jovial Christmas Night and giving himself a little extra indulgence. He was last seen by Mrs Brattle at about half-past six, sitting by a blazing fire, with a couple of unopened bottles of port on the table and a box of cigars. He had a book in his hand and two or three newspapers lay on the floor by his chair. Shortly after this, Mr and Mrs Brattle went out on a visit to Hornsey, leaving him alone in the house.'

'Was there no servant?' asked Thorndyke.

'The servant had the day and night off duty to go to her mother's. That, by the way, looks a trifle fishy. However, to return to the Brattles;

they spent the evening at Hornsey and did not get home until past three in the morning, by which time their house was a heap of smoking ruins. Mrs Brattle's idea is that Bland must have drunk himself sleepy, and dropped one of the newspapers into the fender, where a chance cinder may have started the blaze. Which may or may not be the true explanation. Of course, a habitually sober man can get pretty mimsey on two bottles of port.'

'What time did the fire break out?' asked Thorndyke.

'It was noticed about half-past eleven that flames were issuing from one of the chimneys, and the alarm was given at once. The first engine arrived ten minutes later, but, by that time, the place was roaring like a furnace. Then the water-plugs were found to be frozen hard, which caused some delay; in fact, before the engines were able to get to work the roof had fallen in, and the place was a mere shell. You know what an oil-shop is, when once it gets a fair start.'

'And Mr Bland's body was found in the ruins, I suppose?'

'Body!' exclaimed Mr Stalker; 'there wasn't much body! Just a few charred bones, which they dug out of the ashes next day.'

'And the question of identity?'

'We shall leave that to the coroner. But there really isn't any question. To begin with, there was no one else in the house; and then the remains were found mixed up with the springs and castors of the chair that Bland was sitting in when he was last seen. Moreover, there were found, with the bones, a pocket-knife, a bunch of keys and a set of steel waistcoat buttons, all identified by Mrs Brattle as belonging to Bland. She noticed the cut steel buttons on his waistcoat when she wished him good-night.'

'By the way,' said Thorndyke, 'was Bland reading by the light of an oil lamp?'

'No,' replied Stalker. 'There was a two-branch gasalier with a porcelain shade to one burner, and he had that burner alight when Mrs Brattle left.'

Thorndyke reflectively picked up the proposal form, and, having glanced through it, remarked: 'I see that Bland is described as unmarried. Do you know why he insured his life for this large amount?'

'No; we assumed that it was probably in connection with some loan that he had raised. I learn from the solicitor who notified us of the death, that the whole of Bland's property is left to a cousin—a Mr Lindsay, I think. So the probability is that this cousin had lent him money. But it is not the life claim that is interesting us. We must pay that in any case. It is the fire claim that we want you to look into.'

'Very well,' said Thorndyke; 'I will go round presently and look over the ruins, and see if I can detect any substantial evidence of fraud.'

'If you would,' said Mr Stalker, rising to
310

take his departure, 'we should be very much obliged. Not that we shall probably contest the claim in any case.'

When he had gone, my colleague and I glanced through the papers, and I ventured to remark: 'It seems to me that Stalker doesn't quite appreciate the possibilities of this case.'

'No,' Thorndyke agreed. 'But, of course, it is an insurance company's business to pay, and not to boggle at anything short of glaring fraud. And we specialists, too,' he added with a smile, 'must beware of seeing too much. I suppose that, to a rhinologist, there is hardly such a thing as a healthy nose—unless it is his own—and the uric acid specialist is very apt to find the firmament studded with dumb-bell crystals. We mustn't forget that normal cases do exist, after all.'

'That is true,' said I; 'but, on the other hand, the rhinologist's business is with the unhealthy nose, and our concern is with abnormal cases.'

Thorndyke laughed. '"A Daniel come to judgment,"' said he. 'But my learned friend is quite right. Our function is to pick holes. So let us pocket the documents and wend Bloomsbury way. We can talk the case over as we go.'

We walked at an easy pace, for there was no hurry, and a little preliminary thought was useful. After a while, as Thorndyke made no remark, I reopened the subject.

'How does the case present itself to you?' I

311

asked.

'Much as it does to you, I expect,' he replied. 'The circumstances invite inquiry, and I do not find myself connecting them with the shopkeeper. It is true that the fire occurred on quarter-day; but there is nothing to show that the insurance will do more than cover the loss of stock, chattels and the profits of trade. The other circumstances are much more suggestive. Here is a house burned down and a man killed. That man was insured for three thousand pounds, and, consequently, some person stands to gain by his death to that amount. The whole set of circumstances is highly favourable to the idea of homicide. The man was alone in the house when he died; and the total destruction of both the body and its surroundings seems to render investigation impossible. The cause of death can only be inferred; it cannot be proved; and the most glaring evidence of a crime will have vanished utterly. I think that there is a quite strong *prima facie* suggestion of murder. Under the known conditions, the perpetration of a murder would have been easy, it would have been safe from detection, and there is an adequate motive.

'On the other hand, suicide is not impossible. The man might have set fire to the house and then killed himself by poison or otherwise. But it is intrinsically less probable that a man should kill himself for another person's benefit than that he should kill another man for his own benefit.

'Finally, there is the possibility that the fire and the man's death were the result of accident; against which is the official opinion that the fire started in two places. If this opinion is correct, it establishes, in my opinion, a strong presumption of murder against some person who may have obtained access to the house.'

This point in the discussion brought us to the ruined house, which stood at the corner of two small streets. One of the firemen in charge admitted us, when we had shown our credentials, through a temporary door and down a ladder into the basement, where we found a number of men treading gingerly, ankle deep in white ash, among a litter of charred wood-work, fused glass, warped and broken china, and more or less recognisable metal objects.

'The coroner and the jury,' the fireman explained; 'come to view the scene of the disaster.' He introduced us to the former, who bowed stiffly and continued his investigations.

'These,' said the other fireman, 'are the springs of the chair that the deceased was sitting in. We found the body—or rather the bones—lying among them under a heap of hot ashes; and we found the buttons of his clothes and the things from his pockets among the ashes, too. You'll see them in the mortuary with the remains.'

'It must have been a terrific blaze,' one of the

jurymen remarked. 'Just look at this, sir,' and he handed to Thorndyke what looked like part of a gas-fitting, of which the greater part was melted into shapeless lumps and the remainder encrusted into fused porcelain.

'That,' said the fireman, 'was the gasalier of the first-floor room, where Mr Bland was sitting. Ah! You won't turn that tap, sir; nobody'll ever turn that tap again.'

Thorndyke held the twisted mass of brass towards me in silence, and, glancing up the blackened walls, remarked: 'I think we shall have to come here again with the Divisional Officer, but meanwhile, we had better see the remains of the body. It is just possible that we may learn something from them.'

He applied to the coroner for the necessary authority to make the inspection, and, having obtained a rather ungracious and grudging permission to examine the remains when the jury had 'viewed' them, began to ascend the ladder.

'Our friend would have liked to refuse permission,' he remarked when we had emerged into the street, 'but he knew that I could and should have insisted.'

'So I gathered from his manner,' said I. 'But what is he doing here? This isn't his district.'

'No; he is acting for Bettsford, who is laid up just now; and a very poor substitute he is. A non-medical coroner is an absurdity in any case, and a coroner who is hostile to the medical profession is a public scandal. By the way, that gas-tap offers a curious problem. You noticed that it was turned off?'

'Yes.'

'And consequently that the deceased was sitting in the dark when the fire broke out. I don't see the bearing of the fact, but it is certainly rather odd. Here is the mortuary. We had better wait and let the jury go in first.'

We had not long to wait. In a couple of minutes or so the 'twelve good men and true' made their appearance with a small attendant crowd of ragamuffins. We let them enter first, and then we followed. The mortuary was a good-sized room, well lighted by a glass roof, and having at its centre a long table on which lay the shell containing the remains. There was also a sheet of paper on which had been laid out a set of blackened steel waistcoat buttons, a bunch of keys, a steel-handled pocket-knife, a steel-cased watch on a partly-fused rolled-gold chain and a pocket corkscrew. The coroner drew the attention of the jury to these objects, and then took possession of them, that they might be identified by witnesses. And meanwhile the jurymen gathered round the shell and stared shudderingly at its gruesome contents.

'I am sorry, gentlemen,' said the coroner, 'to have to subject you to this painful ordeal. But duty is duty. We must hope, as I think we may, that this poor creature met a painless, if in some respects a rather terrible death.'

At this point, Thorndyke, who had drawn near to the table, cast a long and steady glance down into the shell; and, immediately his ordinarily rather impassive face seemed to congeal; all expression faded from it, leaving it as immovable and uncommunicative as the granite face of an Egyptian statue. I knew the symptom of old and began to speculate on its present significance.

'Are you taking any medical evidence?' he asked.

'Medical evidence!' the coroner repeated, scornfully. 'Certainly not, sir! I do not waste the public money by employing so-called experts to tell the jury what each of them can see quite plainly for himself. I imagine,' he added, turning to the foreman, 'that you will not require a learned doctor to explain to you how that poor fellow mortal met his death?' And the foreman, glancing askance at the skull, replied, with a pallid and sickly smile, that 'he thought not'.

'Do you, sir,' the coroner continued, with a dramatic wave of the hand towards the plain coffin, 'suppose that we shall find any difficulty in determining how that man came by his death?'

'I imagine,' replied Thorndyke, without moving a muscle, or, indeed, appearing to have any muscles to move, 'I imagine you will find no difficulty whatever.'

'So do I,' said the coroner.

'Then,' retorted Thorndyke, with a faint, inscrutable smile, 'we are, for once, in complete agreement.'

As the coroner and jury retired, leaving my colleague and me alone in the mortuary, Thorndyke remarked:

'I suppose this kind of farce will be repeated periodically so long as these highly technical medical inquiries continue to be conducted by lay persons.'

I made no reply, for I had taken a long look into the shell, and was lost in astonishment.

'But my dear Thorndyke!' I exclaimed; 'what on earth does it mean? Are we to suppose that a woman can have palmed herself off as a man on the examining medical officer of a London Life Assurance Society?'

Thorndyke shook his head. 'I think not,' said he. 'Our friend, Mr Bland, may conceivably have been a woman in disguise, but he certainly was not a negress.'

'A negress!' I gasped. 'By Jove! So it is. I hadn't looked at the skull. But that only makes the mystery more mysterious. Because, you remember, the body was certainly dressed in Bland's clothes.'

'Yes, there seems to be no doubt about that. And you may have noticed, as I did,' Thorndyke continued dryly, 'the remarkably fire-proof character of the waistcoat buttons, watch-case, knife-handle, and other

317

identifiable objects.'

'But what a horrible affair!' I exclaimed. 'The brute must have gone out and enticed some poor devil of a negress into the house, have murdered her in cold blood, and then deliberately dressed the corpse in his own clothes! It is perfectly frightful!'

Again Thorndyke shook his head. 'It wasn't as bad as that, Jervis,' said he, 'though I must confess that I feel strongly tempted to let your hypothesis stand. It would be quite amusing to put Mr Bland on trial for the murder of an unknown negress, and let him explain the facts himself. But our reputation is at stake. Look at the bones again and a little more critically. You very probably looked for the sex first; then you looked for racial characters. Now carry your investigations a step further.'

'There is the stature,' said I. 'But that is of no importance, as these are not Bland's bones. The only other point that I notice is that the fire seems to have acted very unequally on the different parts of the body.'

'Yes,' agreed Thorndyke, 'and that is *the* point. Some parts are more burnt than others; and the parts which are burnt most are the wrong parts. Look at the back-bone, for instance. The vertebrae are as white as chalk. They are mere masses of bone ash. But, of all parts of the skeleton, there is none so completely protected from fire as the back-bone, with the great dorsal muscles behind,

318

and the whole mass of the viscera in front. Then look at the skull. Its appearance is quite inconsistent with the suggested facts. The bones of the face are bare and calcined and the orbits contain not a trace of the eyes or other structures; and yet there is a charred mass of what may or may not be scalp adhering to the crown. But the scalp, as the most exposed and the thinnest covering, would be the first to be destroyed, while the last to be consumed would be the structures about the jaws and the base, of which, you see, not a vestige is left.'

Here he lifted the skull carefully from the shell, and, peering in through the great foramen at the base, handed it to me.

'Look in,' he said, 'through the Foramen Magnum—you will see better if you hold the orbits towards the skylight—and notice an even more extreme inconsistency with the supposed conditions. The brain and membranes have vanished without leaving a trace. The inside of the skull is as clean as if it had been macerated. But this is impossible. The brain is not only protected from the fire; it is also protected from contact with the air. But without access of oxygen, although it might become carbonized, it could not be consumed. No, Jervis; it won't do.'

I replaced the skull in the coffin and looked at him in surprise.

'What is it that you are suggesting?' I asked.

'I suggest that this was not a body at all, but

merely a dry skeleton.'

'But,' I objected, 'what about those masses of what looks like charred muscle adhering to the bones?'

'Yes,' he replied, 'I have been noticing them. They do, as you say, look like masses of charred muscle. But they are quite shapeless and structureless; I cannot identify a single muscle or muscular group; and there is not a vestige of any of the tendons. Moreover, the distribution is false. For instance, will you tell me what muscle you think that is?'

He pointed to a thick, charred mass on the inner surface of the left tibia or shin-bone. 'Now this portion of the bone—as many a hockey-player has had reason to realize—has no muscular covering at all. It lies immediately under the skin.'

'I think you are right, Thorndyke,' said I. 'That lump of muscle in the wrong place gives the whole fraud away. But it was really a rather smart dodge. This fellow Bland must be an ingenious rascal.'

'Yes,' agreed Thorndyke; 'but an unscrupulous villain too. He might have burned down half the street and killed a score of people. He'll have to pay the piper for this little frolic.'

'What shall you do now? Are you going to notify the coroner?'

'No; that is not my business. I think we will verify our conclusions and then inform our clients and the police. We must measure the skull as well as we can without callipers, but it is, fortunately, quite typical. The short, broad, flat nasal bones, with the "Simian groove", and those large, strong teeth, worn flat by hard and gritty food, are highly characteristic.' He, once more, lifted out the skull, and, with a spring tape, made a few measurements, while I noted the lengths of the principal long bones and the width across the hips.

'I make the cranial-nasal index 55.1,' said he, as he replaced the skull, 'and the cranial index about 72, which are quite representative numbers; and, as I see that your notes show the usual disproportionate length of arm and the characteristic curve of the tibia, we may be satisfied. But it is fortunate that the specimen is so typical. To the experienced eye, racial types have a physiognomy which is unmistakable on mere inspection. But you cannot transfer the experienced eye. You can only express personal conviction and back it up with measurements.

'And now we will go and look in on Stalker, and inform him that his office has saved three thousand pounds by employing us. After which it will be Westward Ho! for Scotland Yard, to prepare an unpleasant little surprise for Mr Percival Bland.'

There was joy among the journalists on the following day. Each of the morning papers devoted an entire column to an unusually detailed account of the inquest on the late Percival Bland—who, it appeared, met his death by misadventure—and a verbatim report of the coroner's eloquent remarks on the danger of solitary, fireside tippling, and the stupefying effects of port wine. An adjacent column contained an equally detailed account of the appearance of the deceased at Bow Street Police Court to answer complicated charges of arson, fraud and forgery; while a third collated the two accounts with gleeful commentaries.

Mr Percival Bland, *alias* Robert Lindsay, now resides on the breezy uplands of Dartmoor, where, in his abundant leisure, he, no doubt, regrets his misdirected ingenuity. But he has not laboured in vain. To the Lord Chancellor he has furnished an admirable illustration of the danger of appointing lay coroners; and to me an unforgettable warning against the effects of suggestion.

We hope you have enjoyed this Large Print book. Other Chivers Press or Thorndike Press Large Print books are available at your library or directly from the publishers. For more information about current and forthcoming titles, please call or write, without obligation, to:

Chivers Press Limited
Windsor Bridge Road
Bath BA2 3AX
England
Tel. (01225) 335336

OR

Thorndike Press
P.O. Box 159
Thorndike, Maine 04986
USA
Tel. (800) 223–2336

All our Large Print titles are designed for easy reading, and all our books are made to last.

